CIRCLE OF HONOR

a novel

CAROL UMBERGER

The scottish crown series

INTEGRITY
PUBLISHERS®

NASHVILLE, TENNESSEE

CIRCLE OF HONOR

HELPING PEOPLE WORLDWIDE EXPERIENCE *the* MANIFEST PRESENCE *of* GOD.

Published in association with the literary agency of
Alive Communications, Inc., 7680 Goddard Street,
Suite 200, Colorado Springs, Colorado, 80920

Cover design: David Uttley
Interior: Inside Out Design & Typesetting

Library of Congress Cataloging-in-Publication Data

Umberger, Carol
    Circle of honor / by Carol Umberger.
      p.   cm.
    ISBN 1-59145-005-5
    1. Scotland—History—War of Independence, 1285–1371—Fiction.
    I. Title.
PS3621.M35 C57 2002
813'.6–dc21

2002069074

Printed in the United States of America
02 03 04 05 06 LBM 9 8 7 6 5 4 3 2

DEDICATION

To the memory of Richard V. Umberger
With love to Betty J. Umberger

Acknowledgments

THANKS AND PRAISE to God for the gift of storytelling and for giving me the courage to pursue a dream.

Thanks to my friends and mentors in Pikes Peak Romance Writers for their support and encouragement.

A special thanks to Angel Smits, friend, walking partner, and brainstorming genius. We did it!

And thanks to my constantly patient, always supportive husband Tom, and to our sons, Dan and Dave, who understand when I'm "lost" in another century.

Author's Notes

Eva macpherson and angus mackintosh were indeed married in 1291, uniting Clan Chattan with the Mackintosh clan and causing a Mackintosh to become chief of this federation. Although Eva's uncle is thought to have petitioned Robert the Bruce to prevent this, the fact is that for over six hundred years the federation was led by a Mackintosh. In 1936, the clans became separate entities, with never a drop of blood shed between them.

Robert the Bruce did, sadly, kill John Comyn in Greyfriars Church. And although Bruce was unusually forgiving toward most of his enemies, he was ruthless in his treatment of the Comyns. If you would like to read more about this incredible period of history, I can recommend Ronald McNair Scott's book *Robert the Bruce, King of Scots* (Carroll & Graf Publishers, Inc. 1996) as being highly readable and informative.

Clan Chattan supported Bruce at Bannockburn, but to my knowledge, Angus wasn't wounded, nor did he die until 1345 when his son William became laird. I have also taken liberties with the timing of certain events, in order to tell Adam's fictitious story. I hope the reader will forgive any trespasses upon historical fact and will enjoy this story about what *might* have happened if a MacPherson had challenged his laird.

May Gwenyth and Adam's story inspire you with the sure belief that God controls everything and that victory always belongs to those who do his will.

ONE

Dumfries, Scotland
February 10, 1306

ADAM MACKINTOSH tied his horse's reins to a post and followed his liege lord, Robert the Bruce, into Greyfriars Church. They stopped just inside the door, cautiously allowing their eyes to adjust to the weak wintry light filtering through the stained glass behind the altar.

Blowing on his numbed fingers, Adam thrust his hands under his armpits; the church was little warmer than the frosty morning outside. Robert motioned Adam to stand guard at the rear of the sanctuary, but Adam hesitated, silently questioning the earl with his eyes.

He didn't trust the man waiting by the altar, and Robert knew it. Not that Adam's opinion mattered. A moment later, the earl walked toward Sir John Comyn, lord of Badenoch. *The two most powerful noblemen in Scotland.* If it wasn't so dangerous, if treachery didn't hang in the air, this meeting would be cause for celebration. Instead, the two greeted each other with cordial nods and stood face-to-face, hands at their sides. Both had high aspirations: Robert to the Scottish throne, Comyn to power and wealth, however it might be obtained. They had come to blows before, and Adam inched closer, the better to react quickly at the first sign of trouble. Comyn's own sentry stood in the shadow of one of the towering columns.

In the quiet of the church, their voices clearly carried. "We had an agreement, Sir John. You agreed to renounce your family's claim to the throne. You promised to support my claim in return for my lands in Carrick. Is that not so?"

Adam heard the controlled temper in the earl's voice. After their misadventure last night, Adam wanted to throttle John Comyn himself. He admired his liege's determination to seek a peaceful resolution, despite the man's treacherous act.

Comyn said nothing.

Robert pulled a document from inside his tunic. Unfolding it in hurried, jerking motions, he then jabbed it with his finger. "Is this your seal or is it not?"

John Comyn glanced at the parchment. "You know it is."

Robert's voice rose. "Then why have you betrayed me to Edward of England?"

"What proof have you that I've done such a thing?" John protested. But he nodded ever so slightly to the shadowy figure standing opposite Adam. Robert noticed it too. Adam laid his right hand on his sword hilt, ready to act should the need arise.

Bruce took a menacing step closer to Comyn and practically shoved the paper in Comyn's face. "Because this is your copy, Lord Badenoch, taken from the men who nearly captured me last night."

Sir John's expression hardened. "My cousin, Edward Balliol, is the rightful heir to the throne of Scotland. Not you. You tricked me into signing that scurrilous agreement, and I renounce it. My brother and I hold land and castles from one end of Scotland to another, enough to withhold the crown from you and put Balliol on the throne. And we shall do so."

He pushed Bruce, trying to shove the earl aside. But Bruce stepped back in front of Sir John, blocking his way. Sir John withdrew his dagger and, at Adam's shout of warning, chaos broke out. Comyn's sentry raced toward Bruce, but Adam intercepted him and intercepted the man's sword just short of Bruce's exposed back. They fought for several minutes, the sentry's sword coming uncomfortably close to Adam's neck. But he drove the man back and back until he slipped and fell, and by a stroke of fortune, hit his head, and was knocked unconscious.

The sounds of fighting had alerted the others waiting outside the church, and they all came running, immediately taking up arms against their foe. The sanctuary's stone walls rang with the sounds of cursing, the clash of swords, but Adam had but one thought: *Bruce.*

Panting, he whirled and rushed back to defend the earl. But there was little he could do but stand aside and watch.

Sir John swiped his dagger at Bruce again and again, missing his target, becoming more and more careless with each thrust, his anger and frustration building. Bruce's aim was better. After three quick jabs, John Comyn clutched his chest and sank to the floor.

Although a seasoned warrior, Bruce looked down at John Comyn in shock. Adam grabbed Bruce's arm and nearly dragged him through the doorway toward safety. Adam urged the earl to mount his horse, which he did slowly, as if his body carried heavy armor. By now the brief skirmish was nearly over. Roger Kirkpatrick, who had remained outside with the horses, asked, "My laird, what happened in there?"

"I think I have killed John the Red Comyn," Bruce said, numbly staring ahead.

"Do you doubt it?" Kirkpatrick shouted. "Then I'll make sure the traitor is dead!" He dashed back inside, followed closely by Adam.

Kirkpatrick reached Sir John first and stabbed him with his sword. Comyn's body jerked and he breathed his last. Despite the heady rush of battle and John Comyn's part in his own downfall, Adam regretted the man's death. Nothing good would come of this day.

Comyn's men had already lowered their weapons, looking at one another in mute disbelief. As Sir John's men gathered around their fallen leader, Adam and his compatriots returned to the earl.

"He is dead, my lord," Fitzpatrick announced quietly. With the encounter over and reason returning, they realized the gravity of killing a man in a church.

Adam looked to where the earl sat his horse. "What next, my lord?"

Glancing at his bloodstained hands, the earl of Carrick seemed at a loss. Adam knew Robert's options were few. All was lost with King Edward of England, who no doubt viewed Robert's agreement with Comyn as treason. Nothing could be done to restore that relationship now. Comyn's treachery had destroyed any peaceful means to the restoration of Scotland's throne.

They sat on their horses, not knowing whether, or where, to flee.

Kirkpatrick asked, "Is it Norway, then? Shall we seek shelter with your sister and her husband the king?"

Still the earl did not answer. But Adam knew. He knew with a certainty born in serving with Bruce during these past difficult months. They would rebel against the English tyrant and fight for freedom. And he, Adam Mackintosh, heir to the chieftain of Clan Chattan, would willingly follow Robert the Bruce to the ends of the earth.

His face grim, Bruce broke his silence. "It begins. We will stay and fight. Starting now. My friends, this day we commence to cleanse our land of the English. Gather our men together. We will begin by taking Dumfries Castle."

"And what banner shall fly over Dumfries when we have taken it?" asked Kirkpatrick with glee.

"Find the royal standard of Scotland, friend. The treasured Lion Rampant of red and gold. For this day, I, Robert the Bruce, earl of Carrick, claim my rightful inheritance, the throne of Scotland. I stand before you as your liege lord, Robert, king of Scots!"

The group hushed. Even Adam was stunned. He knew they would have to fight, but he never dreamed Robert would so boldly claim the crown. Especially knowing that Comyn and Balliol were firmly united against him.

Adam recovered his wits. 'Twas a daring move completely in character for the compelling nobleman! Raising his sword high, he shouted, "God save King Robert! God save the king!"

The entire company raised the cry in a delirium of excitement and emotion. All about them, from the church to the far reaches of the town, the word spread. The townspeople joined in the cry, then grabbed one another and began to dance in the streets. After ten years of English rule, Scotland once again had a king of Celtic blood. Adam glanced at his fellows, and all wore mighty grins, echoing his own joy.

Amid the exultant confusion, Bruce and his men dismounted. One by one the men knelt before their king to swear their allegiance. When Adam's turn came, he took Robert's hand between his own and made his pledge. Then the new king surprised Adam by asking him for his sword. Adam handed it to him.

As Adam continued to kneel, Robert tapped each shoulder with the flat of the blade, saying, "I dub thee knight. Be thou a true knight and courageous in the face of your enemies. Rise, Sir Adam."

"Thank you for this honor, my lord. I shall fight by your side to the end."

"And fight we shall, sir knight."

LADY JOAN AND HER YOUNGEST DAUGHTER sat in front of the massive fireplace in the main hall. A crackling fire took the chill off the cold February afternoon and gave sufficient light for handwork. The young woman deftly knotted her embroidery thread and surveyed her work, a scene of Daniel in the lion's den she'd designed herself. She rose from her chair and presented the nearly finished tapestry for her mother's inspection.

"Nicely done, daughter. Why did you choose this particular story to illuminate?"

Gwenyth smiled, pleased to share her knowledge of the Bible. "Because Daniel tells us that victory always belongs to those who do God's will. No matter how difficult the situation, you must trust God."

"Your life will be blessed if you keep that thought close to your heart. Now, tell me more of your visit to Ruthven. I detect a note of wistfulness when you mention certain of your cousins."

Gwenyth felt her face grow warm. "I did enjoy their company, Mama."

"I'm sure you did. With your sisters and brothers all married and gone, it is very quiet here at Dalswinton." Lady Joan laid her hand on Gwenyth's arm. "'Tis understandable if you miss them, lass."

"Aye, Mama." She was especially close to the Ruthven cousins for she'd spent her fosterage with them. In those six years her Aunt Isabella had taught her all she would need to know about caring for a castle and a husband. Her husband.

"And I suspect there is one cousin who is missed more than the others."

Gwenyth smiled. Edward Balliol, a distant cousin and contender for Scotland's throne, had been a frequent visitor at Ruthven during Gwenyth's recent stay there. Just yesterday he'd come to Dalswinton and offered for her hand in marriage. If Papa gave permission, she might be queen of Scotland one day. To have handsome Edward for a mate and to be a queen surpassed her fondest dreams.

Having composed her expression, she asked, "When will Papa be home?"

"You are anxious for his answer, aren't you? Then you must be pleased with Edward's suit."

"Oh yes. Yes I am. Do you think Papa will say yes?"

"I believe he will. You are sixteen—'tis time for you to leave the nest as well. Your father and I will miss you, but Edward is an excellent match." Her mother's smile quickly faded.

"You are worried about the politics surrounding such an alliance."

"Aye."

Despite her affection for Edward and excitement at the prospect of becoming his betrothed, she, too, had misgivings. News of an alliance between the Balliol and Comyn families would further divide the loyalty of Scotland's nobility. If Papa were to accept Edward's offer, then he must also agree to withdraw his support of Robert the Bruce's quest for Scotland's throne. She could only imagine Bruce's anger at being denied the crown. "Papa will do what is best."

"And his women will suffer the consequences."

She stared at her mother. She'd never heard her criticize Papa.

Lady Joan paced away, then turned to face her daughter from the other side of the hearth. "Don't look so surprised. Your father often makes decisions to obtain land and power without thought to the cost to his children or me. I say this not in bitterness, but so that you will be prepared for your own marriage. Your father and Edward are much alike in this regard."

Her face must have betrayed her doubts. Mama came to her and put an arm around her shoulders. "I didn't mean to dampen your joy, lass. Edward is a fine man, albeit ambitious. All you can do is love him and pray for God's blessing. You shall certainly have mine."

She kissed her mother's temple. "Thank you, Mama."

"Enough serious talk. Finish your embroidery while I see that the servants prepare warm food and a hot bath for your father's return." She smiled. "I shall await him in my solar, and I promise to encourage him to give you his answer soon."

After Mama left, Gwenyth stared into the fire, her needlework forgotten. Their conversation had given her much to think about. She was certain that Edward was more interested in her as a person than as a political tool. Wasn't he?

Hours later, a commotion in the bailey signaled her father's return. Still clutching the tapestry, she hurried to her mother's solar. Papa might be persuaded to give his answer yet this evening if she requested it of him.

But instead of her father, she found Edward holding her sobbing mother. "Edward, where is Papa?" she demanded.

"Hush, lass. Come and comfort your mother."

Fear paralyzed her. "Why is she crying?"

"I'm sorry to bear bad news, Gwenyth. The villain Bruce has killed your father."

For a moment Edward's words didn't make sense. Papa couldn't be dead—he hadn't given them permission to marry. "You are wrong. It isn't true."

Edward held her mother with one arm and offered his other hand to her. "Come here, lass."

She ignored his offer of comfort. "How? How did my father die?"

"Bruce stabbed him on the altar at Greyfriars Church."

A fierce pain gripped her heart and she stared at the tapestry she still held in her hands, at Daniel calmly accepting his fate, trusting God. And she knew that she had nothing in common with Daniel, for she would not accept her father's death as being God's will. Nay, it had been Robert the Bruce's will and ambition that had killed him.

While Edward continued to console her mother, she walked to the solar's fireplace and threw the needlework into the flames. Then she hugged her mother and led her to a chair before asking Edward, "Does our betrothal still stand? Did Papa give you his permission?"

He stood before her but looked into the fire as he answered, "Aye, he did." Then he rested his hands on her shoulders and looked her in the eye. "But this is not the time for a wedding. You must take time to grieve. I must leave for England and France to strengthen our alliances in case Bruce actually manages to be crowned king. I will come for you when all is ready, I promise."

"And will you kill Robert the Bruce?"

"His death is assured."

"Then I will wait for your summons."

ADAM LOOKED ON as Robert the Bruce knelt at the tomb of St. Fillan of Glenlochart, the revered Scottish saint who'd founded a church on this spot in the sixth century. The sacrilege of killing a man on the altar of a church weighed heavily on Bruce. Adam had frequently seen the newly crowned king of Scotland on his knees, praying to his Savior, in the months since that day. Now he knelt on this sacred ground to pray for forgiveness and receive the blessing of the local bishop.

Just two months ago, before the battle of Methven, Bruce's army had numbered forty-five hundred soldiers and nearly one hundred knights. But the battle was a disaster, Bruce was nearly captured, and all that remained were the five hundred men and a handful of knights that watched as the bishop blessed him this hot August afternoon.

Bruce had become a hunted man in his own country. They had spent the last few days in relative safety with a laird loyal to Bruce. The respite had refreshed Bruce's wife, daughter, and two sisters, who were traveling with them. The presence of the women added to the vigilance of Bruce's men.

But last night Adam had rebelled against the months of tension, against the constant need for vigilance, and against the constraints of his knightly vows to shun the sins of the flesh. In high spirits he'd celebrated his twentieth birthday with an excess of strong drink and a willing tavern wench.

Today the late summer sun seemed overly warm and his head ached. He hoped Robert would soon move into the shade and safety of the trees. And he hoped they'd move before Adam embarrassed himself by succumbing to the dizziness that plagued him.

As the king prayed, Adam struggled to stay alert. St. Fillan's tomb lay on lands owned by the lord of Lorne, son-in-law of the murdered John Comyn and one of many who schemed to avenge the man's death. Despite the danger, Robert had insisted on a pilgrimage to this shrine. The sooner Robert and his troops were gone from here the better.

Finally, to Adam's relief, Bruce indicated they should mount up. Once they were through the narrow pass at the head of the valley they would be relatively safe. Adam fought fatigue and dizziness, berating himself for his foolishness. He would be wise to withstand such temptation in the future and vowed to do so if his head would just return to its normal size immediately.

The horse's movement gainsaid any relief from the shade, and Adam rode in misery. Just as they reached the narrowest part of

Dalry Pass, a screaming swarm of Lord Lorne's highlander warriors descended on them. The surprise of the attack immediately split Bruce's troop in half. The attackers slashed at the bellies and legs of the horses with their long Lochaber axes, succeeding in unhorsing several of Adam's comrades before his befuddled brain could make sense of the noise and confusion.

Adam watched in horror as three highlanders pursued his friend and comrade, Gordon MacNab. Adam's mind and body seemed to work in slow motion as he fought his way toward Gordon. Too late. Gordon's horse went down, and Gordon with him. The highlanders swarmed upon him.

Adam fought off the man nearest him, turned around, and saw Robert in a desperate effort to divert the attackers from his women. He heard Bruce yell, "Retreat!" Others gathered around the king, but another of Lorne's men was already upon Adam. With leaden arms and a sluggish brain, Adam slashed and hacked at his assailant.

A glimpse of Gordon's body, alone in a motionless heap, gave him pause. Adam struggled to focus through the fog in his aching head. Sudden pain seared through his left arm, and he looked in shock at the gaping wound that ran from shoulder to elbow. Robert appeared beside him then, viciously attacking and slowly making way, pushing Adam's mount toward the pass and safety. Cowed by Robert's determined feat of arms and somewhat appeased by their retreat, their pursuers slowed their assault, and Robert and Adam rejoined the rest.

The women were safe, for now. A number of men were slain along with Gordon MacNab. Of the men who remained, James Douglas and Gilbert de la Haye were among the wounded along with several others, but none as seriously as Adam. Now he wished for the oblivion of his earlier headache instead of the pulsing, searing pain in his arm.

When they gained some distance, the group paused in a hidden glen, forming a protective circle around the wounded so they could be tended before resuming their flight. Kirkpatrick pulled off Adam's hauberk and ripped what was left of his shirt.

"The women . . ." Adam muttered.

"They are well," Kirkpatrick replied. Neither man spoke of their fallen comrades as Roger wrapped Adam's arm tightly in a bandage before shoving him back on his horse. The hours until they reached Loch Dochart and safety seemed like days, and Adam cried out in agony when they finally lowered him from the horse.

He must have passed out, because the next thing he remembered was lying on a pallet of heather as his somber comrades made camp. When all was in order, Robert knelt beside him and shook his head.

"I'm sorry, my laird," Adam whispered through parched lips. "I was of little use to you today."

"Aye, you made a bad decision last night and paid the price."

"Gordon. I couldn't help Gordon." Tears threatened, hardly knightly behavior. But tears weren't the worst of it. His behavior had led to the death of a friend—it could have been Bruce! *What kind of knight am I?* Forcing himself to look Bruce in the eye, he asked, "Do you believe God will forgive me?"

Robert didn't flinch. "Aye, I do."

Adam grimaced with pain. When it passed he said, "And you, my king. Can you forgive as well?"

"I can, Adam. Indeed, I already have."

"Then I swear to you that I will avoid strong drink for the rest of the days given to me."

Bruce laid a hand on Adam's arm. "Watered wine will be fine when you are well again, son. But now is no time to be heroic. Whiskey is all we have for pain unless we can find a healer."

The pain pulsed through him with each beat of his anguished heart. "You may be right. You've been right about many things. Forgive me for failing—"

"I do. Now waste no more of your breath. You've a grievous wound. Best repent of your sins and pray for God's forgiveness. And his mercy." Robert gazed at the ground before continuing. "Morogh will take you home."

To die. Adam had not thought his wound mortal until now. But the man was right. Few survived such a wound as this. Robert was too good a friend to say the words. But the thought of home, of rest from the constant flight and battle, was enough to allow unconsciousness to overtake him.

THEY LEFT AT DAWN, and by the time he and Morogh reached Moy, Adam didn't much care what was poured down his throat so long as it took away the pain. As he slowly, miraculously, recovered at home, he heard of the capture and hanging of Robert's brother Nigel, of the imprisonment of Bruce's wife and young daughter, and of Robert's escape to Rathlin.

On a chilly December evening, Adam sat before the fireplace in his room at Castle Moy, cradling his useless arm and staring into the flames. He wanted to be at his king's side, sharing his exile and planning Bruce's campaign to retake Scotland from the English tyrant. How he regretted that night of sin and temptation, a night that nearly cost him his life and the life of his king!

If he hadn't been wounded, could he have made a difference? Might he have been able to protect Bruce's family from capture? Moreover, had he not imbibed that fateful night, had he slept in camp instead of in a stranger's bed, would he have detected the attack and saved Gordon and the others?

God may well have forgiven him, as Bruce had said. But Adam would live the rest of his life with the guilt and shame of his failure at Dalry Pass.

TWO

Scottish Highlands, 1308

THE SINS OF THE FATHER," Adam Mackintosh muttered as he sat down in one of two massive chairs on the dais. But his father hadn't sinned; he merely made a brilliant marriage all those years ago.

Of course, the brilliance of the match depended a great deal upon one's perspective.

The great Clan Chattan, for hundreds of years proudly and rightfully led by the Macphersons, now unwillingly followed a man with the surname of Mackintosh. Macpherson resentment had simmered for twenty years, ever since Adam's mother—the Macpherson heiress—had married the Mackintosh chief.

Adam Mackintosh, newly named to succeed his ill father as chieftain of this unstable federation, feared that resentment neared the boiling point even as he listened to the toasts raised in his honor this evening. The main hall of the Macpherson keep resonated with the sounds of revelry. Trestles laden with food and pitchers of ale abounded as men in varying degrees of intoxication toasted the new laird. If anyone detected a note of falseness in their praise, none remarked on it.

Leod Macpherson, seated next to Adam, raised his tankard.

"Come, my laird. One sip of ale to toast your continued good health."

For a brief moment Adam considered ignoring his vow to avoid strong drink. But then he thought of all he'd lost, and might yet lose, because of that night near Dalry Pass, and the temptation faded as quickly as it arose. "I'll gladly toast to my health and to yours. With water." Adam saluted his host, all the while wondering how long Leod would wait to challenge him for leadership of the clan. Truth be told, Adam was surprised the man hadn't done so already.

Adam leaned back in his chair, the one his host's wife would have occupied if Leod were married. The lack of a woman's touch was evident throughout the hall—there were no cloths on the tables, and traces of dried food clung to the surfaces of tables and benches alike. The rushes on the floor gave off the odor of rotting food and undisciplined dogs. Tattered tapestries hung on the walls, in need of a mistress's needle and thread.

The contrast to his own home gave Adam reason to be thankful for his mother's conscientious stewardship of Castle Moy. Grateful his rank afforded him the luxury of a seat with a back to lean on, Adam absently massaged his damaged shoulder. This visit to his clansman's keep was one of the few times Adam had left his own castle in the nineteen months since he'd been wounded. His ailing father had insisted that a show of strength was needed.

And that Adam could do, he considered ruefully, so long as no one challenged him to pick up a sword. He picked up his tankard of water instead and sipped from it. He knew Leod would be serving excellent ale, and again came the temptation for just a sip. *Keep me strong in my resolve, Lord. There is too much at stake to repeat the mistakes of the past.*

Once more the man urged, "Come, Adam. Share a drink with me. 'Tis an occasion for celebration." Leod signaled for one of the serving girls to replenish his ale and to bring Adam a cup. Did Leod sense his weakness?

When she set the cup before him, Adam tried to remember if he'd seen this particular girl before. She must be new, for he was certain he'd have remembered such a winsome face. A wee bit of a lass, she hardly seemed suited to the heavy work of carrying food and drink.

"Thank you," he said, though he had no intention of giving in to Leod's taunt. He pushed the cup to the side and met her gaze for a moment. Her golden brown eyes betrayed a sense of wariness, but he had no time to discern why, for Leod yanked her into his lap. She was no match for his great size, but instead of squealing and flirting like the other wenches, Adam saw fear and panic cross her features. She struggled against him.

"Be still, you little queen," Leod demanded.

She fought all the more, and Leod slapped her, hard enough to loosen the cap on her head and send a cascade of deep russet hair falling about her.

Adam bit his tongue to keep from chastising Leod. This was, after all, Leod's hall, and Adam didn't wish to create any more animosity between them. The disturbance caught the attention of several nearby revelers, and they moved closer to watch the display. Two of Leod's men-at-arms took seats beside Leod, pounding his back and making lewd comments about the lass.

To Adam's relief the confrontation ended as the girl quieted and Leod let her go. "You live and breathe at my pleasure, wench," he warned, "and you'd do well to remember it."

Her downcast gaze and posture seemed to appease Leod's temper, and he dismissed her. But as she turned from Leod, hastily pinning her hair as she walked away, Adam was astounded at the flash of anger her eyes revealed.

Something was amiss here. He turned to Leod. "I don't remember that lass, Leod. Who is she?"

"My men came upon her yesterday, near Nairn."

"She was traveling?"

"Aye, and her companions deserted her in the melee. Those who didn't escape have made excellent servants."

"Unwillingly, no doubt." She did not strike Adam as a woman used to the rigors of servitude.

"The unwilling ones are the very best kind." Leod and his companions roared.

Adam laughed, pretending to enjoy the jest. Then he asked, as casually as possible, "What is her name?"

"Well, if you're that interested, my laird, you may enjoy her at your leisure."

Adam quickly regretted his query, for Leod jumped to his feet and went after the girl before Adam's protest left his lips. Leod dragged the lass to stand before him and shoved her at Adam. Caught off-balance, she toppled into Adam's lap, and her head connected with his shoulder. Judging from the smirk on Leod's face, Adam's sharp hiss of pain did not escape notice, and his mood darkened.

Hoping to forestall a repeated blow, Adam pulled her against his chest with his good arm. Her tiny frame supported surprisingly generous female curves. He gentled his hold, and yet still she moved. It wasn't fight he sensed in her, but fear. She trembled.

What was this?

Her actions were not those of a coarse wench used to this give-and-take with men, but rather those of an innocent. She would not remain so for very long, not in this keep. Her vulnerability and petite frame appealed to his protective nature, and on an impulse, Adam said, "I accept your offer of the wench, Leod. I shall take her to Moy as a token of your esteem."

The maid tensed again in his arms, and Adam released her. She leaped from his lap and stood rooted next to his chair, her posture a jumble of defiance and dismay.

"She is yours, my laird," Leod grinned.

Adam didn't trust Leod, and the unease he'd felt all evening intensified. He looked back at the girl, but she had masked her emotions. Oddly, her stoic reaction compounded Adam's desire to see her safely from this place.

Adam said to the girl, "What is your name?"

"Gwenyth, my laird."

Her voice sounded much more cultured than a servant's ought to be, but now was not the time to question her. Best to get her, and himself, safely to Moy first. "Then Gwenyth, come the morrow, you shall leave with me to serve at Castle Moy."

She looked at him and asked, voice trembling, "And tonight?"

Bending close to her ear, he assured her. "Nay, lass. You shall sleep alone."

"As you say, my laird."

Leod cleared his throat. "Show Adam to his room, girl."

Adam shook his head. "That isn't necessary."

Stepping closer, Leod gestured to the inebriated men who remained in the hall, including the two leering drunks sitting at their table.

"She appears to be an innocent maiden, Adam. I can't guarantee she'll still be one in the morning."

Adam shot Leod a heated look. "Then perhaps it is I who must provide protection, if you won't."

"It matters little to me what you do with her, Adam." His gaze left Adam's to roam in a leer over the girl, then came back to Adam as if to say Adam wasn't man enough. Adam's hands clenched, and he itched to drive his fist into Leod's sneering face. But if his ability to wield a sword was questionable, his chances in hand-to-hand combat were even less encouraging.

Seeing no other choice but to escort his new servant from the hall, Adam took her arm and led her to the bottom of the stairs. He turned to her and said, "You may spend the night in my chamber, lass, if you'll feel safer there."

She shook her head.

"Then show me the way to your quarters."

She hesitated, clearly unsure if she could trust him. "I can find my own way."

"I'm certain you can. But I will rest easier knowing you are safely abed."

With a sigh she capitulated and led him to the cramped space she shared with several other servants. She turned to face him. The torchlight reflected reddish highlights in her hair and golden flecks in her eyes. By heaven, she was lovely.

She was the first to speak. "Thank you, my laird. You have no doubt saved my virtue, at least for this night."

"Your virtue is safe with me, lass. We'll leave early on the morrow, so gather your things tonight."

"Aye, my laird."

GWENYTH STARED AT THE HANDSOME MAN who'd so gallantly rescued her from Leod. High cheekbones, deep-set blue eyes, and curly blond hair almost made him pretty, but a strong jaw and masculine nose saved him from such description. Deep smile lines at either side of his mouth were clearly visible on his clean-shaven face.

He appeared to be a man of honor, and she was grateful that tomorrow he would take her from this keep. His twinkling blue eyes assessed her as well and she wondered what he saw—the noblewoman she was or the servant she pretended to be?

"Good night, my laird."

"Good night, Gwenyth."

She watched him walk away, admiring his long-legged stride and the width of his shoulders. His shoulder. She'd bumped his left shoulder and heard his sharp intake of breath. As she straightened her pallet and prepared for bed, she wondered if the injury was old or new. Perhaps she could use her healing skills to help him.

Such foolishness. Crawling under the covers, she admonished herself. She wouldn't remain in Scotland long enough to help him. Best to remember who she was and that Edward awaited her once she regained her freedom.

A SINGLE TAPER lit the narrow passageway where Leod leaned against the wall. The damp, ripe odor of decaying refuse assailed his nose. Not the most appropriate location for a tryst, but then the tryst had not been . . . appropriate.

He grinned despite the smell and moved toward cleaner air and away from the woman's sobs. By the time he reached the top of the dungeon's stairs, his own breathing and the scurrying of rats were the only sounds.

His men-at-arms had easily overcome the man Adam had sent to guard the woman and had dragged her from her pallet and down the steep stairs, into the dark room where he waited.

The Mackintosh fool's honorable behavior had cost this woman dearly. No matter that she was only a servant; highland folk did not take kindly to the despoiling of any woman, and the laws were very explicit. Leod would take advantage of the legal means now open to him to have Adam killed.

He sneered as he conjured up a vision of the outrage he would feign. He, the powerful and just, would vow to find the man who dared to commit such a crime under his very roof. And he knew just whom to blame.

As long as the woman cooperated. And she would, for in the morning he would tell her he had arrested the rapist. She couldn't know for sure who had attacked her, and he would promise to free her after she accused Adam. He would make perfectly clear the price she'd pay if she failed to name Adam as the rapist or dared to accuse Leod, the rightful laird of Clan Chattan. Aye, fate had indeed been kind, and his resolve hardened. By this time tomorrow, with Leod's rival dead, justice would be restored.

Leadership of Clan Chattan would be his.

THREE

Thou shall not bear false witness.
But only a lie will save me!

$\mathcal{G}$WENYTH PRAYED FOR DELIVERANCE, but God seemed very far away. She raised a trembling hand to her mouth and winced when her salty finger touched the split in her lip. Aye, God had finally deserted her for good. Last night, amidst darkness and terror, someone had assaulted her. The windowless cell she'd been dragged to was pitch dark, but the man hadn't needed any light to find and take what he came for.

Even now, in the light of day, she shivered at the memory of his beard brushing across her bared skin. A bearded face was the only thing she knew for certain about her assailant, aside from his brutality. She wrapped her arms across her chest, in an effort to still her quaking, for it disturbed her bruised ribs.

False witness.

She lifted her gaze to the tall, clean-shaven man who stood on the other side of a table placed between them. Adam Mackintosh. How could it have been him? Even in her current state of confusion, she was certain her assailant wore a full beard, not the day-old stubble on Adam's face. See how the sun had kissed his cheeks and chin with color. That was proof, wasn't it?

And why would the gentle man who'd seen her safely to her pallet return later and accost her? She shoved the painful memories aside. Somehow she must see this through, find Daron, and leave her accursed homeland for Edward and safety.

Her gaze locked with Adam's, and she marveled at his arrogant stance. Gone was the kindhearted man of yesternight. He seemed to dare her to go forward with this deceit. He could not know that the lie that would condemn him would deliver Gwenyth and her kinsman from further danger.

The priest, her judge, stared hard at her. "Gwenyth of Buchan, you must identify the man who wronged you."

Another lie, this name she'd given. If she revealed her proper name, or even that she belonged to the Badenoch side of the family, she might very well leave here in chains. This Leod who'd captured her thought her to be a servant, for that was the story she and Daron had concocted to aid their escape. Now their web of deceit threatened to ensnare yet another soul. Was Adam an enemy or a possible ally?

Foolish question. Daron was her only true friend. And yet Adam's kindness had held promise of shelter, of gentleness. His smile could not have hidden a brutal nature, could it? Gwenyth no longer trusted her own judgment. She would be safer to believe she had no allies here in this keep.

And only a distant, unresponsive God to call upon. He'd deserted her the night her father had been killed. This feeling of separation from God tormented her nearly as much as her physical pains, but she didn't know how or if she could ever bridge the chasm. And last night had only pushed him farther away.

In increasing despair, she forced herself to look at Leod Macpherson. He'd been so solicitous and kind this morning, but more than a hint of evil clung to him. Despite his promise to free her, she would not entrust her life to him just yet. She asked him, "Why do you accuse this man?"

With barely concealed impatience, Leod responded, "I've told you. This is the man who raped you, woman."

She winced at the sound of that ugly word spoken before this gathering of men. If only she could hide her battered body somewhere safe until she healed. Not just her body, but also that inner fragment that even now screamed in outrage and anguish. It took every bit of courage she could muster to harness her emotions. Swallowing her humiliation, she asked, "Aye, so you have said. But what evidence have you?"

"Everyone saw you leave the hall with him, lass. 'Tis obvious that when you didn't give to him freely, he took what he wanted." His dark gaze bored into her, reminding her of their agreement. "Now all we need is your accusation."

Despite Leod's black glare, she refused to comply until she was sure. She asked Adam Mackintosh, "Are you truly laird?"

The blond warrior leaned across the crude wooden table that stood between them. "Aye, that I am. Lord of Clan Mackintosh and soon to be captain of the Chattan federation of clans."

Gwenyth backed away from the man's overbearing presence. Laird. Her assailant had said the word like a litany all through . . . Laird.

Adam was laird.

Leod shoved the man back from the table, then moved around it to stand next to her. She flinched when he gripped her arm in a gesture meant to intimidate, not console. She was beyond consolation, but her temperament did not easily bow to intimidation. And she would not give way to her emotions or the cry of her body to retreat, collapse, until she was safe. Nor would she accuse Adam or anyone else unless she was sure of his guilt. She fought to focus on all that was transpiring about her.

Leod's silky voice sickened her. "Mackintosh and Macpherson are united under one chieftain, Angus Mackintosh."

"Aye, that's true, as far as it goes." Adam turned to her, his earlier arrogance displaced by obvious distress. "My father is gravely ill, and I am his successor."

Confused, unsure who to believe, she sought answers to the questions crowding her mind. "So you are acting in your father's place?"

"Aye."

She turned to Leod. "And you are not laird."

A feral gleam came into Leod's eyes. "Nay, I am not. Come, Gwenyth, just name the man and be done with it. All these questions change nothing."

She was being used as a pawn in some deadly game between these two men. Why else would Leod Macpherson dare to accuse his laird's son and heir? Suddenly Gwenyth's faith in Macpherson's promise of freedom plummeted.

She was being asked to condemn a man she believed to be innocent, most likely to further Leod's ambition to lead his clan. How could she trust Leod if he showed so little loyalty to his laird? What if she kept her part of the bargain and accused the Mackintosh man, and Leod broke his word to her?

In vain she tried to remember something, anything, about her assailant. But the beard remained her only clue. Many men in the hall wore beards, including Leod. Which of them had it been last night? Who among them was capable of such cruelty? She couldn't even be certain which of them had dragged her to the dungeon.

Gwenyth panicked as dawning awareness of her future gripped her. Leod would not release her, would not help Daron as he'd

CIRCLE OF HONOR

offered. She would be forced into an unholy relationship that would send her to purgatory. And her stay in hell would begin while she yet lived.

She cried out in pain and fear as Leod grabbed her arm and pulled her to his side.

His voice was harsh and low enough for her ears only; his hand crushed her flesh. "We have an agreement, Gwenyth. I will help you and your cousin find passage to England, and you will name this man as a rapist and choose the punishment we agreed on. Is that not so?"

His rough treatment brought pain to her ribs and tears to her eyes. Enough. She could not take any more of this impossible situation.

"Aye," she whispered at last, feeling faint.

He hauled her back to stand before Adam. Desperately she prayed that God might still be near, might guide her decision. Lives were at stake—hers, Daron's, and that of the Mackintosh man. A man who had shown her nothing but kindness. Now that he knew of her ordeal, would Adam still treat her tenderly? Would any man? Had she lost not only her innocence, but the hope of a husband's love? Edward. Edward would still love her, wouldn't he?

False witness.

Her gaze riveted on Adam Mackintosh, and she saw that he held his left arm stiffly, protectively close to his body. A man with only one good arm was at a definite disadvantage in a fight, yet Adam showed no fear or even anger. Indeed, the lines in his face bespoke a man who laughed often and well. But not today. Today she found his visage hard, his gaze frosty, which did nothing to encourage her in choosing a course of action.

"My lady." The cleric's voice took on a note of impatience, no doubt inspired by Leod's deepening scowl.

The fair-haired laird dropped his gaze to the table before them, and Gwenyth did likewise. There the judge had laid a small piece of rope fashioned into a hangman's loop, and a ceremonial sword. And next to them lay her own dead mother's wedding ring, taken from Gwenyth's finger before the trial began. No doubt Leod would have preferred not to give her that third choice, but he could not openly circumvent the law without drawing suspicion.

These are my choices.

The significance of the items displayed there couldn't have escaped Adam. Which would he prefer—death, or marriage to a ruined liar and enemy of his king?

Aye, both Leod and Adam were her enemies and could not be trusted. She'd already taken Leod's measure and found him lacking. What of Adam Mackintosh? Once again she looked into his eyes. What kind of man was he? Would she be safer with him? Had his kindness last night been genuine? There were no answers in those icy depths.

Only two things she knew for certain—she would die herself before she would condemn an innocent man. And she would never be safe in Leod Macpherson's keep.

She looked once again at Leod and caught her breath. Pinned to his left shoulder was the brooch that held his plaid. Her assailant had collapsed heavily upon her, leaving a peculiar bruise. A bruise that matched the shape of Leod's pin.

Her gaze shot to the brooch on Mackintosh's shoulder to find an encircled rampant cat. Until she knew if Leod's pin was unique, she couldn't be positive that he was guilty. But she could be absolutely certain that Adam Mackintosh was not.

Should she accuse Leod? No. If she were foolish enough to do that, Adam might be allowed to leave, but she would not. Leod had made that point very clear.

She released her breath, saying a silent thanks for what must surely be a sign. Perhaps God was watching over her after all. For the first time, she felt as if she had some control over her situation. Putting her trust in heaven and Adam Mackintosh, she pressed forward.

God forgive me for this lie.

With a prayer for the strength to see this through, she answered the judge's question. Her voice quavered as she said, "'Twas Adam Mackintosh who raped me."

"The woman is lying!" Adam's shout sounded harsh, cold.

The judge cleared his throat. "The woman has been examined by our physician, and I assure you, she tells the truth."

Gwenyth cringed, remembering the humiliation of the examination. She nearly strangled on the sob caught in her throat at the reminder she was ruined—no man would want her for a wife now.

Perhaps the Mackintosh man saw her discomfort, for although he continued to stare, his voice was less strident. "She may have been ill used, but 'twas not by me, and she knows it."

Despite Adam's protest, the judge pronounced him guilty, and Gwenyth wondered if Leod had included the man in his wicked plot.

Indeed, the judge looked nervous as he said, "Lady Gwenyth, you have the right to choose his punishment."

Glancing at Leod, she was momentarily terrified by his menacing glare. No doubt he expected a servant to be easily intimidated. Well, she was not a servant; she would not lose heart or all would be lost.

The Mackintosh man's stare bored through her as well. Silently she beseeched him to trust her. She must leave this keep and find a way to ensure Daron's safety. And Adam would live. He might hate her, but he would not die because of her.

"Get on with it, Gwenyth," Leod exploded. "What will it be—a hanging or a beheading?" Belatedly he added, "Or a wedding?"

The priest hurriedly left the hall, as if afraid to be further tainted by such proceedings.

For a moment, fear and comprehension registered on Adam's face, but he quickly regained control. Gwenyth considered the ramifications of thwarting Leod's plan. She doubted that her choice would change anyone's opinion of the Mackintosh laird—others would believe what they wished in regard to his guilt or innocence. Indeed, even if they thought him guilty and she chose to marry him, they would consider it just punishment.

Leod, on the other hand, would profit no matter what, for she realized that, should anyone discover her identity, her marriage to Adam might well weaken his rule as captain of the Chattan federation. Marriage or death. There was really only one choice.

"I choose the ring," she declared, watching Adam for a reaction. She saw his shoulders slump momentarily in relief, but his expression remained glacial. Still, Gwenyth knew she'd made the only possible decision, although she doubted he would thank her for it.

In her preoccupation with Adam, Gwenyth failed to notice Leod closing in upon her. "Nay, you impertinent wench." His face contorted in rage and he tried to hit her.

Adam stepped between them, deflecting the blow and pushing Leod away. "Leave the woman be. Judging from that bruise on her face, it would appear she's already sampled your hospitality, Leod. And it appears she didn't care for it."

"So she runs to a cripple for protection."

Adam's jaw tightened, but he said only, "Well, I'll not fault her loyalties just now, Leod. She at least is wise enough to see she can't expect much in the way of loyalty from you."

"The council still must approve you as captain, Adam."

"Which they will do, and well you know it. Tell me, why did you not simply knife me in my sleep? Or put poison in my food? 'Twould have been much less chancy than depending on the whims of a woman."

"Obviously I thought her suitably subdued." Leod's evil sneer repulsed Gwenyth. "I'll consider your methods next time."

Clearly, a challenge had been issued and accepted. How would she ever find the safety she craved in such a place as this?

Leod glared at her, but his words were for Adam. "Your wife-to-be is damaged goods, Adam."

"You sound overly familiar with the proceedings, Leod. Perhaps you were a witness." Adam's voice had an edge as sharp as a Damascene sword.

"Nay, my laird. One only has to look at her to see she's been well initiated."

Gwenyth had had enough of Leod and his odious behavior. *She must leave this place.* She tugged at Adam's arm to get his attention, realizing too late it was the injured arm. She heard Adam's intake of breath, and she quickly let go. Despite his pain, pain she had caused him, he nudged her to stand in front of him. Now she faced Leod, with Adam's strength to bolster her.

Adam said, "Release my men, Leod. They have been noticeably absent during this mockery of a trial."

Leod turned to a man-at-arms. "Release the Mackintosh men. Then send that miserable excuse for a priest back in here."

"We don't need a priest."

Gwenyth's knees threatened to buckle.

Leod smirked. "Judgment has been pronounced. You can't escape punishment, Adam. Would you prefer to have the priest administer last rites instead of the sacrament of marriage?"

Gwenyth swallowed. Had she obeyed Leod, the priest would have shriven Adam and possibly her, as well.

"I've no doubt you were planning on my death, Leod. It was a brilliant plan, all very legal, but luckily the lady has discerning tastes. Still, there's no need for a priest."

No need? Gwenyth's head spun. He must be daft—surely he didn't prefer death to marrying her? Gwenyth turned to him and laid her hand on his sleeve. "We must have a priest to—"

"Enough." He brushed her hand away. The blue of his eyes turned more frigid than a highland blizzard. "I'll not make the honest vows of the church with a deceitful woman." He glared at her, again daring her to react.

"But the lie saved your life," she whispered.

His gaze gentled, but his voice remained cold. "Aye, so it did. And I'm mindful of it, lass. But I'll not enter into a binding marriage founded in dishonesty."

Lord help me when he learns the full measure of my deceit. She cast a fearful glance at Leod, who watched her closely. She reminded herself that Leod stood to gain, no matter how this turned out. She returned her gaze to the Mackintosh warrior, silently pleading with him to cooperate.

Whether he read her entreaty or merely played a role himself, she didn't know, for his next words startled her.

"We will handfast. Marriage for a year and a day is all you will have of me, Gwenyth of Buchan."

Gwenyth's heart hammered. The custom of handfasting, while not officially sanctioned by the church, did provide for an acceptable union until a priest might be found for more formal vows. Most handfasts became permanent marriages, but if the parties agreed, they could part in a year and a day.

She could insist on a proper, binding marriage, but Adam was right. Handfasting fulfilled the spirit of the law and gave them both their freedom, eventually. Could she hide her identity long enough to get word to Edward? To assure Daron's safety as well as her own? Her brave cousin deserved that much from her. And Adam would not be bound to his king's enemy.

Bowing to the inevitable, she said, "As you will, my lord."

Adam's men strode into the hall, looking and smelling as if they'd spent the night in Leod's dungeon. Adam turned to speak with one of them, and from the corner of her eye, she saw Leod move toward her. Gwenyth watched him warily, steeling herself for another confrontation with this man she hated.

Leod lowered his mouth to her ear even as she moved away. "You may very well regret your treachery one day."

"Not as much as I would regret dying, or worse, becoming your mistress," she retorted, only loud enough for him to hear.

Leod eyed her closely, and she glared back, unwilling to cower before him. Adam's protection sustained her, gave her the strength she needed to finish this. But only just barely.

"'Tis your word against mine, lady." He grasped her chin and forced her to meet his gaze. "I'll enjoy watching Adam raise my son to be the next laird."

Leod's threat struck like a dagger. The thought of bearing Leod's child nearly undid her. Rage welled in her at this man who'd stolen what she should have willingly given to her husband. She slapped him—a good measure of how close she was to losing control altogether, for she'd never before raised her hand in anger to another.

Stunned, Leod lunged for her, and then yelped in pain as Adam gripped his wrist.

"Keep your hands off her." Once again Adam thrust his big body between Leod and Gwenyth. "The woman's been badly used.

The Macpherson keep harbors a rapist, Leod. You had best protect your women. But I suspect you know that best of all."

"Little hope she'll have of protection from a one-armed—"

Leod's words were choked off as the Mackintosh laird grabbed the neck of his tunic with his good right arm and pulled Leod to him, nose to nose.

"One is all I seem to need for the likes of you," he snarled. Adam shoved Leod away, and then scowled at Gwenyth. "Come, let's say the words and be gone from here." His face was an icy mask.

This was not the time for talk. He obviously wasn't happy at being forced to marry, but neither was she. Best just to have it done. In a numb stupor, she slid her mother's ring from the table and moved to the side of her soon-to-be husband.

One of the Mackintosh men acted as witness while first Adam, then Gwenyth, recited the handfasting vows. None of it felt real, and it was far removed from the dreams of her childhood. Bruised and battered and wearing a torn work dress, she stood beside a man she didn't know, reciting vows that bound her to him, gave him dominion over her for the next year and a day.

She shivered, then clamped down on her apprehension. She would think of his kindness, holding it in her heart like a talisman.

Adam turned to her, and Gwenyth hesitated. She was grateful to be rescued from Leod's clutches, for this gift—unbeknownst to Adam—of safety and freedom for her and for Daron. And Adam's insistence on handfasting opened a previously closed door—when they separated, there would be no stigma upon either of them. She could be welcomed as a wife by any man.

Unless there was a babe. In such a case, the parents must stay together. Then she and Adam would never be free of each other. She shoved the unwanted worry aside, to be dealt with when the time came. Too many other problems were more pressing at the moment.

She owed this man as great a debt as he owed her, and now a way came to her to show her gratitude. Although rings were not normally exchanged in a handfast ceremony, she wished to remind herself, and the man, what she owed him.

She placed her mother's band in his large, callused hand.

He inclined his head. "You wish to wear a ring?"

"Aye, my laird, if it pleases you. I ask to wear this ring as a reminder of my loyalty to you, and only you. For a year and a day."

Not surprisingly, mistrust and disbelief clouded his eyes. *Will it always be so between us?* Gwenyth shook her head. Such thoughts were not appropriate—all she needed from him was his promise of safety.

Despite Adam's unwilling participation in the ceremony, he looked down at the ring with its intricately carved pattern of intertwining circles, picked it up, and reached for her hand.

"With this ring, I pledge the protection of my name," he said, slipping the band on her finger. "'Tis all you may expect from me, for a year and a day."

At his words her heart eased. Protection and safety were what she needed—she had a year to ensure her future. A year in which she would rest in refuge, heal, and prepare herself to move on. "Thank you, my laird."

She had little else to offer. Judging from the look on his face, he didn't believe her sincerity. But he had promised to protect her, with his body and blood if need be, and she took comfort from his vow.

"Will you seal your vows with a kiss?" Leod prompted with a snarl.

Adam didn't hesitate. "I think not."

With a heated glance at Leod, Adam motioned to her. "Gather your things. I would be gone from here before more mischief arises."

"I have nothing."

"Nothing?"

"All was lost when I was taken into custody."

Adam rounded on Leod. "Return her possessions at once."

Leod scowled before giving the order, and Gwenyth dimly wondered that he obeyed. The Mackintosh man was unarmed and his men were outnumbered. If she had condemned Adam to die—well within the limits of the law—Leod needn't have feared retaliation. But to kill one's laird or his appointed successor outright would bring immediate deadly justice. For now, Adam was safe.

Her musings were interrupted when a servant arrived with her belongings, which upon inspection proved to have been rummaged thoroughly. Gwenyth didn't care what might be missing—she only wanted to be gone.

Now that her immediate safety was assured, Gwenyth became increasingly aware of her body's aches and pains. Her bruised ribs protested with every movement. But the desire to be gone from Leod's presence overruled any thought of seeking a healer to tend her wounds. Gwenyth supported her ribs as she slowly made her way to the bailey where her husband waited.

A feeling of dread overcame her. No matter that the vows only bound them for a short while—they would be man and wife, legally bound, with all the rights and privileges of marriage. She knew what to expect of him, but what did he expect of her?

FOUR

ADAM OBSERVED THE BAFFLING WOMAN as she walked across the courtyard toward him. He was struck by the hatred she displayed toward Leod for a brief, unguarded moment. Had Adam read it wrong? If, as he suspected, she and Leod had conspired to entrap him, why did she hate the man? Or allow it to show? And why on earth had she chosen marriage when it was obvious Leod wanted him dead?

He would have answers, Adam vowed.

The half-dozen men who'd accompanied him to Leod's keep had retrieved their weapons and horses, as well as an extra horse for the woman. He'd have to ride bareback, as he'd instructed them to put his saddle on her mount to ease her riding. Adam helped her mount, wincing as his damaged shoulder protested the upward movement. He ignored the pain, pulling himself astride his own horse.

His men's guarded countenances told him they shared his urgency to leave this place. Clenching his hands into fists, Adam stifled his frustration. If not for this worthless crippled arm, he would have challenged Leod to fight and put an end to their dispute once and for all.

He cleared his head with a shake. Foolish thought—even as a whole man he wouldn't have done such a thing where he and his men were so outnumbered.

Reason slowly returned, and he set his thoughts on more immediate concerns. He stationed a man on either side of the woman, then took the lead, signaling his kinsman, Morogh, to bring his horse up next to him.

Once clear of the castle, Adam asked, "What did you learn?"

"Just as ye thought, Leod is telling his people ye aren't fit. 'Tis clear he wants to take over the federation."

"He very nearly got his wish."

"Aye, God be praised for such a brave lassie."

Adam stared at Morogh. Apparently Gwenyth had won herself an admirer. Well, it would be churlish not to be at least somewhat grateful to her.

Adam knew others shared Leod's opinion of his fitness to lead, but few were bold enough to say it to his face. The wound he'd suffered was nearly healed, but he feared the arm would never regain its former strength. A laird had to protect his people with a swift sword and unswerving justice.

The day would come when Adam would be tested, and he dreaded it.

Adam rubbed his eyes. He'd had a short night's sleep, and the morning had been difficult. But it would seem easy compared to what he faced at Castle Moy when he arrived with a handfast wife in tow. And a servant at that.

Renewed anger at being forced to marry threatened to over-whelm him. But to give in to his anger would not help. Instead, he reined in his temper and focused on discovering what he could from Morogh.

"What did you learn of the woman?"

"She and some kinsmen were headed to England when Leod seized her. One of those kinsmen was Daron of Ruthven, a warrior good with a sword and loyal to Balliol."

"So, I may assume my new wife is no friend to my liege lord, Robert. Where is this Daron now?"

"No one knows. He and several others disappeared."

"I should just give her food and some coin and send her on her way."

Morogh said nothing.

But Adam couldn't just send her away. Her kinsmen had evidently deserted her, and someone in Clan Chattan had ravaged her. She'd suffered enough, and even though the assault had taken place in Leod's keep, Adam, as captain of the Chattan federation, felt responsible. No woman, whether servant or highborn, deserved such treatment.

He should have insisted she come to his room last night where he could have personally ensured her safety. Well, he'd tried to make up for it by giving his word to protect her from further harm. Thankfully, he only had to honor the vow for a year, not a lifetime.

"Morogh, do you think she conspired with Leod in that farce of a trial?"

"Aye, she did. But I think she figured she couldn't depend on Leod's word and hoped for better from ye."

"You may have the right of it, friend. But I'm not sure I trust her."

"Nor should ye. And ye shouldn't ride out again until this is settled with Leod."

"You think I should crawl into my keep and lick my wounds? How will it look if the laird hides behind his castle walls?" The volume of his voice must have risen, for the rest of their company glanced nervously in his direction.

Lowering his voice, Adam said, "I must be out where my people can see I am well and strong, Morogh."

"Aye, well, and I say ye'd do better to just send word and stay out of Leod's reach for a time."

"I'll think on it."

"Do that."

Adam hated to admit it, but Morogh was probably right. However, it wouldn't do to give in so easily, so he changed the subject.

"Do you think Leod ravished the woman?"

"Could be. He's a mean one."

Adam nodded in silent affirmation. His sense of propriety was deeply offended by what Gwenyth had suffered, and he meant to find the culprit.

Still, the woman was the last thing he needed. She seemed of good breeding, but he planned to marry someone who would enhance his holdings and his position. Furthermore, Gwenyth was an unwelcome intrusion in his personal life. For more than a year he'd managed to push aside the pain of his failed betrothal, but this battered woman and her dependence on him opened the floodgates.

Memories poured through him—memories of Suisan's rejection . . . The pain from that wound remained vivid; it hadn't healed nearly as well as his shoulder. He'd nearly lost his arm and his life—he should be thankful all he'd forfeited was the woman his father had chosen for his son to marry. There had been times early in his convalescence when he'd been nearly overcome with guilt. But God had spared him, and Adam was now wise enough to be thankful for his life.

Aye, and thankful his betrothed had refused to marry an invalid, for his torment over her betrayal had been the catalyst to his recovery, a recovery far beyond what the healer predicted.

As it was, far too many Mackintosh and Macpherson clansmen shared Suisan's opinion—a man who was not a prime warrior should not be laird of the federation. And now their damaged chieftain was handfasted to . . . Gwenyth of Buchan, a serving girl.

He pushed aside the sense of unease that stole over him, and he turned to his companion.

"Well, then, Morogh. What shall I do with such a wife?"

"Ye might credit her for saving yer hide."

"You needn't keep reminding me." Adam tried to suppress his impatience with Morogh's admiration of the lass. True, it had taken considerable strength of character to stand up to Leod, but he didn't want to admire her. He wanted to be rid of her.

Although part of him empathized with her, he didn't want a wife, nor did he want a woman who would lie under oath. These noble thoughts warred with the knowledge that her willingness to lie, to accuse him, had saved both their lives. He conceded it would be difficult to remain angry with her for long, under the circumstances.

For a moment he recalled the feel of her in his arms last night and her shy smile. Dark, arched eyebrows framed a gamine face and warm brown eyes.

Morogh interrupted these agreeable images. "I think the clan will forgive her for being no more than a handmaid when they learn how she stood up to Leod. But if not, the marriage is only handfast—ye can put her aside in a year."

Adam scratched his ear. "Aye, I suppose so."

They rode on in silence.

"If ye plan to be rid of her, ye best not touch her, Adam. She may already carry a babe. If 'tis ye that gets her with child—"

"I know, I know." Adam pounded the pommel. Morogh was absolutely right. But Morogh worried needlessly about Adam siring a child with the woman; he would not accept her as his wife unless and until proper vows were spoken before God.

Morogh drew apart, as if to give Adam time to reflect on the consequences of this marriage that wasn't a marriage.

God had been good to Adam, restoring him to life and giving him the strength to avoid temptation. *God, give me wisdom in the matter of this woman. Wisdom to know what she needs to be able to heal.* Adam wondered how a woman dealt with such an invasion of her person. Surely she would fear the intimacies of marriage. She might never welcome a husband's touch.

The thought saddened him.

How was he to deal with her? Even though Adam was determined that this marriage would be temporary and chaste, it would be difficult to live with a woman who feared him.

Gwenyth's behavior, aside from her lying, said much about her character, Adam reflected as he pulled his plaid close to ward off the heavy mist. Despite her physical pain and emotional distress, she had reacted with calm assurance and well-masked emotions. Indeed, her stamina amazed Adam. Such attributes made for a formidable enemy, and despite her pretty avowal of loyalty, Adam would watch her closely.

Adam looked back at the woman. She had tied the ends of the reins together and left them drooping upon the horse's neck. Her arms cradled her chest, and distress etched her features, the very picture of misery.

Belatedly he wondered if she was unaccustomed to riding. From her tense posture, he surmised she feared what lay ahead at Castle Moy. He could only guess that her reception would be less than warm, although no one would be outright cruel. The laird's offer of hospitality bound each clansman to civil behavior, at least.

Anxious to begin questioning her about her collusion with Leod, he reined in his horse, allowing hers to catch up. When it was nearly abreast of him, the beast stumbled, pitching Gwenyth forward. He saw her bite her lip, but a sob escaped and tears filled her eyes.

"Halt," he ordered, and his men reacted quickly. Her animal stopped, more in response to the other horses than from her command.

Her distress unnerved Adam, for he could not abide another's suffering. He dismounted, chastising himself for not taking the time to assess the extent of the woman's injuries.

She lifted her head, and the bruise on her temple fairly glowed, it was so vivid. He quickly dispelled conjecture on her other injuries, willing away the sick feeling that accompanied the thought.

Golden brown eyes gazed at him with not a little trepidation. He sensed a deep-seated wariness and pain. He had experience in dealing with suffering in the aftermath of violence against his person. Her body would mend, given time, but he knew only too well the mind healed slowly, if at all.

He would punish the man who had done this.

Adam reached for her hand, but she jerked it back. In her haste, she took a deep breath and cried out in agony, clutching at her rib cage.

"I'm sorry, my lady. Do not agitate yourself." He called to one of his men to help her dismount, knowing his own clumsy efforts were likely to injure her further.

The other man set her on the ground beside Adam, then gathered her horse's reins and stepped aside to give his laird privacy. "You've some damaged ribs?" he asked.

She nodded, all she seemed capable of.

"Did you bind them?"

She shook her head.

Disgusted with himself for not thinking of it sooner, he ordered her to stand still. He went to his horse and pulled a section of cloth from the saddlebag. After folding it into a triangle, he walked back to her. "Which side?" he asked.

She whispered, "The left."

As gently as he could, he placed the cloth beneath her arm and then tied the two ends together behind her neck.

"Rest your arm in this sling."

When she complied, he took a second cloth and wrapped her arm firmly to her side.

"This will give the ribs support." He took a deep breath. "The man who did this to you should die. Do you know who it was?"

She hesitated, and he knew she would lie. "I can't be certain. But it doesn't matter who it was, my laird. I would not trouble you to seek revenge on my account. It would grieve me to see you come to harm because of me."

He didn't expect her to answer, but he asked anyway. "Then why did you accuse me?"

She remained silent but appeared close to tears, as if it distressed her to deny him.

But he needed to understand why she'd behaved the way she had. "You know that by not naming him you protect your attacker from punishment?"

"Aye, but he would not help me."

"And you believe I will?"

She nodded. "When I locate the cousin who was accompanying me, and when I am well enough, I should like to continue my journey to England. Will you help me?"

He smiled. "Aye, lass. I will."

"Until then, I am grateful for your offer of sanctuary."

He indicated his damaged limb. "I'm not certain how well I'll be able to provide that safekeeping."

"You have no use of the arm?"

"Some."

She gazed at him, and in her lovely features he saw fear and desperation war with hope. But not a trace of the pity he had feared to find.

"I am willing to take that chance, sir, for no one would have protected me . . . there." She waved weakly in the direction of the Macpherson stronghold. "Laird Mackintosh, perhaps this marriage is a good bargain. You question your ability to protect as a man should. I must be equally honest. I'm not certain I'll ever be able to . . . to be a wife to you."

She was so tiny, so weak; he feared a strong wind would blow her over. Stunned by an overwhelming wave of tenderness and a fierce desire to shelter her, Adam cupped her cheek. "It wasn't your fault, lass. Whatever happened, you are not to blame."

She closed her eyes and surprised him by leaning into his hand for comfort, as if she needed to believe those words.

"Perhaps not. But there'd be no one to blame but myself if I had stayed there and Leod . . . I had to leave . . ." The tears that had threatened earlier now raced down her face as her iron control cracked. "He would have killed you," she whispered. "I had to lie, to keep us all safe . . . I'm sorry."

She had accused him to save him. She'd known Adam was innocent and lied to him. Adam didn't know how to respond.

Opening her eyes, she backed away and wiped her face with her unbound hand, as her composure returned. "I did what I had to, even though it meant binding myself to a man who doesn't want me." Her chin rose with those last words, daring him to wound her pride further.

So, she had defied Leod and accepted the consequences. And saved Adam's life in the process. His opinion of her softened. He tried to envision her face the way it had looked without the bruises, red-rimmed eyes, and deep-seated hurt. She was easy enough to look at, even now. His gaze lowered, and he saw her squirm at his obvious perusal.

But something more than physical attraction drew him. Though she was weakened and vulnerable just now, Adam sensed strength of character as well as determination in the woman. Strangely enough, her acceptance of his disability made him feel . . . competent.

"Angry as I am at being forced to wed, I much prefer it to your other choices, Gwenyth."

His rueful humor wasn't lost on her, and she offered a weak smile. "I'm certain you do."

He would not trust her; he would not be a husband to her. But he could not deny her safe haven.

Blast his soft heart. "Come. You are safe now."

He prayed it was true.

FIVE

W AS THIS CONSIDERATE MAN the same angry laird Gwenyth
had handfasted with barely an hour ago? She welcomed the
change, for his kindness held hope, and hope was an anchor that
might carry her safely through the storm. An anchor that might
constrain the despair that threatened to overcome her.

She tried to avert her face, but his hand gently held her chin
fast, forcing her to meet his eyes. His earlier frosty gaze had
warmed considerably.

"'Tis the devil to ride wounded, especially on a clumsy beast, is
it not?" he asked.

"Aye." No doubt he spoke from experience, and tears threatened at his compassion. Gwenyth willed her unruly emotions to be
still, for veiling them had always been her favored form of self-
protection. It had stood her well this morning, and now she needed
that ability more than ever.

"Come, ride with me. My mount has a smoother gait, and I will
support you. 'Tis only another hour or so to my home."

"But, your arm, my laird." Unfortunately she hadn't mastered her
tongue as well as her emotions. "Will you—"

"I'm not an utter cripple." He glared at her. "You would do well
to remember that, Gwenyth."

His warmth disappeared like the sun in a sudden highland

mist—apparently his benevolence had limits. The thought of his touch alarmed her, but he'd promised refuge, and she clung to that assurance as if he alone offered salvation.

How would he arrange to hold her and guide his mount? She didn't ask. It was enough to be given comfort, and she cared not how he managed the horse.

While one of his men held the animal still, Adam stood upon a large rock and mounted. Gwenyth fought the urge to push away the hands that gently lifted her to sit in front of him. 'Twas not very dignified to sit astride in a dress, but the skirt was full enough to allow sufficient modesty.

Then one of his men laid his plaid across her lap, draping and tucking it to keep her legs and feet warm. Adam drew her close with his good arm, and she stiffened at the contact before allowing her head to rest against his broad chest. He loosened the brooch that held his plaid at the shoulder and pulled the excess cloth around them both. The heat of his body and the smell of man, leather, and damp wool soon encircled her, consoling her bruised spirits. Somehow, God seemed closer with Adam near.

She wanted only to sink into oblivion, but the tangled workings of her mind held her prisoner. *My husband.* She shivered in apprehension. The thought of the intimacies of marriage raised bile in her stomach, and nausea washed over her. *Surely he will allow time for my wounds to heal.* And time to learn if she carried a babe. Leod's words crashed over her like a fist to her heart, and she raised her head so fast she cracked into Adam's chin.

"By all the saints above, be still, woman." He pushed her head down on his chest.

"I'm sorry."

A babe. A child should be conceived in love within the cradle of a marriage sanctioned by God. Such a union would bring joy, not memories of violence and pain. The headache that had been plaguing her now blossomed into full force.

Breathing deeply, Gwenyth calmed herself. In the time it would take to know for certain, she could locate Daron and take her shame with her to England. There it would be easy to pass herself off as a widow and no one would be the wiser.

But a babe was definitely not part of the plan. Edward waited for her in England and he would not welcome another man's child. Nor would he be pleased by the delay this handfast marriage entailed. Already she had postponed sailing in order to bury her mother, who had taken ill at Christmas and died a few weeks later. Gwenyth must hasten to find Daron and get word to Edward.

Aye, Adam would not dare to touch her until he knew if she carried a child. The thought summoned tears she could not prevent, and they dampened Adam's sark. Her sobs did not go unnoticed, for his large hand stroked her hair and he crooned in soothing Gaelic, abandoning the French of daily discourse. He didn't press her to learn why she cried, and she was grateful for his forbearance and willingness to console.

Gradually the tears diminished. Her only solace was the satisfaction that an illegitimate child would be freed from her dangerous birthright—the crown of Scotland.

Of course, if God was kind, there would be no child, and Adam would not learn of her identity until long after she'd reached England. In any event, she would be spared Adam's advances for now. She allowed that thought to ease her and willed her mind to consider other matters.

But her thoughts remained on Adam. He'd been right about his horse—this animal walked with a smoothness hers had lacked; and she found her aches and bruises less jostled, seated as she was against Adam's strength. His closeness held no terror, only succor.

The gentle rocking of the horse and the man's reassuring support soon lulled her to doze. As her consciousness drifted, she offered a silent prayer of thanks for her deliverer.

It seemed no sooner had the prayer been formed than a deep bass voice rumbled in her ear. "Wake up, lass. We're home."

"Home?" The sound of a male voice and the feel of a male body pressed against hers awakened her terror, and she thrashed wildly.

"Be still, woman, before you fall." His arms tightened around her and she cried out, even as she was coming to her senses.

"Hush, lass, hush," he soothed. "You're all right, 'tis only me, Adam."

Adam's soothing voice and gentle stroking of her back calmed her. She stilled and his grip relaxed. He settled her back against him. "We're home, lass. Welcome to Castle Moy."

He stopped the horse on a rise of land, and she looked to where he pointed. The morning's mist had lifted, allowing an unobstructed view. Despite her disappointment that they looked upon Castle Moy and not Dalswinton, her breath caught at the sight, for there on an island in an aquamarine lake rose a castle of surpassing beauty. The gray stone gleamed in the sunlight, a perfect foil to the stand of timber at the far end of the island.

A stone causeway connected the isle to the lakeshore, providing access into the bailey. The outer curtain wall followed the shape of the land, and two sturdy round towers graced the wall, one at either end. Within the walls a few sheep and goats grazed to keep the grass short. A majestic keep with a high-pitched stone roof rose from the center, and a flag depicting a rampant cat flew from the ramparts.

"This is your home?" Her cares were momentarily forgotten in the splendor of the scene.

"Aye, Loch Moy and its castle."

"'Tis uncommonly beautiful."

"I'm glad you share my opinion. 'Tis not only beautiful, lass. It is also virtually unassailable. You will be safe here." He made to spur the horse, but she stayed him.

"Let me look a bit longer." Knowledge of what faced her behind the fortress's walls unnerved her, for despite its beauty, this castle harbored his clan, people loyal to her enemy.

"Another time. You need to have your wounds properly tended." There was no trace of the earlier tenderness in his voice, only the sound of a man used to being obeyed. And she owed two-fold obedience to him—both as laird and husband. She shivered in dread.

Repositioning his plaid around her shoulders, he said, "You will soon have a warm room and food and my mother's healing skills." He must have signaled the horse, for it began to move.

Again she thought of facing the man's mother and kin, and her heart began to pound. Would she need to sleep with her door bolted? His family could easily kill her and none would be the wiser—such was not unheard of in forced marriages.

And when they learned she was Gwenyth Comyn—daughter to a man they considered a traitor—her life would surely be forfeit, despite Adam's promise of protection.

Gwenyth's imagination took flight and her agitation increased as they crossed the causeway and entered the bailey. Not only were these her enemies, but soon she would suffer the humiliation of having them know she'd been raped. And she would have to face their anger at her false accusation of their laird. She feared Adam's promised safety was naught but an illusion.

Strangers reached for her, and she shrank away from them.

Adam gently pushed her toward them. "'Tis all right, lass. My kinsmen only wish to help you from the beast. I'll not allow you to come to harm."

She slapped at the hands that reached for her as hysteria threatened.

"Gwenyth!" Adam shouted. "Cease." But there was no anger in his voice, only concern for her. He leaned toward her ear and said quietly, "I keep my promises, woman. Now dismount."

Reluctantly, she allowed one of the men to help her down, then stood there trembling as Adam dismounted. He brushed off the inquiries of the curious castle inhabitants while he surveyed the crowd. Gwenyth followed his gaze until it rested upon an older woman, framed in the keep's doorway.

He bent his golden head until his lips were again at Gwenyth's ear. "My mother will tend you. I trust no one else." Before she could answer, one of Adam's men picked her up and headed for the woman, with Adam close behind.

Wounded, frightened, and too weary to care, Gwenyth made no more protest. Instead, she wondered what Adam's mother would think of her son bringing a bedraggled and obviously injured woman into her keep.

CLIMBING THE STAIRS to the women's quarters, Adam hoped his mother would save her questions for later. With relief, he watched her expression change from curiosity to distress when she saw Gwenyth's bruised face.

They entered a bedchamber and his mother drew back the heavy drapery around the bed, then pulled back the quilt. Sim, the man holding Gwenyth, laid her on the clean linens and Eva Mackintosh said to him, "Fetch my healing satchel and bring more wood for the fire."

"Aye, my lady," Sim said and took his leave.

Eva set about heating water, then joined Adam beside the bed. Gwenyth's eyes were closed. Poor thing was probably exhausted from all she'd been through, Adam thought. As he reached to unfasten the makeshift sling, his hand thoughtlessly brushed Gwenyth's breast. Her eyes flew open and she cried out.

Eva slapped his hands away. "What do ye think yer doing? Find something more suitable to do with yer hands."

"I have every right . . ." *to touch my own wife.* He couldn't finish the thought aloud. *She is wife in name only.*

He would do well to remember it.

He stepped back while Eva examined the woman, their murmured voices mingling. Eva crooned in obvious sympathy and Adam began to relax, knowing that Gwenyth was in capable hands. Sim returned with the medicines and wood; Adam dismissed him and built up the fire.

With the fire satisfactorily producing heat, Adam turned to watch his mother as she bent over the small form on the bed—the better to hear what Gwenyth said. Eva gasped and sat upright, and Adam knew she'd learned of the worst of Gwenyth's injuries, the one that would take longest to heal.

In the voice that would have sent him scurrying when he was a child, Eva said, "Leave the room, Adam. She has wounds I must tend and ye cannot be here."

"I'll stay." At his mother's black stare, Adam conceded, "But I'll turn my back."

Eva's expression clearly indicated displeasure with him. "Yer behavior is most curious, son."

Obviously his mother wanted an explanation. "I need to know the full extent of her injuries, Mother. Tend the girl." When she made no move, he softened his tone. "'Tis not the first creature I've brought home for you to heal."

"Nay, 'tis not." The corners of her mouth twitched. "But usually they are four-legged and furry. Or feathered."

He smiled. "And I always help you."

"Aye, but this is not the same."

With a guarded glance at the woman on the bed, he said, "Nay, 'tis not. This time the unfortunate one is a woman who has been beaten and raped. A woman who accused me of the crime."

Eva's face went pale. "And you bring her to me to heal?"

"I had little choice since she forced me to marry her."

"Marry?" Eva made the sign of the cross before glaring at the bed's occupant.

Gwenyth's shame and pain glowed in her eyes, and Adam's emotions warred between anger and the need to console. Anger prevailed, and he gestured his mother to the other side of the room. There he recounted how he came to return home with a handfast wife.

GWENYTH WATCHED WITH TREPIDATION as Adam spoke with his mother. The woman had been kind in her questioning and compassionate in her touch. But Adam's news had obviously distressed her, and Gwenyth worried how Eva would treat her when she returned to finish her ministrations.

If only she could rise from the bed and leave. Leave this place and the man who both comforted and frightened her. Leave her homeland, this accursed country that had brought rack and ruin to her and her family.

And now this final humiliation. Gwenyth turned her anger on the God she believed had deserted her so completely. She sobbed quietly, for the loss of that source of comfort was more painful than her physical wounds.

As her tears fell, she listened to the rise and fall of voices on the other side of the room. Adam's voice. How it had soothed her earlier today when she'd soaked his shirt with tears. Now as she listened to the cadence of his words, she was once again soothed and her sobs stopped. Since God had abandoned her, she would cling to the comfort Adam supplied. Gradually the warmth of the room and the medicinal tea Eva had given her lulled her into much needed sleep.

WITH THE TELLING, color returned to his mother's face. Adam glanced to where Gwenyth lay. She'd fallen asleep, and he and Eva moved back to the bedside.

Adam gazed down at Gwenyth, observing her dark lashes fanned against pale skin, and the trace of fresh tears on her cheek. For a moment he allowed himself to think how it might have been if they'd met under more auspicious circumstances. She was a pretty thing, and he admired her courage.

"She's got spirit," Eva said.

"Aye, she does. If not for that, I'd be dead."

"She'll need courage and more to come to terms with what has been done to her. I'll say a prayer for the lass."

"As will I." Adam rubbed his shoulder, remembering that the people of Buchan were Robert the Bruce's enemies. "I'm grateful to the lass for saving my life, but she's of Buchan. Better than being of Badenoch, but I'm not overfond of either branch of the Comyn clan."

The fight at Greyfriars, then Dalry and Adam's injury at the hands of the Comyns were never far from his mind.

"Surely a maidservant's loyalty lies with whomever she serves, Adam."

"Aye, but she's not a servant any longer; she's my wife."

"And a wife's allegiance lies with her husband."

Adam recalled the maid's pledge. "Let's hope she remembers that. As a precaution I've sent Seamus to see what he can learn from Bryan."

Eva nodded. "'Tis well to be cautious in such unsettled times." Her foster son, Bryan Mackintosh, served with Robert the Bruce and could be trusted to provide wise counsel.

Adam forced his thoughts back to more pressing matters. "Mother, I will break the news to Da." Anguish at his father's precarious health washed through him. "How is he today?"

"He's stronger than ye give him credit, son. Having ye assume the duties of laird has prolonged his life." She sighed. "Ye say she's a maidservant?"

"Aye."

"Not exactly what yer da had in mind when he encouraged you to marry."

"Well, the matter is not settled—'tis why I insisted on a handfast union. And why the union will remain chaste for the foreseeable future."

"For the foreseeable future, she'll not welcome a man's touch, I'd wager. Only God knows what time will bring. Lay it in his hands, son." Eva gave him an encouraging smile. "You need time to puzzle this through. Talk with your father tomorrow. He's resting, and I'll see no one disturbs him so you may be the one to tell him."

He acknowledged her words with a rueful smile before looking down on the sleeping maid. "You will tend her?"

"Not Nathara?"

"I'm in no mood to explain all this to the healer." He hesitated. "I promised this poor lass sanctuary, Mother. She deserves that much, and I give it willingly."

"As ye wish, my laird." She smiled again, and some of Adam's tension eased.

"I will find the man who did this and make him pay. I'll not harbor such within my domain."

Eva nodded, "By God's grace, may it be so."

Rubbing his aching shoulder, Adam knew he shouldn't make such promises, not to anyone, not even his wife.

ADAM AWOKE with the first stirrings of the servants. He'd spent a restless night, and yesterday's events remained unresolved in his mind. He pushed aside the bed hangings and climbed down from his bed, pulled on a linen sark, and kilted his plaid about his hips, securing it with a wide leather belt. Pulling the excess material over his shoulder, he pinned it fast with a brooch. As was the habit of any prudent man, even within the safety of his own walls, Adam sheathed a dirk in the top of his stocking and grabbed his short sword before making his way to the kitchen.

The others wouldn't break their fast until after morning mass, but today Adam would forsake the formal ritual and seek God's counsel in private. He took some bread and cheese and a flask from the kitchen and ate as he walked the path to the east end of the island, where lay his favorite spot for pondering life's perplexities.

Here the land gradually sloped toward the loch, making this the castle's most vulnerable spot, except that the loch was deepest on this side. A round tower stood guard on this wall, ready to deflect any attack. The tower housed a small, well-fortified gate, which provided access to a fine, sandy beach where he often strolled. But that was not his destination this morn.

Instead he headed for a grove of aspen and poplar trees on this side of the wall. The trees sheltered an area of rock formations whose fanciful shapes had enthralled his imagination as a child.

Steam rose in wavy fingerlets from the warm water of the hot spring nestled among the stones. He found a submerged ledge to lie on. These days Adam sought out the warm water when his shoulder ached from cold or overexertion. Or sometimes, it was his soul that required the soothing feel of the sulfurous liquid.

As the warmth assuaged him, he remembered days in his youth when he'd come here with his cousins. They had not been interested in the restorative properties of the water. A thick twist of worn rope still hung from a branch where he and his foster brother, Bryan, had swung before dropping into the deep end of the pool.

Childhood memories faded, replaced with the cares of a man responsible for the well-being of several hundred souls. Those burdens had grown increasingly heavy these past months, as it became apparent he would never regain his former prowess as a warrior. He would be forever vulnerable, forever uncertain of himself.

Only recently had he begun to come to terms with the legacy of his failures at Dalry. Robert had told him to forgive himself, but in the year and a half since, he hadn't been able to do so. Would he ever be able to?

A twig snapped. Adam moved instinctively to where he'd left his weapons and clothing. Dagger in hand, he crouched at the water's edge, motionless, until a familiar female figure came into view. He laid the dagger back on the shore and moved into waist-deep water.

"Hello, Nathara."

"You didn't come to see me when you returned," she pouted prettily.

How am I going to explain Gwenyth's presence to Nathara? Stalling for time, he splashed water on his arms and torso before answering. "I wanted to bathe first."

Nathara began loosening the pins that held her abundant, wavy black hair, letting one coil fall prettily to her shoulders, and then another. Her intent was clear—Nathara accomplished everything with effect in mind, often using her substantial womanly wiles to pull him closer. And she was still clearly determined to become his wife. Seeking distraction, he began to bathe in earnest as he called to mind his relationship with the clan healer. Nathara's skills had been sorely tried in saving Adam's life. But he had lived and she had even managed to save his arm. It didn't work well, but he hadn't lost it to the knife.

She had stayed by his side constantly until he'd been out of danger. And so it was that Nathara had been with him the day his intended bride had looked upon his withering body with shock and refused to formalize the betrothal.

Having observed his humiliation at Suisan's rejection, Nathara had offered to heal his spirit with her woman's touch. He'd resisted, continued to resist, but she wasn't easily dissuaded. As if to accentuate the point, she now reached for the hem of her dress, and he caught his breath and turned his back as she pulled it over her head.

Although he'd never made any promises to her, he owed Nathara—she'd healed his body and salvaged his pride. But what she offered was against God's commandments and Adam's vow.

He heard the splash as she entered the water and walked to him. "Go, Nathara." He gently pushed her away, relieved to see that she'd had the decency to leave her chemise on to cover herself. She thought he was playing and reached for him. But he waded quickly to shore, determined to make the break now.

"Adam, where are you going? Come finish what we started."

"We started nothing, Nathara. There is nothing between us." The words came out more gruffly than he'd intended. He walked toward his discarded clothing and she splashed her way to stand beside him. With a wicked smile, she enticed him. "Stop teasing. We haven't even begun."

He gently removed her hand from his arm. "What we began was friendship, nothing more." He drew a deep breath, bracing himself. "I am handfasted, as of yesterday."

If he hadn't been staring at her face, he would have missed the brief wounding revealed there. Regret pierced him; regret that she had seen more in their friendship than he did.

But Nathara hid her feelings well, and anger replaced hurt in an instant. "Handfasted? With whom, may I ask? And how dare you do such a thing without even discussing it with me first? Do I mean nothing at all to you?"

He pulled on his shirt. "Nathara, I've never promised you anything beyond the day, is that not so?"

Her charms faded fast when her will was contested. Her voice became shrill. "You can put me aside this easily?"

Adam stooped and picked up her gown as he explained. "I owe you much, 'tis true. If you hadn't tended to my wounds . . ." He handed her the dress. "You saved my life, Nathara, and I am truly grateful. I had not thought to marry—"

"Then why did you?" She clasped the gown to her chest but made no move to put it on.

"I had no choice." Briefly Adam described the circumstances of his marriage to Gwenyth.

Nathara donned her clothes. "You admit the woman was forced on you—at the end of the year put her aside." She twined her arms about his neck. "I will wait, Adam."

Adam lowered his head, mesmerized by the sultry tone of her voice. He reached for Nathara's hair and stroked it. Saints above, she was so tempting, and so willing. He would need God's help if he had any hope of fighting this temptation while chastely handfasted to Gwenyth.

He had pledged the protection of his name, and the vows he'd spoken clearly announced he would honor Gwenyth with his word and his body. The words were no less binding for the year and a day than the church-spoken vows of a lifetime.

Resolved to seek out Father Jerard as soon as he returned to the castle, Adam removed Nathara's arms from his neck and backed away. "Nay, Nathara. I am not happy to be bound to Gwenyth against my will, but I will not break my pledge to her, either in thought or in deed."

Nathara's facial features hardened and Adam saw the beginning of animosity and anger. Gone was the seductress and in her place stood a woman accustomed to getting her way. Perhaps he shouldn't have been so forthright with her.

He knew that she wasn't chaste; she made no secret of her conquests. That alone made her inappropriate as a wife. He'd made it clear he wasn't considering marriage with her, and she'd seemed content with what he was willing to give. Until now. The look on her face at the moment gave Adam reason to doubt just how well she was taking this news.

"She is nothing more than a servant, not fit to be wife of the Chattan captain. You want to remain laird, don't you?"

"Aye."

"She'll be no more help than I would. Probably less, since she's from outside the clan."

"Don't concern yourself." Adam was growing tired of the discussion. His time in the healing waters had been far too brief to soothe either his shoulder or his mind, and Nathara had only increased his agitation.

"Nathara, I'm sorry."

"I am, too, Adam. Sorry you feel compelled to honor vows that have no meaning and can bring you nothing but trouble. Sorry that you will not honor the unspoken vows between us."

So, she had hoped their friendship would end in marriage. Adam anticipated tears but saw a vengeful woman instead.

Nathara spun on her heel and strode away, leaving him to wonder just what trouble he could expect from her.

He finished dressing, irritated that his dilemma remained unresolved. He returned to the castle, and after a long talk with the priest, sought his mother.

He found her in Gwenyth's chamber. Eva put her finger to her lips, and Adam walked quietly across the room. Looking down at the sleeping woman, he was struck again by her beauty. Her thick auburn braid lay across her shoulder, disappearing beneath the cover. He wanted to touch it—to feel the texture instead of imagining it.

Stop. He must not look upon her without reminding himself of the lie that had bound them together. And touching was out of the question.

For a moment he considered his conversation with Nathara and his decision to honor the vows with Gwenyth. Surely he held no warmth toward her. But a man whose fighting ability was questionable had only his word to show for his honor.

His word was all he had, and by God's grace, he would not forfeit it.

SIX

GWENYTH LAY QUIETLY, aware of Adam's presence by her bed. She could not bear any more of his concern and kept her eyes closed, feigning sleep, until she heard the door close behind him. The shutters had been drawn in the chamber and a single candle burned on the table next to her bed. Adam's mother sat by the large stone fireplace, gazing into the flames.

The serenity of the scene did not penetrate Gwenyth's spirit. Waves of despair washed over her and her teeth chattered despite the fire and the warm bedding. Her body ached all over, but the worst was her heart. What once had felt warm and expectant now felt cold and empty.

Leod had stolen her innocence. Aye, though she would not admit as much to Adam, she knew it was Leod. And because of him she would never invite any man's touch; to do so might unleash such a beast once again.

More likely, no man would want her now, especially not one as kind and good as Adam. Or Edward. *Oh, Edward. What will I do now?*

At least she need worry no longer about a babe; her courses had come as she had hoped they would. But despite that welcome news, hopelessness filled her, and she craved the oblivion of sleep.

A sob escaped, and Eva hurried to her side. In her shame Gwenyth could not look the woman in the eye.

"There now, lass," Eva crooned, stroking the hair back from Gwenyth's face much as her own mother might have. "You are safe now from everything but your own fears."

Gwenyth closed her eyes as tears rolled down her cheeks. Her mother was only recently buried, her father and brothers dead at Bruce's hand or in battle against him. Who knew where Daron was? Alone—unloved, unlovable, abandoned even by her God—she bowed to despair. Shunning Eva's condolence, she wanted nothing more than the privacy to grieve for all she'd lost.

As her world spun out of control, she searched frantically for something to hold fast to. Something to anchor her in the tempest that threatened to destroy her sanity. And out of the chaos, out of the pain, came a bright guiding light of kindness and hope.

She found Adam's smile.

ADAM STOOD OUTSIDE his father's chamber, preparing himself for the sight of his once-robust sire, now reduced to a bedridden old man. His knock was met with a surprisingly hardy "Come in."

Angus sat propped up in his bed. The swelling of his hands and face was less noticeable, and for a brief moment, Adam allowed himself to hope that Nathara was wrong about the condition of his father's heart.

"You're looking fit today," he said.

"Aye, and feeling fit too. Come, lad. Bide awhile and tell me of yer visit to Macpherson."

Adam sat on the stool next to the bed and took a deep breath. "It did not go as planned."

"He challenged ye outright? Already?"

Adam hesitated—he must tread carefully. Nathara had warned them not to allow Angus to become upset. But he knew his father hated to be treated like an invalid as much as Adam hated keeping things from him.

"Come, lad. 'Tis not likely I'll leap from my bed and beat ye over bad news."

Chuckling at that image, Adam replied, "Aye, he challenged me. But his plan miscarried."

As Adam debated the best way to tell his father about Gwenyth, his father scowled.

"All right, Da, I'll finish. But you must promise to calm yourself."

"Calm myself." Angus yanked at the bedcovers. "Fine. I'm calm."

Adam knew better than to believe it and felt himself cringe even as he said, "I returned with a handfast wife."

The old man's face flushed scarlet. Through gritted teeth he said, "And just how did ye manage that?"

Adam jumped to his feet. "You'll have mother in here clucking at you if you don't quiet down." He stalked to the table and poured his father a dram of whiskey in hopes of calming him. He returned and gave the goblet to his father. "Here."

Angus took the drink and quaffed it in one swallow. "Thanks to ye." He leaned back against his pillows and motioned Adam closer. His color returned to normal, much to Adam's relief.

"I doubt if Nathara would approve of the whiskey," Adam said as he sat down, "or my method of breaking news."

Waving the thought away, Angus replied, "She means well, but I don't have time to be coddled, Adam. I want to leave with my affairs in order, and I can't do that if ye hide things from me."

Adam nodded. "I'll tell you the rest now, but another outburst, and I'm done."

"Aye. Speak yer piece."

He pulled his stool even closer to the bed and told of his trial and subsequent punishment, carefully observing his father all the while.

However, Angus listened without interruption until Adam finished. "Well, I wanted to see ye marrit before I die, but I thought to have ye choose. Does she suit ye?"

"She's a servant."

"She isna comely, then?"

Adam smiled as he envisioned Gwenyth as she had defied Leod. Bruised and battered, still the fire in her eyes had given him a glimpse of the woman hidden beneath the pain, the woman she might become again when time had healed her.

He collected his thoughts and answered, "Nay, her appearance is not the problem. 'Tis her name that troubles me."

His father gave a quizzical look. "What's wrong with her name?"

"She is Gwenyth of Buchan, a lady's maid and no doubt loyal to Balliol."

"Ye haven't asked her?"

"Da, we haven't had time to discuss politics."

Adam observed his father for signs his anger was returning, but Angus only stared at his son. Thinking he'd said quite enough, Adam waited for his father to resume the conversation.

"Yer handfast, you say?"

"Aye."

"Ye were smart not to take the binding vows, Adam." Angus paused, and a grin lit his features. "Still, we canna fault her wisdom in saving yer life, now can we?"

"Nay, I'd say not." He captured his father's gaze before going on. "But there's still the matter of her accusing me of rape."

Angus sobered. "I can understand yer anger at being falsely accused."

"'Tis hard to stay angry under the circumstances. I've given her my protection and promised to help her reach England. That much I owe, and nothing more."

"Aye, the sooner 'tis done, the better, although I doubt that anyone who knows ye believes for a minute ye would force a lass."

Reluctantly, Adam nodded. "Aye, the lasses are most willing to marry the laird's son, even when he has only one working arm."

"Yer charms as a man and laird go beyond physical strength, Adam."

So, they were back to this argument again. "And that isn't the most important thing?" Adam wished he could believe his father's words. "The clan will follow the strongest man."

"Nay, Adam, they will follow the man who will fight as hard in battle as he will fight to lead them safely in times of peace. Leod isna that kind of leader, boy. The only ones who stand for him now are those as greedy and power hungry as Leod himself."

"But what of a man's character? Gwenyth has besmirched even that with her accusation."

"Those who know ye will know 'twas a false claim."

Adam steered the conversation back to Leod. "So, you think 'tis a small group that follows Leod?"

"Aye, I don't believe he has near the support ye credit him with."

Mustering his patience, Adam asked, "What if you are wrong, and I must fight?"

"Then ye will fight and win," Angus said with conviction.

Adam stifled the urge to leap from his stool. If he allowed his anger to show, Angus would feed off it and they'd be yelling again. When Adam felt able to continue, he replied, "Perhaps. But I would rather avoid confrontation. I want no more of my clan's blood to be shed."

"Ah, see. That is just what makes ye a better man than Leod Macpherson will ever be. He doesna think of others, only of himself."

But Adam worried that the real reason he wished to avoid bloodshed was his belief that in pitched battle, he would lose, would be shown to be incompetent as a warrior as he had been at Dalry. It wasn't death he feared so much as being remembered as a weak and tragic figure. No man wanted the bards to sing of him as anything but a mighty hero.

His father's misplaced faith frightened him. "I value your opinion of me, Da. But I'm afraid this marriage to a servant with questionable ties to the Comyns gives Leod needed fuel to gain further support."

"Perhaps. Ye can send the woman away."

"I've thought of that, but the vows are binding for a year."

"Surely you can come to an agreement—she can leave as long as neither of ye marry within the time."

"Aye, I suppose so. But I may not be able to get rid of her as soon as I'd like." *And if she stays too long, I may very well be tempted to change my mind.*

"Why is that?"

"Because—" Adam caught himself before he answered the wrong question. Gwenyth could not be his wife; duty demanded he seek a wife who would strengthen the federation, not weaken it. Still, he had always been one to protect and help the defenseless, and Adam felt most protective toward the lass.

Protection or attraction? Was it her beauty or her vulnerability that called to him? Or something more—a core of inner strength and dignity that drew him? Again he wished to have met her under other circumstances, to be free to know her better.

Aye, he wanted her. Adam shook his head to clear it of that last, dangerous thought. Intimacy was the last thing Gwenyth needed just now. Such thoughts were best kept well hidden for many reasons. Not the least of which was his determination, sealed during his heartfelt discussion with Father Jerard, that he would not lie with Gwenyth or any other woman until God and the church sanctioned the union.

Hoping his face did not betray his mind's wanderings, he looked up to see his father studying him carefully.

Angus spoke softly. "Ye've a lot on your mind, boy. And I think the maid is not the least of it. Send her to me."

"Nay, father. She is fragile just now. Do not add to her burden."

"'Tis ye I worry about, son. I admire yer tender heart, 'tis a good thing for a laird to be concerned for those in his care. But ye cannot let it lead ye where ye shouldn't go. I'll not be here for much longer—"

"Nay—"

He raised his hand, cutting off Adam's protest. "'Tis true and we both know it."

Angus assessed Adam, and Adam wondered if he measured up. "Answer me one thing, son. Do ye want to be laird, want it bad enough to fight for it if need be?"

"'Tis my duty and my birthright. I have no choice."

"That's not the answer I want to hear. Do ye want it or no?"

Adam groaned in defeat. "I don't know."

"When are ye going to forgive yerself for what happened at Dalry? Because Leod Macpherson senses yer lack of confidence, mark my words." Angus' voice became more heated as he continued. "'Tis why he is pressing ye, and he will continue until ye stand up to him. What I want to know is this. Shall I name another as my successor, or will ye fight?"

In anguish Adam shouted, "I can't fight, you stubborn old man! I cannot use the shield to protect myself."

"Then find a way to fight—train yer men to protect yer weak side. Do something, but don't just give up without trying!" His voice rose until he, too, was shouting. "Otherwise, ye're not the son of my loins, but some impostor."

Angus had grown red in the face and his breathing became labored. Fearing for his father's well-being, Adam grabbed his hand. "Da, calm yourself. Please, Da, don't vex yourself."

The door burst open. "What the devil goes on in here?" Eva glared at Adam. "Well? Have ye nothing to say?"

"He's angry with me."

"I can see that. What have ye done to stir him up?"

"Eva, leave the boy be," Angus whispered. His color was again returning to normal, Adam noted with relief.

No one spoke as Angus, calmer now, dropped Adam's hand and patted the bed for his wife to sit down. She closed the door and took the seat he offered.

"Our son has a decision to make," Angus said. "Adam, for the good of the clan, I must force this upon ye. If ye wish it, I'll choose another, but we must not linger. I won't live much longer."

Adam's emotions reeled. He rose and paced. First a forced marriage, now a decision that would affect not only his own future, but the future of his people. Could he be what they needed? Could he win against Leod if it came to a fight? And most importantly, could he live with himself if he gave up without trying?

He looked at the man in the bed, his once great frame now

thin except for the unnatural swelling that spelled his death sentence.

"Who would you choose, Father? If I say I don't want to be laird, who would you choose?"

Adam heard his mother draw in her breath.

Angus looked at his wife and son, and Adam saw love and pride outshining anger in his father's eyes. "I will not answer that. I choose ye, Adam. Ye were born and raised to the job. Ye have the moral character and devotion to others that make a good chieftain. If only ye believed it."

"But a laird must also be able to lead in battle!" Adam shouted in frustration.

"And I tell ye that is the least important thing!" his father shouted back.

"Enough," Eva said, raising a hand that stopped them both. "I've heard enough. Two more stubborn men have never graced this earth." She turned to her husband. "Ye said he must make this decision. Then let him. And ye," she pointed to Adam, "take heed of yer father's words and share yer thoughts with no one. If Leod finds out what an uproar ye've caused, he'll have just the advantage he needs to make yer decision moot."

Adam's heart was heavy as he acknowledged her words. "You are right, both of you. You needn't cast about for someone else. I will fight and win, or die trying."

He spun on his heel and just as he reached the door, his father called out, "Send the lass to me, Adam."

Adam heaved a sigh of resignation. "Aye, Da."

ANGUS KNEW, as he and Eva watched their son depart, that she would have her say. She always did, and for that, he was thankful.

71

Eva Macpherson had not been meek as a young maid or at any time in their marriage. If such were not true, he doubted she'd have survived the upheaval their union had caused.

Eva Macpherson had inherited the chiefship of Clan Chattan from her father and thus transmitted it to her husband and son. The sticking point came when Angus chose to keep his own name, rather than become Macpherson. This did not sit well with her male relatives, for chiefship and name were meant to be inseparable.

A compromise had been reached whereby each clan kept its respective name and came together as Clan Chattan. But not everyone had agreed with the decision, and his opponents now saw Adam's weakness as a means to return a Macpherson to the position.

No sooner had the door closed than she turned to him. "Can ye not speak to the boy without shouting?"

"He's no' a boy, but a man. A mighty stubborn one at that."

"Aye, and I wonder where he got that particular trait?" Her smile softened her accusation. "Yer tired, love. Talk with the lass tomorrow."

He ignored her. "Ye've met her?"

Eva nodded.

"What do ye think of her?"

With a sigh, Eva sat closer and took his hand. "I think she's been frightfully assaulted and not likely to welcome a man's touch again in this lifetime."

Angus thought about this for a moment. "Judging from the look on Adam's face when he spoke of her, I'd wager he's thought about touching her, and more."

"'Tis just his tender heart."

"Perhaps." For the first time in months, Adam had shown fire and spirit. Had the defenseless woman brought out Adam's natural inclination to protect and defend? If so, then Angus would fuel that fire and speed his son's healing.

"Are ye mad, ye ol' fool? After Suisan's rebuff, do ye think he'd take on a damaged woman like this Gwenyth and face rejection again?"

"Adam is good at healing hurting creatures, is he not? He is drawn to her. Perhaps 'tis time for someone to heal Adam."

"You want her to heal him so he can fight Leod." Eva's shoulders slumped. "It always comes back to that, doesn't it?"

"Eva, the boy needs more than to regain his fighting arm. He needs the wholeness that only love and forgiveness can give."

She reached for his hand and smiled. "You are right, as usual."

Gently he said, "He will still have to fight, my love. Leod has always acted as if the world owed him something. And he believes he has been cheated of his birthright."

Eva stood and paced the room before coming to stand next to him. "How can we protect our son?"

Angus shook his head, knowing the time had come for Adam to stand on his own. He prayed he'd prepared the boy well. "We cannot, my love. He must use his head, heart, and hands to defeat Leod."

"How much support does Leod have among the clan?"

"In numbers, not many. I'll speak to Ian. I believe the council will approve Adam, despite the lass's accusation. But so long as Leod lives, Adam's life is in danger. It only takes one well-placed sword thrust, one man to do the deed."

"But surely Leod knows he would forfeit any hope of becoming captain of the federation if he kills his laird."

Eva paced again, and Angus longed to pull her to him, to ease her mind and make her forget. Make them both forget the cares of this world in each other's arms. But those days were gone, and now he had to prepare her, and Adam, to go on without him. The thought pained him, but he pushed it away. He didn't have time for such maudlin musings.

"Aye. Who would do Leod's will to the point of killing our son?"

"Who?"

"I don't know. And I fear I'll no' live long enough to be of any help." He saw a shadow pass across her face and again it grieved him to remind her of his impending death. "I've spoken with Adam and he has taken precautions."

"And the girl?"

"We must wait for Seamus to return."

She drew a deep breath. "Will Adam be able to fight, if it comes to that?"

All the worry of a mother for her child lay open in that question. "Whether he can or not, he's going to have to."

She sat beside Angus once more and took his hand. "If belief alone could win the day, yer son would be able to fly." She smiled. "Now then. Ye need to rest, and the lass does, too. Talk to her tomorrow."

"Nay. I don't have the luxury of putting things off, Eva."

"For her sake, then."

He relented. "All right. Tomorrow."

Eva kissed his brow. "Goodnight, love." She stood and walked to the door. "I'll check on ye before I retire." She closed it quietly behind her.

Angus closed his eyes, resting his weary body. The harsh words with his son still rang in his ears, but none so loud as Adam's anguished cry that he could not fight. Angus refused to believe it. Men far weaker in body and spirit had successfully led this clan in the past. He smiled. *Even I.*

With pleasure, Angus thought of his strong, fine son, the only male child of his and Eva's who had survived to adulthood. Those four small graves in the churchyard still grieved him. Although Adam and his two sisters pleased him, those graves were a reminder that only the strongest in body and will survived the harshness of the highlands.

Aye, only the very strongest survived.

'Twas a grievous shame he couldn't climb the stairs and learn for himself if his daughter-in-law was a survivor.

SEVEN

Darkness surrounded her. *Must not fall asleep—stay awake. Nothing to be afraid of, save the rats scurrying through the straw. No light but a pale sliver beneath the door of the damp, fetid chamber. Watch the light; keep your eyes on the light. But the saving light faded as sleep overcame her.*

Now she was warm, lying in a soft bed with gentle voices. Safe.

Nay, not safe. Never safe.

A hand came out of the darkness, clamped upon her mouth, and muffled her screams of terror. She heard them, tearing her soul even as he tore her clothing. She fought, twisting her body and tugging at his beard. But he was so strong. Still she struggled, to no avail. She closed her mind to all thought and feeling. Why were the bedclothes coiled? The screams echoed in the small room and then ended abruptly, leaving her weeping.

"WAKE UP, LASS," a woman's voice crooned. "Come, 'tis only a bad dream. Ye are safe."

As the nightmare and its terror faded, Gwenyth fearfully opened her eyes to see a woman sitting by her bed. Gwenyth touched the covers, to see if they were real and not straw, to know the dream was truly over. The reality of the warm, soft bed and the sweet-smelling chamber sank in and her sobs quieted.

She remembered where she was. And how she came to be here. She was not safe. Not here, not anywhere in Scotland, for he might return at any time.

She raised herself up, eyes gradually focusing on the woman beside her bed. Adam's mother put a pillow behind Gwenyth's back, and she sank gratefully into its softness.

Eva reached to the small table beside her and lifted a bowl. "You should have some broth, lass."

Gwenyth stared at the ceiling. "I'm not hungry."

"I know, but ye need to eat a bit anyway."

Remembering the anger on Eva's face when Adam had explained Gwenyth's presence, she asked, "Why are you being kind to me?"

"I cannot turn my back on one of God's creatures any more than my son can. And I admire a woman who can outfox Leod Macpherson, especially when so doing saves my son's life."

Hearing Leod's name brought back the dream and Gwenyth recoiled. Leod was the man in the dream, the man in the chamber that night. The shudder became a quaking that would not cease as the images from the dream unfolded yet again.

Eva stroked her hair. "There now. 'Twas not yer fault, never was it yer fault. Ye must put it behind ye. Yer safe here."

Gwenyth didn't believe any of it. She should have fought harder, screamed louder, gouged out his eyes. She should have done—

"Nothing ye could do to prevent it, lass," Eva said, as if reading her thoughts.

"I want to go home." Home. She had no home. Robert the Bruce had destroyed it in his retaliatory raids throughout Buchan not six weeks ago. Thankfully, her mother hadn't lived to see it.

Gwenyth didn't even know if Daron still lived and if so, where he was. The trembling overpowered her yet again, and she despaired of ever being in control of her emotions, let alone her life.

Eva patted her hand where it lay on the covers. "Pray for strength, child. God will not fail ye."

Oh, but he had. She had prayed over and over again but her family was dead, Daron was missing, and her dream of becoming Scotland's queen was quickly dying. Aye, she thought bitterly, God had turned his back on the Comyns for sure. Since he would not help, she would hide herself far away from emotion, from pain. And from the world that hadn't protected her. She closed her eyes and sank deeper into the pillow.

A soothing hand brushed Gwenyth's hair off her forehead. She opened her eyes. Again Eva offered her the bowl with the admonition to eat. Eat and restore her health or hide and what? Give up? Two years of planning and patiently waiting for Edward to send for her, to finish what Bruce started in Greyfriars Church?

She would *not* hide, nor would she cower in fear. Gwenyth accepted the bowl and brought it to her lips, drinking deeply of the rich broth. She was strong, strong enough to do what must be done. She needed no one except Daron. Only her cousin knew her plans, only her cousin would help her. She would find him, with or without God's help.

ADAM RUBBED a handful of straw across his horse's gleaming coat. The repetitive motion and the touch of his hands on the silky hide normally soothed him, but not today. He rested his head on the horse's neck, and the animal reached around, nuzzling Adam's side as if to offer comfort. But the nibbling tickled, and Adam gently pushed the velvet nose away. "Stop, Kai."

The big red stallion stomped his foot, successfully distracting Adam from his pensive mood. He reached into the fold of his plaid for the dried apple hidden there and offered it to the horse, which nipped it from Adam's palm with expert lips.

The stable door opened and closed, and Morogh walked over and leaned against the stall door. "Thought ye might be here. Too cursed cold for the hot spring today, even for ye."

Adam stroked Kai's neck. "Aye, winter's taking one last crack at us."

"How's the wee lass, then?" Morogh asked, his voice full of concern.

Adam shook his head. "She insists that she's fine, just sore ribs and a few bruises. And of the other, she refuses to speak of it, even to Mother. She cried when I visited this morning."

Morogh cleared his throat. "Well, for all ye know, those were tears of gratitude for removing her from Leod's keep and further abuse."

"Aye. Or tears of fear at seeing the one man who has a right to her." He said another prayer of thanks that the marriage was only handfast, that he wasn't tied for the rest of his life to a woman who would never invite his touch. For surely her tears gave proof that the very sight of him filled her with fear.

Adam closed the stall door behind him and walked to the hay stacked at the far end of the barn. He grabbed an armful and returned to fill Kai's rack.

"Have ye had any luck in finding this cousin of hers?"

"None." And it had been that admission to Gwenyth that had preceded her tears, now that he thought on it. Perhaps she didn't fear him so much as she wanted to know her kinsman was alive. That made more sense. Adam's mood lifted. He raked up the loose hay that lay on the dirt-packed floor of the aisleway. "He's either left the country or he's holed up somewhere in the hills."

"Aye, or he's dead."

What would Gwenyth do if that were so? Adam's initial anger at her accusation of rape had greatly diminished. And not a one of the people whose opinion mattered to him believed he'd been the one to assault her. She had saved his life, no matter what her motivation, and for that, he and his clansmen were grateful.

Perhaps she deserved more than just his promise of protection, so grudgingly given. It was obvious, though she tried to deny it, that she had suffered a terrible trauma. From the look of her bruises, which were only beginning to fade after five days, she had fought her assailant, else why did he beat her?

How could any man intentionally harm such a mite of a woman? She stood nearly a head shorter than Adam, and though she carried a well-rounded body, her bones had felt delicate as a bird's when he'd held her on his horse.

Women and children, the old and infirm, were to be protected from harm. That was a man's responsibility. A laird's responsibility. That lesson had been easily learned, for Adam had a natural tendency to protect. Hadn't he spent his childhood protecting others from Leod's bullying?

Leod.

The suspicion that Leod had harmed Gwenyth grew stronger each day. It wasn't hard to believe that Leod the bully had gone from torturing animals to assaulting a woman. Adam couldn't prove it, of course. And having accepted the blame himself, he couldn't very well accuse Leod, even if Gwenyth could be persuaded to name him. But somehow Adam would discover the truth. And make the man pay.

Adam shared a strong bond with Gwenyth, the bond of comrades who'd suffered bodily trauma and survived. Aye, she was as damaged as he. Maybe they could heal each other before they parted.

For a moment his mind wandered through the possible forms

such healing might embrace. Yes, embraces, kisses, and all manner of delights a married couple might choose to engage in.

And then the vision of Gwenyth sitting in a chair staring out the window dashed his foolish daydream quicker than a cold highland rain. Teaching her the delights of marriage might well prove impossible.

Aye, they might heal one another, but that was all. She didn't want to stay here—she'd made that clear. And he must make a true marriage that would strengthen the clan, as God might direct.

Morogh dropped a pitchfork, and the clatter brought Adam back to the present. "Yer not thinking of keeping her?"

"What makes you ask such a thing?"

"The look on yer face."

Morogh's black-eyed gaze didn't miss much. Never had, Adam recalled ruefully. "Nay. Perhaps under other circumstances . . . Nay, it's not meant to be."

"That's what I'm thinkin'."

"When the weather clears, I'll search for this Daron. I think it likely he's gone on without her, but if not, we need to settle with him. Or see her safely on her way."

"Aye, all will work out for the best, ye'll see."

LEOD MACPHERSON rode his horse into the woods surrounding the small village, exhilarated and freed from the frustration that had plagued him the past few days. As he entered the seclusion of the trees, he pulled the mask from his face.

Support for his cause proceeded much too slowly. His Macpherson tacksmen were loathe to transfer their loyalty from Adam to him, and he was no closer now to taking the chiefship than he'd been after Adam's visit.

Curse the woman. Miserable, misbegotten servant. Who'd have thought she'd have the courage to stand up to him, Leod Macpherson? Had she told Mackintosh who accosted her?

Women. If Eva Macpherson had married within her own clan, Clan Chattan would still be led by a Macpherson. Instead, Leod was denied the right to be laird, all because that woman had betrayed her clan.

He wanted to howl at the injustice, but caution prevailed. The cattle raid had gone well, and no doubt the village men had been summoned from their scattered chores to chase after Leod's men and the absconded cattle. He had made certain his men wore nondescript plaids and the Cameron plant badge. Word would go out quickly that Cameron raiders had stolen Macpherson cattle.

And accosted a Macpherson woman. Leod hadn't planned on the assault. But she'd caught his eye as they rode through the village, driving the cows before them. Before he'd had time to think, he'd reached down and pulled her in front of him.

Lust and rage warred within as he'd dragged her to the ground, not far from where he now rested. The mask hid his face as he took out his frustration on the young woman. He'd finished quickly and ridden away, not willing to be caught by her outraged kinsmen, careful to ride toward Cameron lands before changing direction.

He laid his heels to the horse and moved to the trail that led home.

The word would travel quickly, and Adam would find himself with angry villagers. Soon the resistant clansmen would see that Adam Mackintosh couldn't protect them and wasn't fit to be their laird. Leod would escalate the cattle raids and put fear in the hearts of the villagers.

Then he would step forward, "find" the men responsible, and show Adam for what he was—incompetent.

WHEN THE FICKLE SPRING WEATHER warmed three days after his talk with Morogh, Adam made good on his promise to search for Gwenyth's cousin. But the man wasn't to be found. Adam renewed his determination to heal her, no matter the consequences. She'd been damaged by someone in Clan Chattan, and he would see her well and healed. His duty as laird required it.

His honor demanded it.

She'd remained hidden in her chamber since their arrival a week ago and this morning he'd discovered why. He had knocked at her door and she bade him enter. She sat in the chair by the fireplace, wrapped in a warm blanket. "Good morning, Adam."

"Good morning. You look well. I wish I was bringing better news, but I wanted you to know I haven't found your cousin Daron."

"Thank you for trying."

"I haven't given up and neither must you." He felt awkward and searched for something else to say. "Morogh's telling of how you stood up to Leod and saved me is a popular subject of late."

She smiled warmly. "I guess that explains these." She pointed to a chest in the corner of the room.

The residents of Moy and its village hadn't even met Gwenyth, yet each day one of them brought another gift for "the laird's wee wife"—herbal tea, a ribbon for her hair, a pastry to tempt her appetite.

They gave, these people who had so little, to a stranger.

To Adam's wife.

"Da wants to meet you—says it's a sorry day when he can't meet his own daughter-in-law."

"Aye, well, I'm not much company just now. Soon."

"Just what I told him." Adam smiled, thinking of his father's frustration at being an invalid. Did Gwenyth share the feeling? "Mother thought perhaps you would enjoy going downstairs today."

"That is very thoughtful. I am ready for a change of scenery, I think. But I have nothing to wear save the dress I came here in." A shadow passed over her face. "I asked your mother to fetch it but she said I must ask you."

Her expression was puzzled.

Adam cleared his throat. "I hope you weren't fond of that dress, because I burned it."

"Burned it?" And then just the inkling of a smile graced her lips. "You burned that dress."

"Aye. I hated that dress and what it reminded me of and thought mayhap you'd feel the same—"

Now her smile lit her face and she held out her hand to him. He walked closer and took her hand in his.

Her eyes sparkled with tears as she looked up at him. "That is quite possibly the kindest thing anyone has ever done for me, Adam."

Uncomfortable with the emotions swirling about them, he cleared his throat again and dropped her hand. "Good, then. I'm glad you aren't angry. I will ask Mother to find you something appropriate to wear so you may join us in the main hall for the midday meal. If you feel up to it."

"I do."

"Then I will return for you shortly."

EIGHT

A BEAUTIFULLY WOVEN TAPESTRY depicting scenes from the Old Testament adorned the wall facing Gwenyth. Smaller weavings hung between the two narrow window openings, shuttered now against the morning mist. They reminded her of the needlework she'd been working on the day her father was killed. Of Daniel in the lion's den. Edward and Daron—all of it came crashing back, strengthening her resolve.

It would take time to heal, and heal she must. For the immediate future, she would put aside her need for vengeance and give her mind and body the gift of time. She would be no good to Daron or Edward otherwise. Still, she was gratified that Adam continued to seek Daron's whereabouts.

Gwenyth ran her hands down the gown Eva had given her. Not a servant's dress, but a lovely kirtle with a surcoat of green wool that complemented Gwenyth's coloring. It was worn but serviceable, and Gwenyth was grateful for the older woman's kindness. Grateful as well for Adam's thoughtfulness.

Tears stung Gwenyth's eyes. Emotions still sat near the surface, ready to overwhelm her at the slightest provocation. Still, she felt stronger, much stronger, than she had in days.

Even when she despaired of ever feeling truly normal again, she trusted Adam, knew he would not hurt her or let any harm come to her. His constancy provided much needed consolation and joy to her tattered spirit.

But as mind and body healed, she saw all too clearly that her obligations to Adam and her need for revenge were on a grievous collision course with destiny.

A knock at the open door startled Gwenyth. She turned to see Adam enter the room. Did her face betray how very glad she was to see him?

Adam said, "You look well, Gwenyth."

"Thank you, my laird. But looks are deceiving—I was afraid to stand to greet you for fear I'd topple over."

His smile warmed and his gaze traveled over her. "I'm glad you feel well enough to leave your room."

He moved to offer his arm, but she drew back.

"You needn't fear me, Gwenyth."

"I'm not afraid." Not of Adam's touch, but of her wish to have him hold and comfort her.

"I understand—even under the best of circumstances a maid is often reluctant to accept a husband's touch." He smiled, a smile to warm the most frightened heart. And her unfaithful heart basked in its glow even as she chastised herself for accepting his solace.

Keeping the subject light, she said, "How do others manage, then?"

He reached for her hand, and she allowed him to take it as he answered, "They take time to know each other, to become comfortable in each other's company."

"But we don't intend to remain together, my laird."

He cocked his head to one side. "Perhaps we'll change our minds. Regardless, Gwenyth, I would help you overcome your fears."

"My fears?"

"I would teach you to trust again."

She pulled her hand from his. "Why?"

He shrugged. "You saved my life." He glanced about, his eyes not lighting anywhere for long, his hands absently straightening a fold in his plaid. "I should have taken you to my room that night and protected you." He stepped closer. "I'd like to make it up to you somehow."

Gwenyth was moved by his offer and terrified at the same time. It would be much safer to keep distance between them. She must not forget that in the warmth of his smile lay a man loyal to her father's enemy. As her strength and health returned, so did her determination to exact revenge on Scotland's king.

Yet Adam's affection and obvious sincerity were difficult to resist, and his generous heart called to newly awakened longings.

He took a deep breath and looked away from her. When his gaze returned to meet hers, he said, "I can never replace what was stolen from you, lass. No one can. And I can't promise that we will remain married beyond the year I pledged. I have duties—responsibility to my clan—"

"I understand, Adam. You promised me safety. 'Tis what I crave just now. As to your offer to help me trust again, you have already done more than most men would have in such a situation. I thank you."

He studied her, as if to determine the truth of her words. "You will not press me to make the marriage binding?"

Gwenyth stifled her assurance, reminding herself that a servant girl, as he believed her to be, would be only too willing to achieve such a marriage. She must blame her reluctance on her ordeal, not a difficult part to play, by any means.

"Nay, my laird. We were forced together, and I don't want a man who doesn't want me. Truth be told, I don't ever want to be touched again." The shiver of revulsion that traveled her spine was not feigned in any measure.

"If I cannot find your cousin, you will need a benefactor."

She dare not tell him she had one. In England. "I don't want a husband. Not you. Not anyone." she added hastily.

"Give it some thought, Gwenyth. We might be well suited."

Cautiously she asked, "Why do you think so?"

"We have both suffered from violence. As a result, neither of us will be particularly sought after as a mate."

The statement startled her to the realization that she could hide her trauma, but he could not. And apparently his wound pained him both in body as well as in heart. "But surely you have your position as captain of the federation. There must be any number of women who would welcome a marriage with you."

"Perhaps. But how do they feel about marrying a cripple? Will they look past my wretched arm?"

So, he craved to be loved for who he was, not for the prestige of his position. Obviously his clan loved him, for they had voiced no objection to the marriage, despite the circumstances. But how could they not love and respect a man like Adam? His kindness and generosity were exceptional for one so young. Surely God smiled on him, and Gwenyth struggled with the necessity to keep distance between them.

"Why do you think I will look past those things?"

"Because you judged me in Leod's hall and did not find me wanting."

"I might have been wrong."

"Were you?"

"Nay."

He strode to the window and looked out.

"You don't find me wanting, but you have no desire to accept me as husband." He turned to her, his emotions unreadable. "Why?"

She longed to tell him the truth, all of it, so he would not think her rejection of him was personal. Perhaps part of the truth would be enough. It would have to be.

"Adam, I cannot stay here, no matter how attractive the thought may become. I must join my family. I have obligations—surely you can understand the duties imposed upon a child."

"You are not truly a servant, are you?"

Gwenyth steeled herself not to panic, for if she misspoke now all was lost. Again she must tell half-truths, and it pained her. "Nay, my lord, not really. I am a distant cousin to the Lord of Buchan. My family fell on hard times and so I served at Dalswinton as Lady Joan's maid."

"I thought you must be gently born. You speak too well to be a simple servant. Since you are so determined, I shall redouble my efforts to find your cousin."

"Thank you, my laird." Gwenyth breathed a sigh of relief.

His earlier warmth left him, yet Gwenyth found herself wishing she were free to consider a permanent relationship with him. To cast off all the lies and half-truths that lay between them. To learn what he might teach about tenderness and love. But she was not free, and only pain and heartache could result if she were to forget it. Still, she must depend on this man to help her, and she did very much need someone she could trust.

"Adam, could we not be friends?" It seemed so little to offer, and for a brief moment she wanted more, much more.

An answering desire flickered in his eyes, quickly quenched. "Friends? Friends trust each other, Gwenyth."

"Aye, so they do," she whispered. He was entirely too handsome and kind for her own good.

He turned to leave, then seemed to think better of it. "Mother says you will not receive Father Jerard."

"I have no need of a priest." *Or of a God who deserts me when I need him most.*

"I'm sorry you feel that way. He has helped me deal with my own misfortunes." He studied her before continuing. "Did you, by any chance, learn your letters at Dalswinton?"

"Aye, I can read."

He walked to her and handed her a key. "This unlocks the chest over by the bed."

Without another word, he left the room.

Gwenyth stared at the key in her hand. The chest Adam had indicated was too small to hold clothing but larger than those used to keep jewelry. Shaking her head at Adam's strange behavior, she walked to the chest.

The key to salvation.

Smiling at her fanciful thought, she inserted the key into the lock and heard a click as it opened. Lifting the latch and lid, she gasped at the contents. Books. Two precious books locked away for safekeeping, for they were frightfully expensive.

Her excitement mounted when she saw that in addition to the Holy Bible, which she suspected was Adam's reason for giving her the key, there was also a collection of poetry and French romances. Although plainly bound in wooden boards, the copy work was exquisite.

Eagerly she carried the poetry to sit beside the window where the light was best. She read an enchanting tale by Cretien de Troyes, then thumbed through the parchment pages until she found the work of Rutebeuf and began to read: "God has made me a companion for Job, Taking away at a single blow, All that I had."

She closed the book quickly before her tears could stain the precious pages. She didn't need a reminder of all that she had lost. What she needed, and had found with Adam, was safety. Blindly she replaced the book of poetry and grabbed the Bible. It was not as ornate and beautifully illuminated as the one her family had owned, but it fell open to what had once been one of her favorite passages: "Whither shall I go from thy spirit? Or whither shall I flee from thy presence? If I ascend up into heaven, thou art there: if I make my bed in hell, behold, thou art there."

Once those words had strengthened her heart. But then she'd become Job's companion. She'd lost everyone, and worst of all she'd lost her faith in God's goodness. Clutching the book to her chest, she bent her head and wept.

THE NEXT WEEK PASSED SLOWLY. Adam hadn't mentioned the books or asked if she'd read them. Gwenyth had learned only too well the pain of seeing hopes and dreams dashed to bits by the hand of men. God could not be trusted to protect her. For now, she would rely on someone she could see and touch for her protection. But how long would Adam protect her if he learned her identity?

She walked a dangerous and narrow path between truth and deceit, between friendship and love, trust and betrayal. A chasm yawned on either side, ready to claim her. Despite the tension of living with the threat of being found out, she strove to live each day as it came. Taking what joy she could, ever mindful that disaster loomed.

As the weather improved, the demands on Adam's time increased. His visits became necessarily brief, and they remained wary of each other. And yet he was attentive in other ways, instructing his staff to see she had whatever she needed. Adam did not press her to leave the sanctuary of her room, nor did he suggest again that she receive the priest. Adam stopped by each day, even if only to wish her good morning.

By week's end Gwenyth soon found herself restless, and more

and more she turned to the Bible in the chest. Although she still resented God's apparent abandonment, she took what comfort she could from favorite passages. Grudgingly she began to allow God back into her life, acknowledging that her grief stemmed not from things God had done to her, but from the evils found in men.

Aye, the evils of men. How could a man as kind and accepting as Adam serve a monster like Robert the Bruce? She might be able to forgive Adam for his misplaced allegiance, but she would never forgive Bruce for killing her father.

Always it came back to that. She sighed and picked up her embroidery just as someone knocked on her door. The abrupt sound didn't startle her half as much as the male voice requesting entrance. Adam. Smiling, she quickly pulled a kirtle over her chemise and tied the laces.

"Come in, my laird."

He entered, leaving the door open behind him, and she glimpsed a man-at-arms guarding the door. Her heart seemed to beat in her throat. Had Adam discovered her true name and posted a sentry to prevent her escape?

"Gwenyth. You look well today."

He seemed sincere enough. Nothing unusual in his greeting, but why the guard?

Her hands began to tremble. She was a prisoner. Just when she'd started feeling normal again . . .

Adam strode to her, taking her hands. "Gwenyth, what is it?"

Her voice caught, and all she could do was nod at the hallway.

"The guard?" Bewilderment showed in his voice.

How could she explain without revealing too much, without revealing things he mustn't know? She merely nodded.

"You are trembling like a leaf in the wind because I've posted a watchman." He pulled her to him, and she stiffened in his embrace. Still, he held her, stroking her back like he might a kitten. The gentle touch soothed her, as it was meant to do, and the tremors gradually diminished.

"I don't know what has you so agitated, Gwenyth. He isn't there to hold you prisoner, but to make you feel safe."

She couldn't tell if he joked or not and she pulled away, crossing her arms on her chest. "Am I in danger?"

He walked to the hearth and poked at the fire. "You can't remain hidden in this chamber forever. I thought that having a companion to watch over you would ease your spirit." He turned to face her. "I can't be with you all the time—you are going to have to learn to trust others as well as me."

Did he truly have no suspicions about her? Was he offering freedom and not imprisonment? His generosity and thoughtfulness touched her. She must find Daron and leave, before her need for this man outgrew her need to fulfill family obligations, obligations that were fast fading in importance the longer she dwelled in Adam's home.

"Gwenyth?"

She brought her wandering thoughts and hammering heart under control. "Aye?"

"If you aren't ready to leave the room, you may request whatever you need to make use of your time—a loom, sewing materials—"

He was trying so hard to please her. She must leave, before she repaid his kindness with betrayal. "I should like to send a message to my cousin."

"Indeed." He stiffened, and his azure eyes feigned an indifference she doubted he felt. "And just where shall I deliver this message?"

She softened her tone of voice. "My laird, I am completely at your mercy. I have wronged you and pray your forgiveness. Neither of us wanted this marriage, so the sooner I am gone from here the better. Do you agree?"

He hesitated. "I agree."

"Daron and I decided upon a meeting place, should we become separated."

"You let me search for him knowing all the while where he is?"

"I don't know he's there for certain—he could be injured or . . ." Her voice wavered, but she refused to believe Daron was dead. "I wanted him to have a safe refuge until I was able to travel. Now that I am well, you can send for him, and I can be gone, no longer a burden to you."

"You don't think he deserted you and headed for England?"

She straightened, offended at the thought. "Never. Neither of us would leave Scotland without the other." The thought that Daron might be dead was simply unbearable. Of this she was certain—her kinsmen would not desert her, not if they valued their lives.

Belatedly she realized that such an assertion would give Adam reason to wonder that Daron would be so loyal to a servant. Indeed, he appeared to speculate as he replied, "Then we must hope his health is good. Your cousin is a man of his word?"

"Aye, he is as honorable as you."

He angled his head as if weighing her words. It seemed this man did not make decisions in haste.

"How can I be certain you won't send me into a trap of Leod's making?"

His words stung and her voice reflected her ire. "You think I would send you—a man who, however unwillingly, married me and promised me safety—you think I would betray you to the man who . . . ?"

The ring he had placed on her finger caught her eye. She thrust the hand in front of her, her voice raised. "You who are so devout in your vows—you should understand that I pledged *my* loyalty, and I will not go back on my word."

Her words rang off the walls, hanging there between them like a gauntlet thrown in the dirt. She watched his face for some sign of his feelings. The slow smile that crept upon his features caught her by surprise.

"My lady, you state your case most eloquently. It would seem we must trust each other, then, if we are to be rid of each other."

"You jest with me."

His face became more serious. "Nay, Gwenyth, I do not. I'm sorry I doubted you. You have no reason to betray me to Leod, but what of this cousin? I know him not. And now you tell me where he may be, after all our searching . . ."

His caution was admirable, if maddening. "Only let me send to him, my laird. 'Tis time. I am well now and ready to travel."

Again he was silent, his expression one of deep contemplation. "How did Leod capture you?"

The abrupt shift of his thoughts caught her momentarily off-guard, but she recovered quickly. "Daron and I and our escort were on our way to Inverallochy to meet the ship that would transport us to England."

"To take refuge there?"

"Aye, along with others who remain loyal to Balliol."

He speared her with a sharp look. "Balliol? You remain loyal to Balliol? Even now?"

She stared at him, wondering what sort of trap he might spring. "I would give my loyalty where it is returned, my laird. King Robert has taken away our lands and home—we have no refuge from persecution in our homeland. And few kinsmen to protect us."

"You could rebuild your life, switch your allegiance, and serve Bruce instead. He is very forgiving."

She nearly gave it all away with a bitter reply. Instead she answered, "I would be an outcast from my loved ones if I did. I have lost enough."

He nodded as if he understood the ties of family only too well. "You are certain Daron and his men haven't gone on without you?"

"I believe they will wait for me. As I told you, I served Lady Comyn, staying behind to nurse her through her final illness." That much was true at least. She had stayed with her mother, promising her to flee to England and take the Comyn's claim to the throne with her. Within weeks of her mother's burial, Bruce had burned Dalswinton, and Gwenyth had fled to Ruthven just ahead of his army. Then she and Daron had watched Ruthven burn before setting out for England so Gwenyth could keep that promise. Now she must find a way to get to England, and this man could be either a help or a hindrance. The longer she remained at Moy, the more likely he would become the latter.

"Lady Comyn, widow of Red Comyn." He regarded her thoughtfully, and Gwenyth fought to breathe normally.

How many lies could she tell and still hope for Adam's forgiveness when the truth finally came to light? All the more reason to be gone.

"Aye." *My mother and the father your king killed.* Remembering Bruce made it much easier for Gwenyth to harden her heart toward this man who supported Bruce's monarchy.

"So where do think this cousin of yours may be?"

"Now 'tis my turn to trust, is it not? You won't harm him?"

"I will not. I give my word."

"They are most likely hidden at Altyre."

His eyes grew wide. "On my own lands?"

Her head came up in defiance. "They are Comyn lands, taken from the rightful owners and given to you as reward." She prayed her belligerence marked her as a very loyal servant, and not a member of the family.

"As you say." Again he seemed to weigh her words. She feared he would take days to make up his mind, but he surprised her.

"I'll send your message."

"Thank you, my laird."

He made as if to reply but turned and strode from the room.

Gwenyth watched him leave, knowing that no matter what she did, stay or leave, in the end she would be forced to betray the trust growing between them. For one weary moment, she considered telling him the truth, now, before someone else did. But the truth would hurt him far more than her lies.

Gwenyth sat on the stool, head in her hands. The past weighed heavy on her, promises and plans. Plans that might very well plunge Scotland into civil war as Bruce's followers clashed with Balliol's. Promises Gwenyth had made to others, to further their ambitions and to seek revenge. Bloodshed. Fear.

And promises made to Adam. Healing. Trust.

If only Daron would rescue her before her conflicting loyalties destroyed all she held dear.

NINE

Gwenyth awoke to what appeared to be early morning light coming through the narrow winnock of her chamber. Memories of her conversation with Adam yesterday weighed upon her, and today did not bode to be much better. Shaking off her dark mood, she resolved to create a new needlework design this day. Perhaps the creative endeavor would salve her melancholy spirit.

She finished dressing. Her maid was about to comb her hair when a knock sounded on the door, and Gwenyth bid them enter. But it wasn't the Lady Eva who came through the door. And this raven-haired woman with the haughty expression could not be mistaken for a serving girl.

Indeed, the woman dismissed the servant with a curt nod. Was this Adam's sister? He'd spoken of his sisters, but Gwenyth had yet to meet them as they lived some distance away with their husbands. She laid down the comb the maid had hastily pressed into her hands and stood.

"Good day, my lady," Gwenyth said.

The other woman stared, her cold blue gaze clearly unfriendly. "I'm not a lady of the house," the other woman snarled. "I'm Nathara, the healer."

Still struggling with the woman's evident hostility, Gwenyth replied evenly, "Then 'tis you I must thank for the medicines Lady Eva has used."

"No need to thank me. Eva saw to you herself."

Yes, and Adam had distinctly said he trusted no one but his mother for the task. Why hadn't the healer been called upon to care for her? Confused and fearful of the woman's intent, Gwenyth looked to the still open door in hopes the guard would come and make this woman leave.

Nathara closed the door before Gwenyth could call out to him. Nathara ran her gaze over Gwenyth, eyeing her from head to toe, and her discomfort increased. She dared not let her fear show, and putting on an air of bravado she said, "Why do you come to my chamber uninvited?"

"To see what manner of woman has taken Adam from me."

The woman's words caught Gwenyth at a disadvantage. "I don't understand."

"He was to marry me."

"Oh." Adam hadn't mentioned a betrothal as one of his objections to marrying her. Had he?

"We had not yet announced our betrothal, but we are very close," Nathara declared.

"I see." But she didn't see. "What is it you want with me?"

Nathara's irritation came across quite clearly. "You're handfasted with him, aren't you?"

"If you know of the marriage, then you must also know it was forced upon us. As soon as I am able, I will leave."

Eyes flashing, Nathara said, "Adam has some ridiculous notion that he is bound by his vows to you." Once again she looked Gwenyth over. "But I can see I needn't worry. He'll forget such foolishness and return to me soon enough."

No doubt Nathara hoped to drive Gwenyth away by disclosing

her closeness with Adam. Indeed it did strengthen Gwenyth's resolve to leave. Until then she would keep a close watch on Nathara, for this woman embodied all the hatred between their two clans.

"I have need of Adam's protection, Nathara." That was all she needed or wanted from him. Yet some perverse part of her was reluctant to admit such to the woman.

Nathara raised her chin. "You will not keep him."

Goading the woman was not a good idea. But Gwenyth doubted anything she said would satisfy Nathara. "Perhaps not. But until the time allotted, he is my husband, and I will accord him all loyalty."

Nathara's gaze nearly crackled with heat. "He would be a fool to keep you. And Adam is not a fool." With that she withdrew, leaving Gwenyth to breathe a sigh of relief as she dropped onto the stool she'd left earlier.

Nathara's instincts were correct—Gwenyth and Adam would not truly be man and wife. Even were she willing, her betrayal and deceit would soon close that door. This was just as well, for she hoped to leave Castle Moy in the coming weeks, by God's grace.

THE SPRING PLANTING was well under way and the lambing nearly over. As he finished his morning rounds, overseeing the work of those who kept the castle fed and clothed, Adam breathed a sigh of relief. Relief that was quickly replaced by anxiety as he remembered that today was grievance day. The day when the laird sat in judgment to settle differences among the folk.

He'd attended many of these quarterly sessions over the years, sitting next to his father. But today he acted as laird in Angus's place, and he prayed for wisdom as he settled various disputes— someone's pig had trampled a new garden, a dog had attacked a child, and the owner refused to tie it up.

Several couples, accompanied by smiling parents, asked permission to marry. All in all, a satisfying day's work and easily handled. By late afternoon the cases dwindled and Adam rose to stretch. Bracing his hands on the lintel above the fireplace, he stared into the newly lit fire and counted his blessings.

Scuffling feet and a male voice raised in anger let Adam know he'd started counting too soon.

He turned to face the entrance as James Mactavish and his daughter walked slowly toward him. The girl leaned on her father's arm, her face averted except for a pain-filled glance at the young man following them. Gavin Shaw moved to her side, but James batted him away with a snarl.

The boy clenched his jaw and his hands twisted his bonnet into an unrecognizable shape. A moment of pure defiance flitted across Gavin's face before he regained control. And then his features dissolved into anguish.

Alarmed at the woman's condition, Adam motioned for Morogh to bring a bench for Tyra. She couldn't be more than fourteen or fifteen, but her face appeared old beyond its years. What manner of evil brought her here today?

Gavin was several years older than Tyra, and if memory served Adam, the two were courting.

And James didn't approve. That explained the animosity between the two men, but not Tyra's demeanor. She appeared as cowed as Gwenyth that day he'd brought her to Moy. Adam hoped his suspicions would prove false, but all the signs were there.

As Morogh helped Tyra to the seat, Adam noticed her bruised eye. She seemed to be in a world of her own making, barely aware of her surroundings. Adam locked gazes with Morogh, and he knew his own scowl matched the older man's.

"Fetch my mother, Morogh." As the man moved off, Adam

motioned for James and Gavin to approach. James was nearly bursting with indignation and scowled at his laird. Gavin had eyes only for Tyra.

Fearing he knew only too well the answer, Adam asked the girl's father, "What has happened to Tyra?"

"Look at her," James bellowed. "Can ye not see the *ghaoil's* been mistreated?" He grabbed Gavin, who did not resist, and shoved him forward. "And here's the beast that done it."

Gavin shook his arm free of James's hold and looked Adam straight in the eye. "I did not harm her. Never. Please, my laird. She needs a woman. She needs—"

"I ken what my own daughter needs, and it isna you," James roared.

A muffled sob from Tyra brought all three men's attention to her. Gavin went to her, fending off James's blows as the enraged father tried to pull the boy away.

"Enough, James," Adam ordered.

The man had the good sense to calm himself, to Adam's relief.

Gavin sat next to Tyra, and she curled into his arms, clinging tightly to him. Gavin crooned words of comfort as the girl sobbed quietly.

Just as Gwenyth had dampened Adam's sark with her tears on the ride to Moy. Perhaps he should have told Morogh to bring Gwenyth as well, for she would understand how the girl felt. But he thought better of it, wanting to protect Gwenyth from unpleasant memories. Adam would spare her such pain and instead, use what he'd learned from her to help Tyra.

But first, he must find a way to prove Gavin's innocence; the boy simply wasn't capable of such behavior. "It's obvious the boy cares for her, and she for him, James. Why do you accuse him?"

"He's been sniffing about since before she came of age."

"Has he asked to marry her?"

"Aye."

"Is she willing?"

"To marry? Aye. But I said she must wait, and being a good colleen, she's denied him, and so he took what he wanted. I'll not let her marry—"

"Da." Tyra's voice barely cut through her father's rhetoric. She had regained control of herself, although she still clung to the young man beside her.

"Silence, daughter."

Adam could see he must settle this quickly, before James ruined his relationship with his daughter and forced her to choose between him and Gavin. "James, why don't you simply have them marry? 'Tis the usual way these things are done."

"Would you give your daughter to a man who would force her? Ach, yer too young to understand."

Adam shook his head. James wasn't thinking straight or he'd remember Gwenyth's troubles. But Adam would not remind him. Surely it couldn't help a woman's recovery if people dragged out the telling of her ordeal on every occasion. Best to stay with the problem at hand.

"Why are you so sure young Gavin is guilty?"

"Who else could it be? He took what she wouldn't—"

"Da." Tyra's voice was stronger this time. "Gavin did not do this."

"Then who did?" her father demanded. "Name him."

Tyra looked to Adam. "He wore a mask."

Before Adam could reply, James said, "A likely story, to deflect the blame from this man you claim to love."

Adam watched as Tyra clutched Gavin's hand. The lad entreated her with his eyes and shook his head.

Tyra raised her hand to his cheek. "Aye, Gavin." She stood with

CIRCLE OF HONOR

his aid, and Adam saw her draw on an inner strength, much as he imagined Gwenyth had done when facing Leod that day.

Gavin shook his head once again, but she ignored him, giving her attention to Adam. "My laird, Gavin would take the blame rather than have me dishonor my father."

"Hush. No more, Tyra," Gavin begged.

She straightened, staring at her father. "He has no need to take what I would willingly give."

James sank down on the bench beside his daughter as realization dawned.

Adam understood how it felt to be falsely accused and he admired the young man for accepting the accusation rather than besmirch his lover's name. Once again a wounded woman came to the rescue of an innocent man. His admiration for the female gender rose several notches. God had certainly crowned his creation with a worthy creature.

Adam cleared his throat. "Clearly Gavin would have no cause to beat Tyra—unless he's done so before?"

Mactavish seemed to be absorbing the honor of the boy's intentions. "Nay, he has not," James grudgingly admitted. "Hard to fault a man who would go to such lengths to protect his woman's honor," he muttered, his anger noticeably abated. "But you shouldna have touched her without the priest."

Relieved to see the tension ease, Adam asked the couple, "Aye, that must be remedied. Are you willing to marry?"

"Aye," Gavin said without hesitation.

In a voice so low Adam barely heard her, Tyra asked, "You still want me? After what has happened?"

"Aye, I do."

Did Tyra feel less desirable, less lovable? Unworthy? And more to the point, did Gwenyth suffer similar doubts?

107

Adam remained thoughtful as he said, "Then, when Tyra is ready you shall." He turned to James. "They will marry—as laird I order it done as soon as Tyra feels up to it."

James said, "As you wish." He gazed tenderly at his child. "I'm sorry for my temper, lass."

Tyra smiled for the first time in these proceedings. "Yer forgiven, Da."

Adam thought it likely that even though Tyra and Gavin would struggle for a time, the support of family and friends might soften the blow.

Tyra laid a hand on his arm. "Could we marry now?"

Gently Adam inquired, "So soon?"

She nodded. "I have need of comfort only Gavin can give me." She regarded her father with a tender smile, and after a brief hesitation, James nodded in scowling acquiescence.

Adam patted James on the back, relieved the older man had come around. Morogh had returned with Eva. "Tyra, go with my mother. She can tend to you before you see the priest. We'll have a wedding before this night is done."

Somewhat subdued, James said to Gavin, "I'm still angry with you for not waiting for the vows. But you'll have to answer to God on that, not me. If you swear you love the lass, I'll not object to you as Tyra's husband."

Gavin appeared visibly relieved. "I do love her, Mr. Mactavish, more than I can say. It would grieve me to come between you and Tyra. I will ask God's forgiveness for loving her without his blessing."

"Aye, well then. Ye best take good care of my daughter." James offered his hand, and Gavin shook it, the bargain sealed.

Adam relaxed. He need not fear for Tyra and Gavin. But he renewed his vow to catch the animal who was ravishing Chattan women.

James and Gavin spoke civilly to one another, if not warmly, while they waited for Tyra. And Adam had reason to hope they would overcome today's heated words in time.

Eva and Tyra returned, and Morogh reported that Father Jerard had gone north to tend a parish there and might not return for weeks. So Adam administered the handfast vows, vows that would bind them until a proper marriage could be arranged. Vows as binding, for a year and a day, as any words by a priest.

The very vows Adam had spoken with Gwenyth.

Adam didn't envy Gavin the task of helping Tyra heal. The boy would need patience.

But at least his wife loved him.

Did Adam want Gwenyth to love him? Her strength of character and temperate disposition would make her an excellent wife for the laird of a fractious clan. Aye, it would please him if she could come to care for him—to care for him as he feared he was coming to care for her.

That revelation drove Adam from the small group of celebrants to the solitude of the parapets. Standing high above the earth, he allowed the stillness of the night to seep into him and soothe him.

The days were growing longer as summer approached. By midsummer's eve, there would only be a few hours of darkness each night. He thought of midsummer three years ago, when he'd first answered Bruce's call to fight. When he'd still had full use of his arm and had taken life for granted.

Like many highlanders, Adam had participated in occasional cattle raids, some of which had met with violence when the kine's owners objected to the lifting of their property. Methven had been his first battle, but Dalry had been his first taste of battle against fellow highlanders where the stakes had gone well beyond ownership of a few cows. And even if he'd returned home whole, he would never thirst for combat again.

Sweat broke out on his forehead as he recalled the sight of horses and men falling—the sounds of their screams and the smell of blood. Gordon's face as his horse went down. The shock of the blow to his shoulder, and how he'd fought on despite the pain. The misery of knowing then, and afterward, that his night of celebration had cost the life of a friend and nearly cost the lives of his king and queen.

By all that was holy, he would do whatever it took to avoid such bloodshed again, not only for himself, but also for his clan. God had spared his life, and Adam firmly believed that he had done so for a purpose. To that end Adam had honored his vows of chastity and refusal of strong drink. In time God's purpose would be revealed.

As his memories receded, Adam became aware of his surroundings. Twilight settled over the loch as he gazed at this land he called home. From this spot on the castle battlements, he could see much of the shoreline.

The noise from the adjacent village did not reach him here, and all Adam could hear was the chirping of crickets and the night calls of birds.

A gentle breeze soothed him, bringing with it the rich smell of water and loam. Newly planted fields and a faint whiff of early blooming honeysuckle completed the scents of late spring.

Away in the distance, a calf bawled for its mother. Her answering call assured Adam the young one was safe.

The ordeal with James Mactavish had sorely tried Adam's patience, but he was pleased with his handling of the problem and with the outcome. Morogh had pulled him aside and praised him, saying Angus himself couldn't have done better. Though Adam was uncomfortable with the comparison, he took pride in the compliment.

Aye, imperfect as he was, God loved him, had blessed him far beyond what he deserved. God had forgiven him; maybe the time had come to forgive himself.

As the sights and sounds of the night drifted to him, Adam knew peace and contentment such as he hadn't felt in months. He rested his hands on the cool stone of the wall and closed his eyes, letting the breeze and God's presence wash over him.

After all she'd been through, would Gwenyth ever find such peace? Could she find it here, surrounded by strangers and reminded constantly by his very person of her ordeal?

Approaching footsteps intruded, but he ignored them, hoping they would turn away.

They didn't.

"Adam?"

Nathara.

He didn't want to hurt or offend her, but neither did he want her company. He hung his head, then realized his mistake when she began to massage his shoulders and neck. Her familiarity chafed him, but he held his tongue.

Nathara leaned closer and her chest grazed his back. "I doubt your wife does this for you—she doesn't touch you at all, does she?"

Adam shrugged her hands away and twisted about to face her. "Enough. My relationship with Gwenyth is none of your concern."

"She's afraid of you, the silly woman. I can see it in her." She sidled closer. "But I'm not," she purred.

He moved away. "What do you want from me?"

Flicking her finger at his sleeve and pouting prettily, she answered, "I should think that is obvious."

He blew out his breath. "Aye, there's nothing subtle about you, is there?" Even her vivid coloring—blue-black hair and ice blue eyes set against pale skin—set her apart as a creature to be reckoned with.

"Not a thing," she crooned, rubbing against him again.

Gently he set her aside. "I have a wife, Nathara. What you tempt me with is wrong."

"What good is a wife who won't share your chambers?" Softening her tone, she wheedled, "You have needs, Adam. And I can satisfy them."

A moment of weakness assailed him, but it departed as quickly as it came, and so did temptation. Perhaps the hours he'd spent in prayer had done some good.

When he didn't respond, Nathara demanded, "What do you see in her?"

A very good question.

But the answer came easily. He saw a beautiful woman who, in unguarded moments, looked at him with longing, as if she wished their situation could be different. He saw a soul in need of healing. A woman he could love, were he brave enough to claim her.

His ambivalence toward her was driving him crazy. He wanted her to go. But he wanted her to stay.

"What do you see in her, Adam?" Nathara repeated.

"'Tis not your concern. The woman is my wife, and I'll not dishonor my vows." No matter if they were for a year and a day, a lifetime, or only until he found her cousin. The depth of his commitment surprised him. He might not be sure what he felt or what he should feel about Gwenyth, but one thing he knew for certain. He would never betray his vow to protect her.

"You are a fool," Nathara spit out.

"That may be so. But I am also your laird, and you'll not speak to me in that manner again."

They glared at one another, and finally she backed down.

"As you wish, my laird."

She walked away, and the provocative swing of her hips told

him this battle wasn't over. He didn't believe for a minute that Nathara would cease her campaign to seduce him. He shook his head. It had been a long day, and he craved the peace he'd found fleetingly before Nathara's interruption.

Adam looked out over the loch, allowing the sights and sounds to color his world once more. As his spirit calmed, he bowed his head and prayed, seeking comfort and guidance.

When he finished and opened his eyes, a full moon rose over the water and with it the promise of the circles and seasons of life and love.

A time to embrace, and a time to refrain from embracing.

Adam smiled as moonlight, peace, forgiveness, and hope washed over him.

TEN

A FULL MOON bathed the landscape with silvery radiance on a rare clear night, beckoning Gwenyth to leave the confines of her room. Grateful for the guard who accompanied her, she walked the parapet, wrestling with her chaotic thoughts.

Generally, when she made up her mind, she was not easily swayed to alter her course. But as a result of her stay in Leod's hall, she no longer trusted her feelings or her judgment. The only thing she knew for certain was that she wanted to leave Moy.

But even that thought was a lie. For despite her fear of intimacy with Adam or any man, a part of her wanted to stay, to know this gentle yet fierce man better. To see if her fascination with him was substantive or only fleeting.

Perhaps it was nothing more than gratitude for his kindness, his willingness to help her heal. Yes, that must be it. She mustn't confuse gratitude with affection. She knew little enough of that emotion, for only Daron's devotion had been a constant in her life. Too many others had feigned friendship and love when all they were interested in was her royal blood and how it might further their ambitions.

She could depend on no one, not even Daron. Even as her frustration rose at his inability to protect her, she prayed for his good health. For without him she couldn't hope to end this marriage to Adam, and end it she must.

Adam seemed to have forgiven her for accusing him of the assault, but even if so, what kind of marriage could they contrive? Once he learned of her parentage, any possibility of a lasting union would be dashed.

Marriage. How could she bear to suffer a man's touch? She could never allow it. Ever. Unless . . . Perhaps . . . Adam's touch was gentle, and his kind heart gave promise. But it could not be.

Marriage to Edward and the royal house of Balliol awaited. Her children would be the future wives and husbands of the rulers of Europe. Perhaps even king of Scotland.

Children.

The conception of children required certain duties. Eventually, she supposed she would have to endure those duties in order to conceive these royal heirs.

For a moment she wished she hadn't sent the message to Daron. Scotland and Adam appealed far more than England and a man whose caress might not be as tender, who wouldn't croon words of comfort in the Gaelic of her childhood as her father had.

Papa. His death had shaken her world.

As had Adam, in a different way, with his warm smile and gentle soul. In any other time and place she could have easily loved him.

Gwenyth gave herself a mental shake. Foolish fantasies. It must be the moonlight playing with her, agitating her with such senseless notions. Gwenyth glanced to where her escort stood at the far end of the narrow walkway. As she was about to wave him toward her, the murmur of voices told her others had taken advantage of the beautiful evening. Wishing to avoid interrupting a tryst, she turned the corner, away from the guard.

Within moments, she heard footsteps behind her. The man

couldn't have reached her so quickly. She ducked into a crenelation, hiding in the shadows as Nathara whisked past, anger and frustration clear in each step. Gwenyth breathed a sigh of relief at avoiding a confrontation with the woman. To be safe, Gwenyth remained hidden to ensure she wouldn't encounter her.

From her hiding place, she watched the moon play tag with the mist rising from the loch. The sight captivated her, and it was several minutes before she stepped back into the moonlight. She collided with a huge, male body.

Slow-witted guard.

The collision nearly sent her crashing into the wall, but strong hands set her upright and a familiar voice said, "What are you doing here at this time of night?"

Adam and Nathara. Had he sent her away because of Gwenyth? Or was there truly something between them? He stood just inches away, hands resting lightly on her shoulders, while she stared and struggled to speak. Words wouldn't come.

Moonlight silvered his hair, and his skin shimmered as if lovingly caressed by individual moonbeams. The planes of his face acquired stronger definition from the shadows, and his eyes captured the very color of the moon's luminescence. Long-limbed and well-muscled, he was altogether too handsome.

Out of nowhere came the unshakable conviction that the God she thought had abandoned her had brought them together for a reason, that theirs was no chance meeting. Had she, through an act of self-preservation, unwittingly bound herself to the one man whom heaven had chosen for her?

Nay. That can't be.

Perhaps she was to help him in some way, as he had helped her. She had saved his life and he had given her refuge. Surely their purpose was accomplished and she was free to pursue her plans for the future.

He removed his hands and waved her guard away. Turning back to her he asked, "Lady Gwenyth, are you all right?"

She shivered, pulling her *arasaid* closer about her shoulders. "Aye, my laird. I . . . you frightened me." And indeed it was true, but not because they'd bumped unexpectedly. "I could not sleep and came out for some air."

He stared at her, as if he thought she might reveal a secret.

Then she remembered Nathara and knew he had been with her. *Why were you with Nathara at all? And why do I care?* "I should go in; it grows late."

"You must be glad to leave your room."

"Aye," she agreed, all the while wishing she could escape his presence by returning to that very sanctuary. She raised her gaze to meet his and found him regarding her closely.

"I sent word to Daron."

"Thank you, my laird."

He continued to study her as they faced each other on the narrow passage. He blocked her way to her room, and she grew increasingly uncomfortable in his presence. She wished he would have his say and let her retire. But apparently he was not one to rush into anything.

Finally he spoke. "Why do I believe that your gratitude will exact further price?"

She looked into his eyes and immediately regretted it. There was no mistaking the warmth that resided there.

Gwenyth broke eye contact. "What price?"

He looked out over the castle wall, and she studied his profile, watching in fascination as he masked his emotions. "You will leave as soon as arrangements can be made?"

"Aye."

He faced her, his expression unreadable. "I could hold you to the full term of our agreement—a year and a day."

"That would not be wise," she whispered, wondering why he would want to keep her, and fearing that he would do just that.

"Nay, it would not."

She could swear she heard regret in his speech. "Then we must hope Daron arrives quickly."

ADAM COULDN'T EXPLAIN WHY her offer to leave didn't cause his spirits to lift. One less obstacle to his tenure as the Chattan chief. One less problem with which he must deal.

She seemed so calm and controlled; her face betrayed no emotions. But her gaze penetrated his very soul. She was at once frightening and intriguing. He appreciated her offer to leave, to sever this unwanted relationship. But he was drawn to her, to her fire and intensity, to her deep, mysterious beauty. To the fragile vulnerability she tried to hide.

A time to embrace. This was not such a time. But could that time come? Had God brought her here, not just to be healed, but to heal?

He feared he was staring and shook off this feeling of being spellbound. "You are free to roam the castle grounds, Lady Gwenyth."

She tilted her head. "Why do you call me lady?"

"You are Lady Mackintosh, wife of the laird of clans Mackintosh and Chattan. I would hope you'd take pride in the title, for however long you have it."

"I do, Adam." For his sake, not because she honored his clan.

"Good. When you feel up to it, you have my leave to use my

horses as well, as long as you take your guard or the man Morogh with you for protection."

"You trust me?"

"Where would you go?"

"Aye, where would I go?" Her voice trailed off, and he fought the urge to wrap her in his arms and offer comfort. But she drew her own arms about her. Which was just as well, he reminded himself.

Head bowed, she murmured, "My laird, I fear I have wronged you in more ways than I thought possible."

"What ways, other than lying?"

Her head shot up, and she truly feared him. He didn't like that at all.

Why do you need to find this cousin? Dare you tell me? Does he own your heart? Part of him wanted to demand she tell him it wasn't so. But part of him didn't want to know, didn't want to give her reason to tell another lie. Didn't want an end, even though it was inevitable.

"You and Nathara."

Her answer caught him unaware, and for a moment, he couldn't form a coherent thought.

Recovering he answered, "You have spoken with her?"

"She visited me and made it clear I am not welcome."

"I'll talk with her." He swallowed hard. "Nathara would like to return to my good graces."

"She said you care for her, that you are close, and yet you have turned her away. Because of me."

"Nathara overstates our friendship. 'Tis a matter of honor. Of vows taken and promises made."

"But you made them unwillingly."

"So I did." He rubbed his injured shoulder. "My word is all I have."

Her face lost its calm composure as she touched the damaged arm. "Does it pain you?"

"Only when moved a certain way. But it lacks strength as well as motion."

She withdrew her hand, seeming uncomfortable with the contact. "How long since the injury?"

Relieved to be rid of the subject of Nathara, he replied, "More than a year and a half."

"Dalry?"

He nodded. He told her how he was wounded, even admitting his drunken stupor. What he didn't mention was that he'd been wounded by her kinsman's warriors, although she surely must suspect it.

"So, that is why you drink nothing stronger than watered wine."

"Aye. I may make my share of mistakes as I live out my life, but I won't make that particular one again." Despite these confessions, the silence that followed felt companionable.

Gwenyth broke it. "The wound has had time to knit sufficiently."

"Are you a healer?"

"I have some skill. May I feel the wound, my laird? Perhaps I can help."

What harm could such a slight girl do? "Aye, but let me sit so you can reach."

He made his way to the stairs and sat down on the top one, giving her access to stand below him and thus reach his shoulder more easily. After a moment's hesitation, her hands gently but efficiently probed.

"The bone was broken?"

"Aye. My arm was a mess."

There was no fear in her touch. She grasped the arm and with surprising strength, moved it about to test it. He yelped when she pushed it beyond its limit.

"I'm sorry, Adam. I just wanted to see how well it moved."

"Now you know," he said through gritted teeth.

When her fingers pressed where the sword blade had cut deepest, he winced, determined not to call out again. She stood close and he was aware of her scent, lavender and woman. A groan escaped him as her fingers massaged the tender spot.

Her hands stilled and withdrew, so hastily it was as if she'd touched something hot. "I did not mean to cause you more discomfort. The muscle wasn't severed, my laird. 'Tis a wonder you didn't bleed to death, though. I think if you were to move the arm beyond where it pains you, you might extend the amount of activity it will tolerate."

She must have become uncomfortable with their closeness, because she retreated up the steps even as he rose so quickly he nearly knocked her down.

He steadied himself and reached for her, but she shrank from his touch. Adam wondered if her aversion resulted from the attack she'd suffered, or if she avoided him for some other reason. He softened his voice in an effort to reassure her. "I will try your suggestion."

Although she stepped back, still she pinned him with an unflinching gaze. "You would honor our vows even if you weren't injured."

Not wanting to see the conversation take this turn, he tried to divert her. "How do you suggest—"

"It's true, isn't it? For that is the kind of man you are."

She spoke with such conviction. What had he done to deserve such allegiance?

"You honor me, Gwenyth, with your confidence in my character."

"Then know that while I appreciate your character, I would not deny you Nathara's company, my laird. Since we two are married in name only."

"As it must be."

She nodded. "Oh, aye. It must. Then we are agreed?"

"Agreed on what?"

She looked at him as if he were thickheaded, which of course, was exactly how he was acting in order to prolong the verbal joust and the pleasure of her company.

But when she bowed her head, his enjoyment ceased. He saw her shiver and draw the shawl closer.

He raised his hand, thinking to touch her chin and bring her head up, but at the movement she startled, and he quickly withdrew. "Look at me, Gwenyth."

When she did, he saw pain and confusion in her eyes.

"You need not fear me, Gwenyth. I do not wish to be your enemy, nor to have you cringe at an innocent touch. I know well enough that you'd not welcome any man just now, and rightly so." Shifting his weight, he studied her a moment. "Come, it is late." He followed her down the stairs, escorting her to her chamber.

At the door, he placed his arm across the opening to halt her. "You are safe with me. And I will keep the vows, Gwenyth."

"Why?"

He shrugged. He hadn't told Gwenyth, or anyone else for that matter, about the tavern wench that night in Dalry. But he would never again cheapen that sacred act just to satisfy his needs. "I told you, my word is all I have right now. And to be honest, I was glad for a means to break off with Nathara."

Her eyes grew wide at his confession. And a wisp of a smile caressed her lips.

He forced his features to be stern. "You find that amusing, do you?" By the saints, he wanted to kiss her, to make that smile ripen and bless him. But it would only frighten her and cause him frustration. Because one kiss would not be enough . . .

"Try swimming, my laird."

"What?"

A warm but tentative smile graced her face. "For your arm." With a whispered goodnight, she entered her room, and he breathed a sigh of relief that the encounter was over.

She is your wife, you fool. Why will you send her away?

The question hung in the air, unanswered.

CROUCHED UNSEEN in a corner of the hall, Nathara watched as Adam stared at Gwenyth's closed chamber door.

Unable to hear the conversation, still she'd seen for herself that he slept alone this night. Nathara stormed to her small cottage, cursing Adam and his blasted sense of honor. She'd been so certain there on the parapets that the lure of moonlight and her charms would make him succumb. But instead he'd sent her away.

Then he'd showered his attention on the wench, even allowing her to touch his wounds, the very wounds Nathara had healed. And from her hiding place at the bottom of the stairs, she'd watched Adam stare at her with longing, with hope, with desire. Enough. The wench must be driven from Castle Moy.

ELEVEN

ADAM PAID LITTLE ATTENTION to the food placed before him as the castle inhabitants broke their fast the following morning. Visions of Gwenyth's hair shining in the moonlight, her lovely skin, the way her eyes sparkled, held far more appeal.

"Good morrow, son."

Eva chuckled when he nearly fell off the bench.

He righted himself. "Mother, I didn't see you there."

"Nay, I don't suppose ye did." She examined him before continuing. "When Angus learns ye were walking in the moonlight with yer wife, ye can expect a summons. And I'm warning, he'll not take no for an answer."

"And this walk I supposedly took, 'tis the talk of the keep already this morn?"

Eva grinned. "When her guard returned to his post he found ye outside her chamber, but he wouldn't say if ye were going in or coming out."

Blast the man. "That wee bit of tact is all that stands between him and dismissal."

"Aye, well. Not much happens in this place without someone knowing of it. And, as I said, yer da will hear of it and demand to meet her now she's well enough to leave her room."

"She's not staying—why must he interfere?"

"Because he's yer father."

As if that explained it, Eva took her leave, and Adam made a halfhearted attempt to eat. The summons from his father came before he'd finished his meal. No sense putting it off. His father would badger him until Adam brought Gwenyth to him. He went to Gwenyth's chamber to retrieve her.

She faced him, confused and fearful. "But why?"

"Just humor him, Gwenyth. We both know you'll not be here long enough to make a difference or to give him the grandchildren he's been demanding."

"Don't your sisters have children?"

"Aye, five girls between them. Da says 'tis my duty to give him the grandson."

For a moment, Gwenyth's features were wistful, and the sight warmed Adam. A grandson for Angus, a child for Adam. He stepped toward her, and she retreated swiftly.

"Why do you run from me, little one? I wish you no harm."

"I fear we will forget our promise to separate, Adam. Please, no matter how our feelings may change, it is best if we don't act on them."

Thinking she still feared a man's touch, encouraged by her admission that her feelings toward him were warming, he made no further effort to touch her. Perhaps she would come to care more for him than for her cousin.

Adam smiled. "Well then. We'd best go tell Angus he'll have to wait a bit longer."

THE KNOCK AT HIS DOOR aroused Angus from dozing, and Adam ushered in the woman at his bidding. Angus watched them walk toward him, apprehension written clearly on the girl's face. Adam must have sensed her discomfort, for he leaned down to whisper in her ear. Did the boy care for her, or did he just show empathy to an injured being like himself? An interesting question that begged an answer.

"You may leave us, Adam."

Anger crossed his son's face. "But—"

"Leave us."

Looking none too pleased, Adam gave the girl's hand a squeeze and said something that made her smile before he stalked out of the room, shutting the door a bit harder than necessary.

Angus pushed his son's displeasure aside and indicated the stool beside the bed. "Come, lass. I don't bite."

She gave him a weak smile as she sat on the edge of the stool, head bowed. She'd recovered from the attack, but it angered him to think of such a wee lass being mistreated. "Ah, lassie, ye've had the worst of it, haven't ye? Ye didn't deserve such treatment, and it grieves me that ye've suffered at the hands of Clan Chattan."

"You don't believe in beating women?" she asked, her voice a cross between sarcasm and hopefulness.

He grinned, testing her reaction. "Well now, there may be times a good thrashing is needed."

She raised her head and her features hardened.

"This is not a laughing matter for ye, nor should it be." He paused. "There are better ways to woo a lass."

"Even if the woman is a servant?"

Ah, she had spirit. Good. "'Tis no way to treat any woman." He studied her. "Do ye wish me or mine ill?"

She fiddled with the ends of her belt, twisting them back and forth. "Except for the man who assaulted me, I wish you and yours no harm. But my kinsmen—"

"Yer kin served those who oppose Robert the Bruce. And they've paid dearly."

"With their lives."

"Aye, and the suffering of their kin." As he approached death, Angus saw more clearly that the sins of the father were too often visited on the child. He himself had married an heiress and done all he could to unite two mighty clans. Now Adam would have to deal with the festering dissatisfaction Angus's own actions had brought about. Angus was certain Adam could accomplish this, if only he believed in himself.

"So, lass, where do yer loyalties lie?"

"In England, with my family. And until I join them, with you and your son. I am most grateful for Adam's protection. I shall not remain long, only until—"

"Aye, I know all about yer plans. Do ye truly wish to leave yer home?"

Her back straightened. "I have no home. All has been taken from us."

"If ye have life, ye have all ye need to begin again."

She met his gaze, and the stab of pity in her eyes revealed her knowledge of the gravity of his illness.

"I know I'm dying, lass. 'Tis to yer credit yer face didna light with glee when ye realized it."

She looked away.

Gently he repeated his earlier question. "Do ye truly wish to leave Scotland?"

"In all honesty, my laird, I don't know what I want except to be reunited with my kinsmen." Her eyes glistened as she whispered, "And to feel safe again."

Her pain moved him, and suddenly he felt very old and tired. And useless. He offered his hand. "Come here, lass."

She rose and, standing close, took his proffered hand.

He fought his drowsiness. "I consider myself a good judge of character, and I see strength in ye. Under other circumstances, I would consider ye a good match for Adam."

Her eyes widened in disbelief. "If I weren't a servant, or if I were still a maid?"

He studied her as his weariness tugged at him. "Your innocence was stolen from you, child. I do not hold it against you, nor would Adam or any man worthy of the name." He rubbed his eyes in an effort to rub away the fatigue. "I'm too tired to debate any more today. Come back tomorrow, and we'll talk of this some more."

She seemed about to argue, then thought better of it.

As she turned to leave, he asked, "Do ye by any chance have the gift for storytelling, lass?"

With a puzzled frown, she answered, "I know the old legends, aye."

"Then ye will recite to me after ye've broken yer fast on the morrow."

She regarded him, then rewarded him with a small smile. "As you wish, my laird." The door closed quietly behind her.

A fine day's work, he thought as he drifted off to sleep.

THE DAY BEGAN as all her mornings began of late—waiting for Daron and praying he was well and as anxious as she to be gone. Hoping to help the time pass quickly, she made her way to Angus, only to be turned away from his chamber this morning by an obviously troubled Eva.

"He's worn himself out."

"I am most sorry, Lady Eva. I hope he is soon recovered."

"'Tis in God's hands," she replied and walked away, leaving Gwenyth to wonder if Eva blamed her for the old man's weariness. She had enjoyed the last several mornings with him.

Disappointed at not having Angus's company, Gwenyth retired to her room, resigned to sewing and needlework as a means to pass the time. She took the midday meal there, alone with her thoughts.

A rap on the door signaled the servant's return to remove the tray, and Gwenyth was startled to see Adam standing in the doorway after the girl had gone.

He held his bonnet in front of him, looking for all the world like a petitioner for alms or some other favor. "My lady?"

"Aye?"

"I thought, well, my father thought you might like to ride today."

Gwenyth glanced out the winnock at the bright sunshine, a welcome contrast to the past several days of gloom. A ride and the chance for fresh air would be wonderful.

"I believe my ribs are sufficiently healed. Aye, I should like that very much, especially if you will accompany me."

Adam actually blushed at her words, and Gwenyth suddenly felt more free and at ease than she had in some time.

He tipped his head. "We'll ride outside the castle walls, if you wish."

"That sounds wonderful. I'll need to ask your mother for suitable clothes. And Adam, I prefer to ride astride, if that won't offend you."

"Well, then. So you shall. Meet me at the stables when the sun is straight overhead. I could use some exercise myself."

He turned and left, and Gwenyth called for a maid to help her change into the skirt Eva sent at her request.

Gwenyth met Adam as agreed, and soon a lovely dun mare was

saddled and bridled for her. Gwenyth loved to ride—loved the tangy smell of horseflesh and the gentle sway as they walked. This ride must surely prove more pleasant than her journey to Moy, when she'd been wounded in body and soul. Within moments of crossing the drawbridge, she felt the weight of her situation depart, and her heart lightened.

They rode through the forest and came to an open meadow. Adam seemed disinclined to converse, and she was happy to ride in silence, observing a golden eagle making lazy circles on the air currents, rabbits scurrying for cover, and the fine, sunny day that had emerged from this morning's fog.

The desire to urge her horse to a canter, to fly over the ground and lose her melancholy in the fleet hoofbeats of the animal, came over her. But remembering her companion, she thought better of her impulse. Unhappy with the necessity to placate her keeper, she drew alongside of Adam.

"I should like to canter—will you join me?"

"Nay, lass, go on ahead."

She couldn't believe what she heard. "You trust me, then."

He looked her straight in the eye. "Until you give reason to do otherwise, aye. Go on, I can see you're impatient with this pace. Stay within sight, lass, and I see no harm."

Flashing him her brightest smile, she set her heels to the mare's side and broke free of her worries as the horse flew along the ground. She glanced back and saw Adam gently lope after her. Heeding his words, she circled her horse back around, staying within his view, grateful for this bit of freedom.

When her animal tired, she slowed it to a walk and drew up next to the other horse. They rode up a hill, and reaching the top, she stopped at an overlook of the loch and the castle in its midst.

"This view is even more lovely than the one from the path."

"Aye, it is."

"What is that building there on the smaller island?"

"'Tis a prison."

Gwenyth suppressed a gasp, wondering if that's where he would put her if he learned her identity. Quickly she changed the subject, wishing to leave this place for the relative safety of the keep. "I don't mean to keep you from your duties."

"I can take the time." He pointed ahead. "We'll walk about the loch—cool the horses."

They walked the horses slowly down the hill and around the loch toward the castle entrance. The sun glinted off the water's surface and a cow lowed in the distance, but the lovely setting did nothing to calm her nerves.

Adam cleared his throat. "My father wanted me to thank you for saving my life, Gwenyth. 'Twas a brave thing you did, defying Leod that way without knowing me from, well, from Adam." He grinned, and she felt her heart leap at the beauty of his features.

She must direct their conversation toward duty, both his and hers. "I may have saved your life, but Leod can still use our marriage against you, can't he?"

"Leod will use whatever leverage he can find. But I don't think marriage to a servant will harm me much. They've called a council meeting three weeks from now to vote."

"And you will have to defend yourself—convince them you aren't a rapist."

"Aye." He was quiet a moment. "Best way I could do that is to have a true marriage with the woman who accused me."

Panic welled in her, panic born not in fear of a man touching her, but of this man's healing touch. She schooled her features and voice to portray a severity she did not feel as she exclaimed, "You don't mean that. I'll be gone by then, Adam." She hoped it was true, for the longer she stayed the more she was drawn to him and away from her hatred. Memories of Edward faded fast in the glow of Adam's smile.

"Aye, you'll be gone."

She halted her horse and Adam's mount stopped beside her, so close their knees brushed. "Will they believe you? About the assault, I mean?"

"Some will, some won't."

Adam pointed to a pile of rocks shadowed by shade trees. "Come, there are things you should know."

They dismounted and, being a good horseman, Adam exchanged their bridles for halters. Then he tethered the horses loosely so they could enjoy the lush grass. Adam led her to a place where they sat with their backs to the sun-warmed rocks. A breeze fondled the leaves, making them glimmer in the sunlight. The peaceful setting belied the nervous twitch in her stomach as she wondered what more Adam had to say.

She didn't have to wait long.

"Angus has told you that I was betrothed?"

She nodded. "Aye, he mentioned it the other morning."

"Aye. Suisan, her name was. She was very young, but I was besotted with her. And Angus wanted the alliance to strengthen my claim to be chief. We were to marry when I returned from serving Bruce."

"But you were wounded at Dalry." By her kinsmen. The thought that someone she knew had wounded Adam saddened her.

"Oh, aye." He picked at a cocklebur on his woolen stocking. "I came home more dead than alive. Praise be, Nathara was there to tend me from the start, or I'd be dead, not just maimed."

No wonder Nathara felt possessive of the handsome young

133

laird. She'd saved his life. "Nathara did an excellent job—the muscle has healed well. And I've seen you fight."

Adam raised an eyebrow. "When?"

Gwenyth smoothed her skirt before admitting, "I can see the lists from my room. Even with your arm, you fight better than many men."

He studied her. "You're quick to come to my defense."

"You have earned my admiration."

"Then I'm a lucky man."

Gwenyth felt her face grow warm. She changed the subject. "So, this Suisan withdrew from the betrothal?"

"There was little hope I would survive, and I must have been frightful to look at. Suisan might have honored her promise, given a bit of time, but her uncle married her off quickly."

"And you are convinced she rejected you because you aren't a whole man."

"You don't believe that?"

"Nay, I don't," she said with conviction.

He was quiet for several minutes. "Her uncle is Leod Macpherson."

"Oh. Oh, my. Leod used her to weaken your claim."

Adam lifted his hand from the business with the now banished cocklebur. "Aye, this didn't start with you, Gwenyth. It's been coming for some time."

Gwenyth stared at him, curiosity aroused. "Why are you telling me all of this?"

"Angus wanted you to know."

To know what? A feeling of unease stole over her. The feeling that she stood on the edge of that chasm again and Adam intended to suggest she jump. "For what purpose?"

He squirmed and avoided her gaze.

"Why do I need to know these things about your past?" she gently urged.

"Suisan's defection turned out to be a good thing. Her rejection angered me and gave me a purpose and drove me to become well. For that, I'm grateful to her."

"And what would you have me do?" Another step closer to the edge.

Adam placed his fingers on her chin and raised her face to his. "You have been the victim of violence, as have I. I have prayed about it and I would have you be my true wife. I think we are well-suited."

She pulled away from his touch, even though she knew he wouldn't harm her. But his request was anything but harmless. The chasm seemed to open at her feet. She jumped up, moving away from Adam. "You are asking me to make the marriage real?"

He rose as well, more slowly. After a few moments, moments in which her heart thudded crazily, he asked, "Would that be so awful?"

No. Yes. Her hands fluttered, and she grabbed the material of her skirt to still them. "You are bold, Adam. Have you no care for my feelings?"

"Aye, lass, I do. You've been deeply wounded. The right man could help you heal. I have prayed on it and I believe this may be God's plan for us."

"But—"

"You don't believe that God brought us together for a reason?"

"I . . . yes, I have had that same notion. But I believe he just wants us to heal each other before we part."

"Why? Do you find me repugnant?"

"Nay, of course not. You are not offensive, my laird. I simply cannot be a wife."

"You wouldn't enjoy caring for a home and overseeing the running of this castle?"

"As if your mother would allow it." She found it difficult to harden her heart against him, despite her need to leave and move forward with the plans that Leod had interrupted.

Adam grinned. "Well, that is a difficulty to be handled with care. But she would yield to my wife, did I have one truly."

He untied the horses and gave her the lead to hers. They walked slowly back toward the castle, horses following behind.

"Why are you pursuing this?" she asked. "You know nothing about me."

"I know you've no dowry, you trapped me into handfasting, and, saved my life. You're a poor prospect for a bride, Gwenyth of Buchan. Still, I would know—what if we had met under more auspicious circumstances? What then? Would you still find me repugnant as a husband?"

"You are not repugnant."

"Ah, but I'm scarred and damaged. You would pass me by, no doubt."

She gave him a weak smile. Evidently the earlier rejection by his betrothed still pained him, if he pushed her so to confirm what he so falsely believed about himself. How could he think that no woman would want him? But weren't she and Adam alike in this regard? Hadn't she wondered if Edward would still want her when he learned she was no longer an innocent maid?

Edward with his ambitions—which would be more important to him? Her emotional and physical well-being or her worth as a political pawn?

She looked at Adam, his beautiful hands, the blue eyes and curling blond hair, the handsome features of his face. She would want him if Leod hadn't ruined her very soul with his cruelty. Surely there would be no harm in admitting her own shortcomings in order to save this gentle man's ego.

"Are you searching for a compliment, my laird?"

"I would have the truth."

"You have a fine manly form and a good heart. A normal woman would be a fool to turn you away. But, I—"

Tears welled and she dashed them away, angry that she should lose control when she'd sworn she wouldn't. But here was this wonderful man, hurting every bit as much as she did, no doubt wondering why his charms failed to heal her. But they did heal. They most certainly did.

They stopped walking and he wiped her tears with his thumb. "There now, lass. I'm sorry to make you cry." He pulled her into his embrace, and she allowed it, surprised at how comforting it felt. When she had calmed, he cupped her chin, lifting it until her gaze met his.

"Gwenyth." He caressed her jaw with his thumb. "Surely you know that what happened to you is not how it is when a man and a woman care for each other."

Amazed that he turned away from his own need so easily to tend to her, she said, "I know no such thing."

"Then let me assure you that what you experienced is not natural. It was violent and had nothing to do with tender feelings."

"You are only saying so to convince me to give in to you."

His jaw clenched, and she knew she made him angry. Yet his reply was calm, reproachful. "I will admit that the thought of . . . well, let's just say that the thought of you occupies far too much of my time lately."

She gasped and tried to pull away, but he held her firmly and with care.

"Gwenyth, I would be a fool to give you my heart when you are so set on leaving."

"Give your heart?"

"Ah, dear one. You see, you know nothing of the bond that can be created between lovers."

"Can be? It isn't always so?"

"There is always a bond formed. The question is, how strong and enduring is it? 'Tis a gamble I'll not risk without God's blessing. So, you see, you are safe with me."

If only she could believe that was true.

Gwenyth was touched by his admission of his need to be loved for himself, and not for his title. A need made all the more important for his physical limitations. She wished she could be that woman for him.

Now where had that thought come from? Shaking her head at the absurdity of such a notion, she said, "I have brought you nothing but problems, my laird. We must both pray Daron is soon found."

"I'm not altogether certain I want to give you up."

She swallowed. "You will have to, my lord."

"If you truly cannot abide a marriage with me, so be it. But I ask you to think on it. Perhaps pray on it as well."

Pray on it? "God doesn't hear my prayers anymore." If Adam knew the truth about her, he wouldn't ask this. How much longer could she live the lies? And did she want to? "You want me to stay. But I can't."

"Why not?"

There was no bridge to span the distance between her and Adam. "I've made a promise I must keep."

"To Daron?"

"Aye." And Edward and all those who supported a marriage between them which would unite half of Scotland against Bruce.

"Fine. Go with your cousin. But while you are here, remember you promised me your loyalty." He turned from her and briskly rebridled the horses, then lifted her into the saddle. They rode the short distance to the causeway in silence.

Gwenyth could not believe what she heard in his voice when he spoke of Daron. Anger at her rejection, yes. But surely he'd sounded jealous. Jealous of Daron. Oh, this had gone on long enough. If Daron didn't materialize within the week, she would ask Adam to provide an escort. She must leave Moy before she hurt this man who'd done nothing to deserve it.

Inside the bailey they halted the horses. Adam reached to help her dismount and she fought the urge to avoid his touch. Adam took her elbow, guiding her into the keep. "Come."

She resisted the instinct to pull away from him.

"Since your cousin continues to elude me, you best reconcile yourself to spending a while longer at Moy." He sounded as if he hoped Daron would remain lost. "You will take your meals in the hall from now on."

With that, he strode away from her, taking all the warmth of the day with him. Something about his vulnerability, his need to be accepted, drew Gwenyth. Here was a just man, a well-favored man who, through an unfortunate accident, must prove what he'd always taken for granted. That he could rule his clan.

Her only hope was that Daron would come for her to set sail for England on the next available ship. But the more she considered the meeting between her cousin and her husband, the more she despaired. For then Adam would learn the truth and the depth of her deceit.

His words, the idea that she might remain at Moy, were both a source of comfort and pain. She felt safe with Adam, dared to dream of Moy as her home. Dared to consider that maybe Adam and Moy were God's plan, as Adam said. Until obligations reminded her of the impossibility of such a notion. Her father would roll over in his very grave if she were to swear allegiance to the man who killed him. And that is what marriage to Adam would mean.

She must not forget her father's death at the hands of Robert the Bruce or the terrible carnage Bruce had waged in Buchan. All those deaths and the destruction of her home must not go unanswered. She and Edward would reclaim what Bruce had taken from them. And Robert the Bruce would regret he'd ever set foot in that church.

TWELVE

Gwenyth went to her room to wash and change clothes and bring her emotions under control. How could she possibly accept Adam's daft notion that God had brought them together to be man and wife? If marriage to Adam was part of God's plan, then his timing was all wrong. She and Adam should have met before Edward had made his claim on her.

Why would God pick a man whose clan and king were her enemies? It didn't make sense.

Remembering Adam's order, she made her way to the great hall to eat the evening meal with the rest of the castle inhabitants. She wanted to arrive early, hoping to draw as little attention as possible to herself. A few who were already seated cast glances at her, but most ignored her, and she relaxed.

Until she saw Nathara seated across the hall and glowering at her. Gwenyth quickly turned her head, her eyes downcast as she walked the rest of the way to the dais. A hushed silence alerted her before she walked into Adam. She looked up as he extended his hand to her.

"Come," he said. "I should have done this long before now."

He tugged on her hand, and she rose to her feet as panic set in. "My people need to be clear about my will in this matter."

She looked to Nathara and back to Adam. "Please, my laird. Nathara already hates me. I need no more enemies."

Adam glanced at the dais and said, "My food grows cold." He indicated for a serving girl to bring food for Gwenyth and gently nudged Gwenyth into motion.

"Why are you doing this?"

He leaned down to whisper, "I told you. I believe God means us to stay together. If I am wrong, there's no harm done if you sit here with me. You will be safer if Nathara and others see that I accept you as wife." When they reached their seats, he lifted her hand to his lips, and she felt her face grow warm.

"And you need your people to believe our marriage is agreeable to strengthen your position as laird."

"Aye. Exactly so."

Adam seated her, then called for attention. Every eye in the place looked to him as he spoke.

"You have heard that Gwenyth of Buchan and I were forced to handfast. Despite those circumstances, we will use the allotted time to see if the marriage suits us. I ask you to continue to treat her with the respect due her position."

His glance around the room settled on Nathara, and he stared at her until she gave him a slight, forced nod. Then Adam sat down and the meal continued, though Gwenyth was uncomfortably aware that the buzz of conversation that ensued no doubt centered on her.

Gwenyth excused herself as soon as she could and fled to her room.

We will use the allotted time. Adam's words haunted her. To learn what he promised to teach about tenderness—yes, it held definite appeal. Throw off her responsibilities; subdue the guilt of having survived when her family had not.

Dare she ask God for guidance? Did she really want to know

his will? Could she trust him to know what was best for her? There were no easy answers.

How could she even think of remaining in the same country, let alone binding herself to a man loyal to the very king who'd killed her father, on a sacred altar, no less?

Only Edward, with the backing of those loyal to him and his father, could possibly take the crown from Bruce. Bruce had no heir other than his brother, and the Comyns hoped that her marriage to Edward Balliol would avenge the wrongs done to her family and return the crown to them. She had only to marry and produce an heir, and those who remained loyal to Edward would rally to depose Bruce.

But she had a husband, a fine highland laird, and she could not deny his appeal.

Somehow, she must. She returned to her room and for the first time in nearly two years, Gwenyth got down on her knees and prayed for God's guidance in her future. "I cannot promise him the full time of our handfast, Lord. You alone know my dilemma," she pleaded. "But I give to you and Adam the time that remains before I leave for England. If he is my intended mate, Father, open my heart. Please, Father, if it be thy will, open my heart."

ADAM'S CLEAR WARNING to the clan that Gwenyth was to be treated as his wife freed her to roam the island. Still, she kept a guard with her, since she remained uncomfortable among people she considered enemies. She feared she might never again feel safe alone. If Bruce had learned of her alliance with Edward Balliol, he no doubt had men searching for her. If a visitor to Moy should recognize her and disclose her identity, her hours would be numbered.

Today the man Sim accompanied her to the tower on the rear

wall. Steps led to the top of it and Gwenyth climbed, curious to see the view from this side of the castle. She reached the top and was momentarily made dizzy by the height of the drop. Once steadied, she noted a path leading to a lovely, small cove.

The blue of the water and its gentle lapping against the rocks brought on a rush of remembrances, and she gave in to them. For a moment, she was ten years old, and her father and brothers were shouting at her. *Come in, we'll teach you to swim.*

And so they had, her beautiful brothers and patient Papa. Some of the joy left her as their voices faded from memory. Gone now, except in her heart. A heart that once had been filled with love and now overflowed with bitterness. The bright happy child she'd been had become a woman estranged from God and caught up in schemes of power and politics.

Last night's time in prayer had barely lifted the barrier she'd placed between herself and God. But she would keep trying, for the priest had reminded her that "Blessed are they who keep his testimonies, who seek him with the whole heart."

Would her heart ever know God's love again?

As she stared at the beckoning water, a fragment of peace stole over her, and instinctively she knew that without faith, lasting peace and love would elude her. "But without faith it is impossible to please him, for he who comes to God must believe that he is, and that he is a rewarder of those who diligently seek him."

Unable—no, unwilling—to look deeper, she returned her attention to the water. It called to her as it had that day with her father and brothers. She closed her heart to the burdensome memories and turned to Sim. "Is there a gate?"

"Aye, my lady." Sim pointed, and Gwenyth hurried down the steps within the tower, even as she asked, "Can we open it?"

Sim nodded.

She followed him, and upon arriving at the bottom, saw that the gate was guarded by two men who sat in the shelter of a lean-to built against the wall. They opened the gate and portcullis, and Gwenyth and Sim walked through. They made their way carefully down the rock-strewn path. Early morning clouds had given way to weak sunlight, and the protected cove beckoned despite the chilly air.

Admonishing Sim to go some distance away and turn his back, she watched until he'd walked far enough to give her privacy. Then she stripped to her chemise and waded in. The water was cold, but she was determined to swim anyway.

Rolling onto her back, she floated, relaxing and drifting in the quiet refuge. The clouds dissipated, and the sun grew warmer. She put her foot toward the bottom just as a strong hand rested on her shoulder.

She screamed, and her attacker immediately let go. She whirled, shouting, "Get away!"

"For heaven's sake, Gwenyth, cease. And stop screaming or you'll empty the castle."

In her haste, she tumbled facefirst into the water, stifling her shouts. Even though she sputtered and thrashed to gain a foothold, the man made no move to touch her again.

"I'm sorry. 'Twas thoughtless of me, lass."

"Adam?" she managed to choke as she regained her footing.

"Aye, and I'm sorry to startle you so. I wasn't thinking."

She wiped water and hair from her eyes. "Why didn't those half-witted guards tell me you were swimming nearby?"

He glanced upward. "I don't know—I guess they are used to me and didn't think of it."

"You swim often?"

He smiled. "Aye, you told me to force my arm beyond its limits, remember?"

She well remembered that night on the parapet and the way the moon had blessed him. Now here he stood, sparkling drops of water clinging to the crisp, blond hair covering his chest. With the sun behind him, the shadow of his face deepened the blue of his eyes. His gaze strayed to her neck . . .

As if aware of the impropriety of his action, Adam jerked his head up, then grinned sheepishly. "Seems I've just compounded my poor behavior, Gwenyth. Once again, I apologize."

She wanted to distrust him. But at every turn, he had proved to be a gentleman, always willing to show his tender heart and to help her heal. Each day it became more and more difficult to deny the attraction he held for her. Or to deny the possibility that he was right about their purpose for being together.

What would it hurt, for just a few minutes, to yield? To just enjoy his company, to hold nothing back and pretend she was someone else. Someone who was free to love where her heart might lead her.

Throwing caution and good sense to the wind, she tossed her head and smiled. "Your apology lacks sincerity, my laird."

"Does it now?" His grin deepened. "Well, then, I'll leave you to enjoy your swim in peace."

Should she bid him stay? Or let him go? What harm . . . ? He waded into deeper water, sliding into the depths, and began to stroke.

"Adam," she called.

He halted, then stood in chest-deep water.

She swallowed. Her mind fastened on the first idea that came to her. "Could I swim with you?"

"It's deep," he warned.

She stepped toward him. "I can swim."

"Do you trust me?"

Pushing aside nagging doubts about the wisdom of her actions, she replied, "I want to." And she did.

"THEN COME." Adam extended his hand, very much aware that Gwenyth had just taken an important step toward defeating the demons set loose during the assault. And perhaps a first step in accepting him as God's choice for her mate. He knew the idea made little sense from a logical standpoint, but then Adam wasn't privy to God's logic. The thought made him smile until he remembered her promise to Daron.

Their fingers touched, and Adam drew her into deeper water. Perhaps by the time Daron showed up to claim her, Adam would have won her heart. He had placed this in God's hands, trusting that God would look out for Adam's, and Gwenyth's, best interests.

They swam toward the middle of the lake, Adam matching his strokes to Gwenyth's shorter ones. They drifted, allowing the gentle current to carry them as they floated.

"We should head back before you tire, Gwenyth. Next time we'll bring a boat and do some fishing." How far did her newfound trust go? "Will you join me one morning?"

"Perhaps."

Not far enough. Best not to read too much into her acceptance of his company today. All in God's time.

They reached shallow water and, in unspoken agreement, recognized a need to lighten the moment. Who splashed whom first was unclear, but soon they were frolicking like children, whooping and dunking and sputtering. Gwenyth seemed to forget her fears and Adam's hands caught her and tossed her into deeper water. She shrieked, but in joy, not fear.

She retaliated by kicking water in his face. Despite the activity, though, the cold water took its toll and Adam called a halt.

"Your lips are blue, my lady. Methinks we should sit in the sun and dry out."

She grinned at his teasing words, and after one last splash, they headed for shore. Adam ran to the guards' shack and produced two large cloths, which they used to dry off before draping around themselves for warmth and modesty. Adam watched as Gwenyth lay back with her eyes closed and pillowed her head on her arms. She seemed at ease with him, and he warned himself not to do anything to frighten her.

But how he wanted to lean over and place a kiss upon her brow! And her lips . . .

She opened her eyes, and his thoughts must have been written clear as day on his face, for her smile wavered. Still, she didn't flinch or pull away as he caressed her cheek, gently sliding his finger across the soft skin. Her eyes closed, and she leaned toward him.

Warm sun bathed them, and he felt as if an air of enchantment surrounded them. Slowly, tenderly, he kissed her, and she responded with an innocence that enticed him. With restraint he softly kissed again, as his hands framed her small face. She opened her eyes, and in their golden depths he saw surprise. And the first stirrings of the very same yearning he felt within.

She didn't resist when he put his hand behind her head, sifting his fingers through her damp hair. Slowly, gently, they explored each other's facial contours. Adam fought to keep his touch light and his thoughts from straying past kissing. He must not breach her fragile trust. Like any wounded creature, she must be allowed to come to him in her own time, in her own way, if he held any hope of quenching his thirst for her.

And despite their forced handfast, despite the possibility she loved another, despite her desire to leave Moy, he most definitely wanted more from her. He wanted love. At that thought he deepened the kiss, only a fraction of what he wanted, yet it must have alarmed her, for she jerked away.

GWENYTH SAT BACK and stared at Adam, astounded at the emotions he'd sparked with a few tender kisses. And even more surprised that he was attracted to her in the first place. These kisses held all the promise she'd sensed in their first meeting in Leod's hall, before Leod had made her unlovable.

Adam frightened her, not because he would harm her physically. He had never frightened her that way. But now that she knew him better, she knew beyond doubt that the promises in his kisses would be her undoing, for he would fulfill them beyond imagination. She must not allow it, for both their sakes. As much as she was willing to open her heart a little, to see what life might be like with this man, she was still promised to another.

He sighed and stood, offering his hand to help her up, which she declined, much to his apparent disappointment. "You trusted me in the water."

It was true, she had. But here on the rock everything had changed. Did he sense it too? She gazed at him warily.

"Then why can't you trust me now?"

She shivered, and it wasn't from the cold. "You are a man." *A wonderful man whom I do not want to hurt.*

He grinned. "Aye, and you are a woman. A very pretty woman, even with your hair pasted to your head." He bent and kissed her lightly on the cheek.

She leapt from the rock and ran to where her clothes lay.

"'TWAS ONLY A KISS," he called after her. Why must she be so upset over a chaste kiss? She was pulling her gown over her damp chemise, her movements hurried, nearly frantic.

As he walked toward her, she backed away, tying her girdle and looking for all the world like a frightened animal.

He put his hands out like a supplicant. "Gwenyth, it was only a kiss. What harm can be done with an innocent kiss?"

"It wasn't just a kiss—it was gentle."

"Aye, as a kiss between friends should be."

"Friends?"

He wanted to place his hands on her shoulders, but knew better than to try. "Can we not allow at least that between us, Gwenyth? Surely friendship is something we both need."

"I admit to a lack of friends, my laird." She regarded him with uncertainty. "We needn't kiss to be friends, though."

"Nay, but you must learn to trust or you will never be comfortable as a wife. That is what I would teach you, Gwenyth. Trust. Nothing more."

"I am not one of those wounded creatures your mother spoke of, Adam."

"Ah, but you are in need of healing."

Her fingers wound through the strings of her girdle. "I fear this healing, Adam. The cure is fraught with temptation."

There was no recrimination, no censure in her voice. Only the truth, plainly spoken.

"You go to the quick, my lady."

"I see no need to avoid what must be acknowledged. If I am to remain, we must come to an understanding."

"I thought we had one."

She twisted her belt ends tighter. "Then perhaps, I'm asking if it still stands."

"Why wouldn't it?"

Her gaze seemed to reach down into his very soul, to see what lay hidden there. As if she knew his secrets. As if she knew of his imaginings of her in his arms—

"You are staring as if I frighten you." There was no alarm in her words, only acknowledgment.

"You do frighten me, Gwenyth." He swallowed so hard he felt certain she could hear for herself just how she affected him.

She blushed, head averted, before bringing her gaze back to meet his. "So, am I correct in thinking we are both . . . drawn to each other?"

Adam groaned and ran his hand roughly through his hair. It was worse than he'd thought. With iron discipline he held himself back from stepping toward her and pulling her into his arms. "Aye. Drawn begins to cover it."

Then he looked at her. She was smiling, and suddenly they were both laughing at the absurdity of the situation. Her laugh was wonderful, light and musical, balm for a weary soul.

"I shall have to give you reason to laugh more often, lady. 'Tis a healing sound."

They sobered, each appraising the other.

Adam glanced down at his hands, hands that, had they a will of their own, would be touching her this very moment. He crossed his arms. "I remain firm in my vow—there can be nothing but kisses between us until we have the blessing of a priest."

"A binding union would be a disaster, Adam. Attraction or no, I am not ready. I have made promises I must keep. There can be no future for us together."

Daron again. He fought the jealousy and calmly said, "I believe we have been brought together for a reason, Gwenyth. Fate, destiny, God's will. I will remain open to the possibility that we were meant to stay together. Will you?"

She didn't answer, but her expression became troubled.

"We are fools, Gwenyth, to think we can avoid God's will no matter what is revealed to us."

She continued to knot the material in her girdle. "And you think it is God's will that we make the marriage a true one?"

"I think we must be open to that possibility, yes."

"Perhaps my cousin will rescue us."

He chuckled. "From God?"

She looked stricken by his words, and he laid a hand upon hers to still them. "And if there is no rescue?"

"Then perhaps you will take me to England yourself."

"And if I refuse?"

"Then I suppose I'll have no choice but to accept you as husband."

Brave words, from a nervous maid. "Then we will not speak of this again." He took a deep breath. "Well, at least one thing has come of this conversation."

She lifted her eyebrows in question.

"At least we know we aren't suffering alone."

Their shared laughter eased the tension between them. He extended his hand. "Friends?"

She squeezed his palm, her petite features serious again. "Aye, friends and fools."

He leaned close, grazing her cheek with his lips.

She backed away from him, begging him with her eyes not to tempt her, grabbed the remainder of her clothes, and fled. Adam started after her, then thought better of it.

His disappointment died to be replaced by a hurt he'd not felt since Suisan's visit to his sickbed. Gwenyth's rejection pierced deep. No, not the rejection, but the betrayal. For Gwenyth had promised someone something, and that promise meant a denial of him.

If she truly loved Daron, then betrayal was inevitable. He must harden his heart—'twas time to set this creature free. Her wound might never heal, and she had far too much potential for wounding him. But he was ready to move into new country, whether it be a mountain peak or a steep chasm that he must face.

THIRTEEN

Disobeying adam's request that she eat in the hall, Gwenyth picked at the hot porridge and bread that had been brought to her just after first light. Yesterday's encounter with Adam had provided her with a terrible night's rest. She felt unsettled and more eager than ever to leave. Thoughts of the kiss they'd shared and the promises held within—promises that must not be kept—assailed her. *Surely you can't want this, Father.*

Pushing aside the food, she fought the sense of abandonment Daron's absence fostered. Why was it taking so long to hear from him? She refused to believe he'd left Scotland without her, but surely the messenger had had enough time to ride to Altyre and return.

Tears threatened. He must be dead, as Adam feared. And if so, how would she leave Moy? Could she convince Adam to take her to England? Not likely. After yesterday's meeting in the cove, it was clear there was an attraction, one she feared was strong enough to make her forget her promise to Edward. But was it strong enough to make her forget that Adam was pledged to the king she hated? Or for him to forgive her deceit?

Seeking a diversion from these thoughts, she left her room with her guard in tow. She made her way to the large bedchamber on the second level of the keep. As she approached Angus's door, Eva Mackintosh stepped from the room.

The older woman frowned a little at the sight of Gwenyth approaching. Eva was generally kind, but she guarded Angus like a lioness. The older woman held the door open and directed a curt warning to her husband. "Don't tire yerself." With a nod to Gwenyth to heed the warning as well, Eva left.

"Ah, I feared ye would choose not to indulge me again."

His teasing banter warmed Gwenyth's troubled thoughts. "I didn't think I had a choice."

"I don't suppose ye did. So, which tale will ye tell this morning?"

His insistence on her company puzzled her. "Don't you have a storyteller to entertain you?"

"We can't afford both a storyteller and a priest, and Adam insists on keeping Father Jerard. Not that I object, mind you. The good Father is welcome in good times and bad."

Gwenyth had yet to allow the priest to hear her confession. She would make her peace with God in her own time and in her own way.

Angus settled himself into the pillows. "Why not start with Finn MacCumhail?"

And so the morning passed quickly. To her surprise she found herself warming even more to the gruff old man as she recounted the ancient tale of Finn and his warriors. Though no doubt Angus had heard the story countless times, he listened with rapt attention.

This was the third such morning Gwenyth had spent with Adam's father, and his company soothed her, perhaps because he was in ill health and posed no threat. Perhaps because she missed her own father and menfolk, men with whom she could feel safe.

"Come, lass. That's the second time this morning ye've lost yer way in the story."

"I'm sorry, my laird." She bit her lip.

"Yer worried about yer cousin, I suspect."

She nodded, and when she was sure her emotions were under control, asked, "Have you heard anything?"

"Only that Adam is searching for him." The fatherly concern in his voice fueled her anxiety.

Laying a hand on her arm, he said, "Come. I've an idea to distract ye. I've a mind to watch my son on the practice field."

"You can't mean to go to the lists?"

At her obvious disapproval, he chided, "Where's yer sense of adventure? Help me dress and let's be out for a bit of a walk."

Gwenyth hadn't seen Angus leave his bed in all the time she'd been at Moy. "Nay, my laird. You'll overtax yourself and Lady Eva—"

"Don't dawdle, child. Fetch my plaid from yonder hook and let's spy on the men in the lists."

The diversion appealed to Gwenyth—anything to take her mind off Daron's lack of reply. But she was certain Angus should remain in bed. "I fear for your health, my laird."

"At this stage, what does it matter, lass? I'm not going to live forever, and I'm tired of this room and bed. Now, help me or call someone who will."

They both knew no one else would indulge his wish. All Gwenyth need do was refuse and he'd have no choice but to remain in his bed.

His beguiling smile reminded her of his son. How did anyone, man or woman, deny these two? That smile, along with the lure of fresh air and the opportunity to watch Adam, overcame her objections and good sense.

With a put-upon air, she joined his conspiracy. "All right, we'll go. But Lady Eva will turn us into haggis for this."

He chuckled. "Aye, well, best see she doesn't find out. Let's be on with it."

Feeling like a bairn playing truant, she helped him from the bed. With a few grumbles from Angus and giggles from Gwenyth, they managed to get his plaid belted fast. As she pinned the extra length to his shoulder, she gave thanks that his long linen shirt provided modesty.

Leaning on her for support, Angus shuffled to the door. "Ye'll need a shawl, lass. Use that small plaid hanging by the door."

She wrapped the warm material about her shoulders before asking, "What about my guard?"

"I'll invite him to join us."

Sim didn't appear too happy with this escapade, but Gwenyth persuaded and finally, Angus ordered, and he relented, turning toward the stairs.

"Nay, not that way," Angus admonished, nodding in the opposite direction.

Gwenyth halted. "Don't you want to go up on the battlements?"

"Can't hear a thing from there, lass. And I've no desire to climb all those stairs. I've a better spot in mind."

Sim nodded in understanding. "You wish to see but not be seen, my laird?"

"Aye."

To Gwenyth's relief, their destination was close-by—a small enclosure that, upon closer inspection, proved to be a balcony. If they remained in the shadows, no one on the practice field would know they were there, and they would be able to see and hear most everything. Angus ordered Sim to keep curious servants from disturbing them.

Gwenyth glanced about for someplace for Angus to sit down, but there was none. "Perhaps this wasn't a good idea. You will have to stand—"

"Aye, none to be done for it. And don't be making noises about returning to my room. I *will* watch my son."

Anxious that Angus would not expire in her care, leaving her guilty of his death in addition to her other transgressions, Gwenyth turned her attention to the grassy field below. Her breath caught; to a man they were barechested, wearing only the small plaid kilted at their waists. Most were barefoot.

The sight was at once frightening and fascinating. As a child she'd watched her father's warriors in similar state of dress, but none had compared to Adam. She swallowed, her mouth and throat suddenly dry.

His torso was heavily muscled, despite what must have been a lengthy convalescence. Broad shoulders tapered to a firm waist and fine-drawn hips. The scar on his left arm, which she'd deliberately ignored during their swim, sliced a vivid purple line from the point of his shoulder, down the muscle of his upper arm. He must have been wearing protective garments—a leather hauberk at the least—when he'd suffered the blow, for otherwise the arm would have been severed. As it was, she thought it a miracle he could use it at all.

But she'd touched the length of the scar, and the muscle had healed well. The damage to the shoulder probably gave him the most trouble, and she doubted he would ever regain the ability to lift the arm higher than his shoulder. Yet he would fight.

Indeed, Adam, Morogh, and several others struggled together in what appeared to be a skilled unit.

Leaning closer, Angus observed. "Ah, see. The stubborn lad took my advice, after all."

"What advice was that?" Gwenyth kept her voice low.

"Why, to work out a system to protect his weak side."

"Really?"

Warming to the subject, Angus explained. "See there, how they guard his left? Adam swings the sword well with his right arm, he always did. But now 'tis difficult to block and parry an overhead blow."

Gwenyth watched, fascinated by Adam's prowess, for he was fearsome despite his limitations. Strong, powerful thrusts drove back his attackers. Their voices echoed off the walls. She could hear Adam urge them on, ordering them to give no quarter. Evidently he wanted them to test him with as much force as true attackers would. The men seemed reluctant, but Adam roared at them, and they attacked his left side viciously, breaking through Morogh's defense and overcoming the others as well.

Having thus foiled their laird and his defenders, the men ceased the attack, and then stood there looking as if they awaited punishment for doing so.

Adam's voice carried clearly. "Well done, lads."

Morogh sputtered. "They bested us, Adam."

"Aye, they did. They fought well and we did not. Now, what must we do differently?"

Angus and Gwenyth watched as Adam and the others devised strategies in the dirt with a stick. Morogh argued, but after throwing a heated look at Adam, he took up his position again, and the skirmish continued.

Gwenyth stretched forward, entranced by the skill and the bravado. Here was a force to be reckoned with, a man who would let nothing stand in his way once he'd determined a goal. She shivered, remembering his willingness to stand by the handfast vows and make the marriage real. Permanent.

She would do well to remember Adam's apparent strength, both of body and of will. For not only would he honor his promises, he would enforce his decisions.

Strain showed on Adam's face, and he grunted in pain when a

particularly well-placed thrust forced his injured arm past endurance. But he did not call a halt, and she realized that if ever he clashed with Leod for possession of the clan, they would fight until the death. She trembled as a vision of Adam, lying bleeding beneath Leod's sword, reminded her that Adam's death would mean the end of her safety. She would again be a servant at Leod's mercy.

Gwenyth sent a fervent prayer for Daron to come quickly. She had no desire to witness Adam's dying or to remain anywhere near the threat of Leod Macpherson's power.

Angus touched her arm, and she jumped. "Sorry to scare ye, lassie. Ye were lost in yer thoughts. But I wanted to know, was it ye who suggested he swim to improve his strength?"

"Aye."

"Looks as though ye were right. He's fighting well today."

However well he'd been fighting, clearly Adam had reached his limit, for he stood aside while the others continued with their training. His breathing was labored, and sweat glistened on his bare chest.

Another warrior strode toward Adam. He soon had her full attention, for the hulking giant had flame red hair and an angry posture. Glaring at Adam, he challenged one of the others and through sheer force and little finesse, easily disarmed him, as well as a second, more skilled man.

Having dispatched them both, he faced Adam. "Come, cousin. Show me what you're made of."

Adam's apparent fatigue fled with a nonchalant shrug of his shoulders. He picked up his sword. "Welcome home, Seamus. You seem in a fine temper this morn, and I've a mind to whittle it down to size."

His acceptance of such a challenge surprised Gwenyth. Perhaps something in the man's aggressive stance and tone of voice offended him, or perhaps Adam was eager to prove himself. Gwenyth thought him foolish, either way.

They fought, and thankfully Adam held his own. But Seamus gave no quarter and Adam fought as if his life depended on it.

Angus stiffened.

"What is it?" She touched his forehead. "Are you not feeling well?"

He pushed her hand away. "I'm fine. 'Tis Seamus—why is he challenging so fiercely?"

Adam must have reached the end of this strength for he called a halt. Seamus stopped swinging his sword as Adam bent over, hands on his thighs, taking great gulps of air.

She took the old man's arm. "Come, Angus, we must go."

"Not now, lass. Not now."

Seamus glared at Adam, but Adam didn't step back from the older man's intense gaze or the sword Seamus still held at chest level. Nor did Adam raise his own weapon. "Seamus, calm yourself. Save your anger for an enemy."

Seamus also breathed heavily from his exertion. He shook his great head as if to clear it. Between breaths, sword still at the ready, he confronted his laird. "And just who is my enemy, Adam?"

"What do you mean?"

Gwenyth wondered what had excised the man to raise his sword to his laird. She turned to Angus, but he hushed her as Seamus continued.

"I have the information you asked for."

Adam nodded. "And . . ."

"I had to go to Bruce himself to confirm it. And you aren't going to like it any more than I do."

Adam's voice remained mild. "We should talk of it then. But first, put down your sword, cousin."

Seamus stared at his sword as if surprised to see it raised against Adam. The other men had backed off several steps.

With relief Gwenyth watched the sword descend. Adam motioned toward the keep. "Come, let's have a cool drink and discuss whatever you've learned."

"I would speak of it here, in front of the others."

"Very well. What has you so incensed?"

"You are handfasted to a Comyn." Seamus nearly spit the last word out.

Gwenyth flinched at the venom in his voice and action.

Adam placed his sword point in the dirt and leaned on the weapon. "I am handfast to a woman who served the Comyns, yes."

"She's no' a servant. She's the youngest daughter of the traitor, John Comyn."

Adam's body stiffened as if Seamus had struck him. Gwenyth felt the blood drain from her face. Did Seamus know the rest of it? She looked at Angus, afraid this news would kill him outright.

"Is it true, lass?" the old man asked.

She nodded, and fear pierced through her.

His shoulders slumped and alarmed, she put her arm about him for support. "I'm sorry. Now you understand why I must go, why I cannot be wife to your son."

He nodded. "Ye should have told us yerself."

She would have argued, but Angus gestured for her to remain quiet, and she returned her attention to Adam.

He lifted the sword and examined the blade. "You are sure of this?" his said, voice taut with restrained emotion.

"Aye, I'm sure. Ask her yourself."

"I most certainly will." He rammed the sword upright in the dirt and strode off with Seamus close behind.

Angus sagged, and Gwenyth moved quickly to bolster him, her fear of facing Adam quickly displaced by concern for Angus. "Come, you've tired yourself and Adam will be most displeased with us both."

Angus's voice revealed his displeasure. "And do you concern yourself with Adam's opinion?"

"I am at his mercy, now more than ever."

"Aye, ye should have told us who ye are. Ye best fear him, lass. There's little I can do to protect you from his anger."

"Why would you want to?"

He made no reply, but his wrinkled face betrayed him.

"Ah," she said softly. "So that is where Adam comes by his good heart." She hugged Angus. "All will be well, Angus Mackintosh. I promise I'll not bring harm to your son."

"Aye, well. Adam is angry, but I suspect he'll be lenient with ye."

Not certain she wanted the answer, she asked the question anyway. "Why do you think that to be so?"

Angus kept his voice low as they walked back to his chamber. "He has always been kind to those who are hurting. And when that unfortunate one is a pretty woman, I suspect his tolerance will be great."

"Why are you not more angry with me?"

Angus stopped and turned toward her. "An old man's folly," he said. "I'd hoped to live long enough to see a child born to my only son."

He looked so very old and tired, as if this admission echoed his acceptance of his failing health.

"I'm sorry, my laird." And the truth be told, at that moment she truly was sorry she would not be able to fulfill his wish.

She took his arm, and they walked to his chamber, each lost in private thoughts. After admonishing the guard to keep this morning's activity to himself, Angus allowed Gwenyth to remove his plaid and help him into his bed.

"You are tired." She fussed with his pillows. "Rest, or we shall be denied our time together." Her voice was choked, and their gazes met.

Angus laid his thin hand on her arm. "That would be a disappointment to me."

"And to me."

Angus patted her hand. "If it comes to that, insist on a visit before ye leave for good, lass."

"Of course. I thank you for your kindness, my laird." She pulled the coverlet up and tucked it about him. "Rest now."

"I will."

Gwenyth closed the door gently, willing her tears into abeyance. It was foolish to contemplate the life Angus wished for her—home and family in Scotland's highlands. Her birth and the twists of fate that had befallen her family now dictated her course.

No matter what her heart might wish for.

FOURTEEN

WAIT, COUSIN. Are you telling me that you knew none of it? That the wench has kept her lineage a secret?"

Adam shook off the restraining hand Seamus laid on his good shoulder, refusing to answer him, determined only to meet face to face with Gwenyth and her treachery. Her refusal to be truthful, to trust him, rubbed like salt in an unhealed wound.

"Adam, listen."

Adam whirled on his cousin. "She will tell me the truth herself. Now."

Seamus grabbed his arm. "It isn't like you to hurl yourself at a problem. Too much is at stake for you to charge ahead without thinking. You've a Comyn in your keep. We have to think, man. Think how Leod could use this against you."

"She's done nothing but lie since the moment I met her! And what have I done? Played the lovesick fool." He'd been so sure of God's hand in bringing them together. But had he heard God's voice or his own desire? Aye, desire could be a siren call that banished years of listening to and obeying God's word.

"Lovesick? Oh, cousin, tell me you haven't consummated this handfast."

Adam walked on. Visions of Gwenyth splashing in the loch like a child, agreeing to friendship and admitting to a growing attraction assailed him. Had he been so desperate, so blind, that he'd allowed himself to believe her? To convince himself that God had chosen her for him?

Disappointment and chagrin gradually replaced his anger. Adam slowed his stride and veered toward the main hall. "You're right, Seamus. I need to sort through this. And no, I haven't touched her."

"But you've wanted to."

In the hall Adam seated himself at a trestle as Seamus took a place across from him. A serving girl brought bread, cheese, and drink, and Adam dismissed her.

Seamus broke off a piece of bread. "You shouldn't have hand-fasted with her."

"I had no choice—Leod forced it on us. I promised her protection and now I must protect my enemy." He ran his hands through his hair. "Seamus, I need advice. And I can't take this to Da."

Seamus nodded. "All right."

"First, did you speak at length with Bruce?"

"He hadn't much time. But before I left his camp he sent this to me for safekeeping." Seamus reached into the folds of his plaid and removed a letter. He slid it across the table and Adam took it.

Bruce's mark sealed the parchment. "I'll read it later."

Seamus pushed the tray of food to Adam. "What advice do you need other than for me to say you can't keep the woman?"

Adam ignored the food. "I will know more how to handle that situation once I've confronted her."

"What else, then?"

"You are right. First we must think on how Gwenyth's identity may affect my dealings with Leod and the clan. I would know what drives him to challenge me."

Seamus broke eye contact and stared at the floor.

"What? No need to couch your words, cousin. If I'm to best him, I must know."

Seamus shifted, then brought his gaze to meet Adam's. "Leod truly believes he is the rightful heir." He paused. "He believes you are physically weak, unable, and unwilling to fight because of your injury. He won't be able to withhold his challenge much longer, not if he learns how well you fought today."

Adam stroked his chin. "He thought I would simply die and all would be his. He must have been furious when I rode into his keep, alive and well."

"Aye. It's God's own truth that we all thought you as good as dead." Seamus studied a knothole in the trestle. "He didn't aid his cause by accusing you of harming a woman—no one believes it."

"So, even the Macphersons don't hold that against me?"

"They do not." Seamus banged his hand upon the trestle. "But that woman is a different matter, Adam. You need to be rid of her. She isn't fit to be the wife of a chieftain loyal to Bruce."

"Hatred for the Comyns runs deep."

"Distrust and hatred, Adam. John Comyn's treachery toward Bruce doesn't sit well. Leod will certainly use that to his advantage. But it's mostly personal, him against you. He thinks he can best you."

"What do you think he'll do next?"

"He'll weaken your position any way he can and then challenge you to fight."

Adam sipped from his tankard. "I think you're right. He can use the woman's family ties, and I suspect he's behind the increase in cattle raids."

"What raids?" Seamus asked, instantly alert.

"On the border with the Camerons." Adam shifted uncomfortably. "A woman was assaulted as well."

"By the saints, Adam. You've got to stop him."

"I have no proof." And Adam feared if he pressed the woman to name Leod, her life would be endangered.

"Then what shall we do?"

"We, good cousin, must stand united. Not just you and I, but all of Clan Chattan. Together we are a force no one will tangle with. I will convince the council that I'm the man to do that. And you shall be my right arm."

A face-splitting grin creased Seamus's face. "Don't you mean left arm, my laird?"

Adam chuckled and shook his head. Only Seamus would dare to make light of his injury. "Aye, then. My left arm. I will propose you as my warlord, Seamus."

"That isn't necessary. I fought you myself today—given time you will fight as well as you ever did."

The compliment pleased Adam. "I will fight well enough, as long as I have a man to cover for me. But you will train the men, Seamus."

"As you wish, my laird."

"Good." Now if only the woman were as easy to dispatch. But this news, Gwenyth's deceit—no wonder she'd been so coy yesterday. Rising anger threatened to overcome good sense. He forced his attention back to Seamus. "Once I locate Daron of Ruthven, I can be rid of Gwenyth, and Leod will have one less thing to hold against me."

"But what if this Daron has left the country without her?"

"If she is indeed Gwenyth Comyn, I doubt the man has deserted her. More likely he's wounded or dead."

"She is Gwenyth Comyn, Adam. You must believe it. And you can't afford to wait too long to act."

"She stays until I can guarantee her safe conduct, either with her cousin or by my own hand. On this I will not be moved. I charge you with her safety, Seamus. No matter who she is, I'll not see her come to any more harm."

Seamus stared hard at him. "I will see to it. Just have a care you don't lose Clan Chattan. Leod Macpherson would be a disastrous chief, and we both know it."

"Thank you for the support—and the warning. I'll take neither lightly."

Seamus left, but Adam remained at the table, sipping his water, knowing he must confront Gwenyth. He had no doubt that she was indeed Gwenyth Comyn, daughter of the man Robert the Bruce had stabbed to death. Betrayal upon betrayal. When would it end?

The truth was supposed to set one free, according to Christ's own words. Somehow Adam found little comfort in the thought. The pain of Gwenyth's betrayal was far greater than Suisan's, for this time, much as he hated to admit it, his heart was truly engaged. And that was why he needed time to think.

How much was lie? How much truth? And why in the name of all that was holy did he care? If this was indeed the woman God wanted for him, why was he making it all so difficult?

Not wanting witnesses to what must be said, and aware that delaying the inevitable would solve nothing, Adam instructed a servant to send Lady Gwenyth to him in his solar. Then he retired there to await her.

While he waited for her, he read the letter Seamus had given him from Bruce. And what he read nearly sent Adam to his knees. The promises Gwenyth had alluded to were not promises of love to Daron. Better that they had been. Her promises amounted to treason. Adam's loyalties were on a disastrous collision course.

His enemy. For so she must be so long as she served Balliol. Perhaps he could persuade her to change allegiance. But why would she? For a marriage and a man she didn't want?

Adam held his head in his hands as he sorted through his tangled emotions. He must be sure both his anger and his daft heart were firmly in control before confronting her. His country's future and his king's very life depended on him.

GWENYTH APPROACHED THE SOLAR with trepidation. What would Adam do now that her identity was known? Could she find Daron quickly and escape before the full truth was revealed? Steeling herself for what would no doubt be a horrible confrontation, she knocked crisply at the door. A moment of silence answered, as if Adam hesitated to see her. His gruff "Enter" did little to assuage her fears.

She opened the door and found Adam standing at the window, his stiff back to her. After what seemed like half an hour but could only have been a minute, he turned to her, his face void of expression.

Inclining her head, she spoke first. "You sent for me, my laird."

"I did, indeed. But just who are you, lady fair?"

Calmly, she replied, "You know well enough, Adam."

"But I would like to hear you say it."

"I am Gwenyth Comyn."

"Finally, you speak a word of truth." He gave her no time to defend herself. "You hid your hatred well beneath your claims that you wanted no man to touch you. And I made it all worse by practically begging you to tell me you were drawn to me."

His face might not betray him, but she heard pain and confusion in his voice.

"You did not beg, Adam. And I spoke the truth—"

"Lies on top of lies. Have you spoken a single word of truth in all our conversations?"

His distress had quickly turned to anger, and she was glad of it. For anger would be much easier to deal with than pain—pain she had caused. "You will believe what you wish. I told you I had made promises that made it impossible for me to remain here."

"You will not leave Moy, nor will your cousin when I find him."

Gwenyth fought rising panic. "Of course I will. 'Tis what we agreed upon."

His expression hardened. "We agreed that Gwenyth of Buchan, a ladies' maid, was free to leave. But Gwenyth Comyn will not leave Moy."

Gone was the laughing, smiling man who'd frolicked in the loch. In his place stood an implacable highland warrior. One look at him and she knew her cause was doomed. But she would not give in without a fight. "You have no right to hold me against my will. I demand that you allow me to leave as we agreed."

His face darkened, and he gripped his hands into fists. "I have every right to do with you as I will, wife."

"'Tis but a handfast—we are not truly bound."

"That can be remedied. I can send for the priest and bind you irrevocably."

Gwenyth felt her face drain of color as she fought panic and denial. "You cannot mean to bind me against my will. And for what end? So that you can hang me at your leisure?"

"To remove the queen that would strengthen any claim Edward has on the crown. If you are my bride instead of Balliol's, Bruce's hold is strengthened." He paused. "I still must consider whether I can stomach a traitor in my keep or whether to collect Bruce's ransom."

"He has placed a ransom on my head?" Gwenyth fought to disguise her despair. Her refuge had now become her prison, for she would much rather take her chances with Adam than with Robert the Bruce.

"Aye. On your pretty head so full of deceit."

ADAM GLARED at this woman who'd captured his heart. She stood before him, head held proudly, her bearing that of a noblewoman. No different than before, only now he saw it ever more clearly and understood why she had seemed more than a servant from the very start.

The king, having learned from Seamus that Adam and Gwenyth were handfasted, gave Adam a choice. Imprison her or marry her. The suggestion that Adam marry her before a priest should have brought him joy. It did not, and he would delay the ceremony as long as he dared. He had much to think through first.

He didn't want to force her to wed, but his choices were fast disappearing. Just as hers had that day in Leod's keep. She had chosen to marry him rather than condemn him to death. Now it was his turn to do the same, for to turn her over to Bruce and imprisonment might very well mean her death.

Hardening his heart against the desire to pull her into his protective embrace, Adam said, "You will be free to move about within the castle walls, Gwenyth. Do not give me reason to confine you further." Ignoring the ache in his heart, he turned his back on her, listening to the rustle of her skirts as she left the room.

When she was gone, he crumpled the letter in his fist and vowed to overturn every rock in Altyre until he found Daron of Ruthven and put an end to Balliol's plan to overthrow King Robert.

DARON COMYN SENT WORD to Moy that he wished to meet with the Mackintosh laird, but not at the castle. A roaring waterfall cascaded over a thirty-foot drop as Adam and his small band of warriors wound their way down a narrow trail beside the tumbling stream. The mist from the falling water settled over him, and he drew his plaid close to ward off the moisture. Already they'd endured a heavy drizzle that threatened to become rain at any minute. The unstable weather echoed Adam's unsettled thoughts as he approached the agreed-upon meeting place.

Bruce hadn't specified what Adam should do with Daron. But Adam's course of action was clear. He must take Daron into custody so that neither he nor Gwenyth could flee to England. Would the man come peacefully or resist? Adam would do all he could to convince the man to come willingly.

With that settled in his mind, Adam called the party to a halt when they reached the edge of the woods that had surrounded them until now.

On a clearer day, Adam would be able to see before him a large, grassy meadow, protected on all sides by forest. Today, the fog hid the far side of the open area from view, and Adam regretted the lack of visibility. Daron Comyn no doubt stood on his side of the clearing, cursing the weather and wondering, as did Adam, if the other man could be trusted.

Nothing to be done for it. Adam doubted the man would do anything that might put his cousin in harm's way. Indeed, he was counting on the other man's loyalty to her as a means for a peaceful solution. He ordered his men to remain in the shelter of the trees while he rode alone into the clearing.

The fog dampened not only the ground, but sounds as well. As he reached the center of the meadow, visibility improved. He halted his horse, and soon Daron walked toward him.

Adam dismounted and strode to within a sword's length of a young man near Adam's age. But there was nothing young about Daron's eyes. The events of the past months had taken a toll that was evident in the wary, and weary, expression in his eyes. And in the nearly healed wound at his temple.

The lad had been lucky to survive the blow. A puckered scar, awkwardly stitched, ran from eyebrow to ear. His gaunt face and loose-fitting sark gave testimony to a recent convalescence. No doubt Daron and his men suffered from lack of shelter and food, as well.

Yet despite those hardships, Daron had remained until he'd recovered sufficiently to retrieve Gwenyth. The man was nothing if not loyal to his cousin.

As they studied each other, Adam realized that had the tide of battle turned differently, it might be him petitioning for his loved one's safety, and not Daron Comyn. The thought sobered him.

Breaking the silence, Adam held his empty sword hand in front of him, palm up. "Greeting to you, Daron of Ruthven."

Warily Daron replied, "Good day to you, Laird Mackintosh. Where is my cousin?"

"She waits in my castle."

Daron fingered the hilt of his sword. "You should have brought her with you."

Adam stepped back, careful to keep his hand away from his weapon. "I kept her safe until I could be certain just who was waiting here in the fog. There are those who would harm her."

Daron dropped his hand to his side. "Perhaps I was hasty in my conclusions, sir." He shifted his weight. "Have her brought to me and we'll be gone."

"There has been a change of plans."

Daron shook his head. "You needn't concern yourself, Mack-intosh."

Adam heard the derision in Daron's voice, and his own temper raised a notch. He baited the man. "You'd best remember who holds the upper hand. I'd just as soon turn you both over for the ransom." He would not do this, but Daron didn't need to know that. Not yet.

Daron's eyes blazed, but in a remarkable show of discipline, he acquiesced. "Then you know who she is."

"Aye. Tell me, how did your lady come to be captured by Leod Macpherson in the first place?"

Daron shifted his weight again, and his gaze dropped momentarily. When he resumed eye contact, the pain reflected in his eyes revealed his despair at failing his kinswoman. "We were set upon—my men were tired and hungry. 'Tis no excuse, but," he touched his scar, "when I was wounded, Gwenyth was taken before my men could rally behind my second in command." He studied Adam. "Your message said she is well. How fairs my lady, truly?"

"She is well, but . . ." Adam hated to say the words, but Daron must be made aware of the danger and come to see Adam as her best protection from the wrath of King Robert. "She was violated and beaten."

Daron swayed, clearly stunned. His face turned white, and he stumbled away from Adam. Adam fought the urge to tend the lad as the sounds of retching echoed in the foggy air. Best to let him regain his composure on his own.

Several minutes passed. Adam could only imagine Daron's thoughts; how would he feel in the other man's place? Anger, frustration, a desire to strike back. Not unlike Adam's own feelings, only much more intense, for Daron would no doubt blame himself.

Daron returned, ashen-faced, his visage murderous. "Who is the man?"

Adam made a note to remember this was a warrior, loyal to another king and heretofore an enemy. And a man who'd just learned that his kinswoman had been raped because he hadn't protected her.

"I have no proof, but when I do, he'll be punished, I promise."

"If I don't find him first." The young man clenched and unclenched his fists. The blaze in his eyes matched the fire of his hair, and Adam realized that a powerful force stood before him.

Daron Comyn made a formidable enemy, and he might well make just as fierce an ally.

Their gazes met, and Adam said, "How will you accomplish your revenge as a broken man, without the sanction of a laird?"

"I am sworn to Lady Gwenyth. Her welfare is my responsibility, and I will not rest until the man is dead." His expression revealed his anguish at having failed his duty.

Adam shared Daron's determination to punish the rapist and to keep Gwenyth safe from further harm. Honor demanded it. Honor and emotions he didn't care to explore. "I, too, am pledged to her. Lady Gwenyth is my wife."

Daron visibly reeled at this second blow. "Your wife?"

"Aye, she accused me of the assault, falsely, as she will readily admit, in order to escape Leod MacPherson's keep. We were forced to wed."

Daron shook his head, as if he hadn't heard right. "Forced to wed. This is all my fault." Daron rubbed his forehead as if to massage away pain. "Why are you telling me these things, and not Gwenyth?"

"Because she would not have, in order to be gone." Somehow, Gwenyth's rejection of him had lost its sting. Especially now that he understood her reasons. He didn't like her reasons; but loyalty, even when misplaced, he could admire.

"She would leave her wedded husband? What have you done to her to make her flee?"

"Nothing. We are handfasted, Daron. I would have set her free, planned to do so."

Daron stroked his chin. "Until you learned she is Gwenyth Comyn."

"Aye."

Again Daron grew thoughtful. "Handfast or no, you accept her as wife?"

Did he? The truth was, until two days ago he'd been agreeable. More than agreeable. "I might have, had she been willing." And less deceitful.

"Ah. You have not . . . you haven't . . . but of course . . ."

"The handfast is not truly binding, Daron, if that's what's troubling you. She does not welcome me to her chamber."

"And you've not been there, welcome or no."

Adam had the feeling he'd passed some sort of test as they gazed at each other in silent understanding.

Once again Daron spoke first. "You have feelings for her."

It was a statement, not a question.

"No more than for any creature in need of healing." *Lies.*

Daron's face clearly marked his disbelief. "I would not like to come between husband and wife."

"But you are pledged to her."

"Aye. But I would see her safe, and she is safer with you, Laird Mackintosh."

"How so? A few minutes ago you were demanding I turn her over to you."

"A few minutes ago I had no idea what she'd suffered already, or what was known. Think what might befall her once her identity is discovered."

"I have thought of it."

"There are factions that want to use Gwenyth for their own purposes." Daron brushed a hand wearily across his face and ended by touching the still healing wound at his temple. "What you have told me about Gwenyth . . ." Daron's voice failed him, and it took a moment to regain control. "Since Bruce's rampage through Buchan we have hidden and lived like criminals."

"Aye, my king has been harsh with your clan."

"That he has. Yet he has also united the highlands as no man has done before. He's even managed to subdue the earl of Ross. I don't believe there is a man alive who can wrest the throne from him."

"But some would try."

"Aye, they would. And they would use Gwenyth to further their cause. But all they will succeed in accomplishing is to weaken Scotland and give the English reason to invade yet again. I have supported Gwenyth's desire to make a new life in England, if it would bring her the peace she craves. But it won't. She will live to see her children used as an excuse for further war and bloodshed."

Adam began to see where Daron's thoughts were headed. "Who is your enemy, Daron?"

Daron spoke quietly. "A good question for every Scot to ask himself. Is it a Scottish king with the strength to keep us free, or the English who would deprive us of our right to self-government?"

Adam nodded. "You would give your allegiance to Bruce?"

"My allegiance is first and always to Scotland. And I have my own doubts about Balliol's ability to wrest the throne from Bruce, even with my cousin as his wife. Gwenyth would lose; we all would lose."

They studied each other. A man whose loyalty lay with his countrymen and not the figurehead who led them was a man to be trusted. Still, there was bad blood between Scotland's king and Daron Comyn's clan.

Adam scratched his head and decided to push again. "So, you would serve Robert the Bruce?"

Daron hesitated then answered. "Perhaps." Daron turned and whistled. Three men as bedraggled-looking as Daron materialized out of the fog.

Adam inclined his head toward them and asked, "Then will you all come willingly to Moy?"

Daron didn't get a chance to answer as a loud bird call pierced the air and one of Adam's sentries burst into the clearing. "Leod Macpherson comes, my laird."

Adam ordered Daron, "Tell your men to put down their weapons."

"What?"

"No time, Daron. Just do it." He would soon see if Daron could be trusted.

Quickly, Adam moved among his own men, giving the order to take Daron's men prisoner while Daron ordered his warriors to surrender.

"Aye, but stay close to your weapons," Adam warned.

Now Daron smiled, and Adam grinned back. He was beginning to like this cousin of Gwenyth's. Daron assumed a pose of surrender, and Adam gave an order for Leod's benefit. Then he strode to face his nemesis.

A dozen warriors accompanied Leod into the clearing. He halted his stallion and surveyed the group before him. Adam and his guards came forward, pushing Daron in front of them.

Leod leaned over his pommel and addressed Daron. "Well, who have we here?"

"Daron Comyn of Ruthven. I caught them raiding cattle."

Leod casually stroked his horse's neck. "And what will you do with him?"

"Didn't you know there's a price on his head?"

"I'd heard something of the sort." Leod shifted in his saddle. "You'll have to take him south to collect."

"Perhaps I'll have you do that for me."

"You'd like to see me gone, no doubt." Flicking the reins lightly on his leg, Leod glared at Adam. "Don't send me on your trifling errands."

"I remind you who is laird and who is vassal, Leod." Adam's voice betrayed his growing anger.

"But for how long? You've not been overly anxious to defend your title, Adam. Do you truly wish to be laird, or are you just playing at it?"

Adam scowled at his enemy, for Leod was more an enemy than Daron or any of Daron's men. He held his tongue, fearing what his thoughts might reveal about his turmoil.

Leod went to the heart of it. "You will have to fight me, Adam. Hand to hand, sooner or later. And if you best me, I will acknowledge you as my laird. Until then, I'll continue to challenge you, and to convince others that I am the rightful laird."

There, it was said, the thing Adam dreaded. For a moment his rage nearly overcame good judgment and he came close to challenging Leod to fight on the spot. Have it over and done. But wisdom prevailed at a surreptitious touch to his elbow from Morogh.

Adam released a breath and sought to diffuse the tension. "Aye, Leod. It will come to that. And you'll learn that day who is the rightful laird. Me." Adam sounded far more confident than he felt.

"We shall see. Good day to you." Leod jerked his mount's mouth and retreated.

Daron stood beside Adam. "I don't trust that one. It was in his keep that Gwenyth was harmed?"

"Aye. But do you trust me?"

"For now it seems the wisest course. I am firm in my resolve to avenge Gwenyth. Besides, there's a price on my head, and I've no desire to meet Robert the Bruce so that Leod can line his pocket." He studied Adam for a moment. "I find it hard to believe Gwenyth would bind herself to the man who injured her."

"I did not harm her." *I only kissed her.*

Glad that Daron was persuaded to come peacefully, Adam gave

the order to return to Moy. Morogh signaled the others to join them, and Adam led his mount so he could walk with Daron. Motioning his men in the opposite direction from Leod, Adam watched as they herded the Comyn men toward Moy, maintaining the pretense of capture in case Leod had posted spies.

The younger man spoke first. "If I were not certain you wouldn't harm her, we would not be discussing an alliance," Daron said softly.

"You are willing to swear allegiance to me? All of you?"

Daron nodded. "I will talk to the others, but aye. We are all sworn to the lady."

"And you'll follow my lead in seeking your revenge?"

"As laird, you must punish the man, so our goals coincide. And I give my word to uphold you as my laird and to fight in your defense."

"Good. We are agreed."

As they walked, the fog began to clear although a light mist still fell. Adam absently massaged his shoulder, which always stiffened in the dampness.

"One question, Laird Mackintosh. Won't Leod use my loyalty against you?"

"Aye, Leod will do whatever it takes to oust me, Daron. Trying to outmaneuver him is a waste of time."

Assured of Daron's intentions, Adam stopped to tighten the cinch on his saddle, then mounted for the remainder of the journey. It wouldn't look right to approach the castle on foot with men who were supposedly prisoners.

A short time later a shout of dismay was heard from the castle guard until Adam signaled to them that all was well. The Comyns and Mackintoshes entered the bailey together.

Adam called Morogh to his side. "See to their lodging. And

from the looks of them, they could use a good meal. We shall continue to treat them as captives for the time being."

"What of their weapons?"

"Have them repaired and ready, but don't allow Daron's men to carry them just yet."

"Aye. I'll see to it."

The castle folk surrounded them when they entered the bailey. "Go back to your work," Adam ordered. "I have given these men sanctuary. Do not give me cause to be embarrassed by your lack of hospitality." The folk dispersed, curious but obedient.

"Daron, get yourself something to eat. I'll send for you."

"Aye, my laird. But first I'd like to see Gwenyth."

FIFTEEN

Gwenyth rushed across the inner bailey toward them, and Adam watched as the two embraced: Gwenyth with obvious exuberance, Daron somewhat hesitant. He handled her as if she were fragile glass, crooning, "The fault is mine, lass."

Gwenyth stiffened, her heated gaze accusing as she pulled away and turned on Adam. "You told him."

He nodded.

"Aye, your husband has told me of your trials, my lady," Daron said.

She faced Daron, hands on hips. "What's done is done. I only want to leave this wretched place."

Apparently she still saw Daron as her rescuer, despite the fact Adam had clearly told her she and her cousin would not be departing. Adam cleared his throat. "Perhaps it would be best if I allowed you and your cousin to speak privately."

"Aye, perhaps you should, Laird Mackintosh." Her voice was a whisper, but that did nothing to take away the sting of her dismissal. He hardened his heart—she could not leave Moy or Scotland, and he dared not allow his misplaced feelings for her any room to grow.

He turned away, but Daron stopped him with a hand on his shoulder. Adam winced but did not turn around.

"Stay, my laird." Daron turned Adam around, and their gazes met and held. "There is more you should know."

THE APPARENT ACCORD between the two men surprised Gwenyth, but Daron's next words surprised her even more. "Your husband seems to care for you."

He cared for her? She shook off the warmth that thought brought. Of course he cared, which was one of the reasons she and Daron had to leave. Today. She must make it clear that she was well and strong and ready to go forward. "My husband?"

"Mackintosh says you are wed."

"We are handfast, but I don't consider the tie binding and neither does he." She glared in Adam's direction.

Daron answered. "Gwenyth, we cannot find passage—by now the word is spreading of your whereabouts, and the secrecy of our movements is gone. I doubt we could find a ship's captain willing to transport you. And the risk in attempting it is too great."

"Surely King Robert doesn't hate me so much?" But she knew better. The devastation of her home and family were more than adequate testament to Bruce's animosity toward the Comyn clan. A sense of doom crept over her.

"Perhaps not. But he has placed a ransom on your head, and his followers may well be tempted to collect it."

With his face in profile to her, Daron's wound became visible. She touched it and he winced. "Oh, Daron. You were hurt."

He pushed her hand away. "'Twas nothing, Gwenyth. I am quite recovered."

Obviously, he didn't want to talk about it. She had seen the look that passed between Daron and Adam, and she feared it did not bode well for her plans.

Laying her hand on Daron's arm, she attempted to move toward his men, who were entering the keep behind them. "I want to leave this accursed place, Daron. Now."

"You will remain with your husband."

"Nay." She fought to hold her emotions in check. And much was at stake. Edward and safety. A home in England, safe from Robert the Bruce. Daron didn't answer, his demeanor stubborn, and she called on the last of her patience. "You are sworn to me, Daron. Why will you not obey my wishes?"

"I cannot put you in further jeopardy, my lady." Clearly it pained him to deny her, yet deny her he did. "And a husband's right supersedes my own oath to you." Setting his gaze on Adam, he motioned him to join them.

"Nay," she cried.

"Aye, Gwenyth." Daron's voice held the sharpness of command, one he had never used on her before. He was barely a year older, and until now had always treated her more as a friend than as a responsibility. But it would seem their roles had changed.

Ignoring her, Daron addressed Adam. "You are her husband. As her sworn man, I offer myself to your service." Daron stared at her before continuing. "I have learned that you are to marry John Balliol's heir to strengthen his claim to the crown. Is this true?"

Defiantly, she answered, "Aye."

A glance passed between the two men, and again Gwenyth feared what it meant.

Adam spoke, his voice harsh. "You know that I can't allow that, my lady."

"Nor will I, Gwenyth."

Daron's agreement surprised and angered her. "Why did you tell him this? Why, Daron? You are sworn to me."

"Edward Balliol would use you with no thought to anything but his own purpose. You won't be safe with him, Gwenyth."

"Come, Daron. You exaggerate. Your lady mother assured me in her last letter that I will be welcomed at court."

"And married off," he said, voice rising with heat, "and bred with an heir to the Scottish crown just as quick as can be arranged."

In desperation she shouted back. "Isn't that what we want, Daron? To bring down Bruce?"

Daron huffed a breath before replying. "What I want, my lady, is your health and happiness. And Scotland's freedom."

"Scotland. The country whose king has taken everything from us. You would betray me, betray our rightful king—"

"You don't believe in Balliol's ability to take back the throne any more than I do. And to support his plot to overthrow Bruce will only increase the likelihood of more war, and death and destruction. I have seen far too much of it. Is that the legacy you wish to leave?"

She was suddenly too aware of the highland warrior standing there listening to this conversation. He would not take kindly to discussions of intrigue to regain the crown of Scotland.

As if to seal her doom, Adam said, "On this your cousin and I are in agreement. This is no game we are playing now. I'll have no more lies, woman." Pointing to her hand, he argued, "You willingly donned that ring, insisted on wearing it as a sign of your loyalty to me. 'Tis time to give what you so pledged or bring the wrath of Bruce down on all of us."

Gwenyth felt her shoulders slump. She realized in her heart that Daron and Adam spoke the truth. Her dreams of peace and safety with Edward were nothing but illusions. Illusions born of desperation when her home and loved ones had been destroyed.

Still she clung to them, for they had sustained her, had continued to do so through the ordeal of the past weeks at Moy.

Adam lifted her chin with his fingers, and the tenderness in his eyes nearly undid her. They were on opposite sides, yet he put his anger aside to concern himself with her well-being. Some of the fight went out of her, as it always did when confronted with his generous nature.

She shrugged away his offer of comfort and turned to Daron. Perhaps he would listen to reason.

But Daron didn't give her a chance to speak. "Look what has already befallen you. The next time it could be death or imprisonment."

"You are safe at Moy," Adam promised.

"Aye, it's a pleasant enough prison," she retorted. "So long as you remain laird."

ADAM'S STOMACH CHURNED. The only way this plot to have Gwenyth mingle her royal blood with that of Balliol could succeed was if Robert the Bruce were dead. Adam must hold Gwenyth at Moy, and Daron must be persuaded to swear his loyalty to Bruce.

Daron looked at Adam. "Mayhap we can be of service to one another, Laird Mackintosh."

"Indeed."

Daron indicated Adam's injured arm. "I've heard there is resistance to your leadership?"

"Some."

"Then additional warriors could be useful."

Adam tipped his head to one side. Perhaps Daron wouldn't require persuasion after all. "What do you suggest?"

"I will pledge my sword arm to your fight, my laird."

Gwenyth sputtered, "What of your pledge to me?"

"By serving your husband, I also serve you."

"You would serve me better by doing what I ask of you. This marriage is only temporary. What will you do at its conclusion?"

Although it pained him to bind himself to a woman who didn't love him, Adam knew what must be done. "We will stand before a priest. You will not sail for England and betray my king. Not today. Not ever, as long as I have the means to stop it."

"You would force me to wed." Her voice sounded wooden, and all trace of animation left her face.

Adam took her limp hand. "Aye, for my only other choice is to send you to Bruce for imprisonment or worse. You once saved me—now it's my turn. We will wed, but I'll do naught else against your will." He lifted her chin until their gazes met. "You have my word."

Even as he said it and meant it, Adam knew he was marrying a woman who would reject him in the most fundamental way of a husband. But he would protect his king, no matter if he and Gwenyth never shared the intimacies of marriage.

Aye, he'd marry her, and then guard his heart like a miser shielded his gold from view.

Then he remembered her response as they'd lain sunning on the rock, and the growing accord between them. She had enjoyed his touch then, and somehow, he would teach her to do so again. God willing. He smiled, and she withdrew her hand.

For now there were other matters to be dealt with. And until she had time to resolve her anger with him and Daron, thoughts of lying next to her and sharing kisses would have to wait.

"What are you going to do?" she asked Daron, her voice devoid of emotion.

Adam hated to see the look of despair revealed upon her features.

Daron backed away and brushed a hand through his burnished hair. "I am going to see that your honor is avenged."

"I don't want revenge for that, but for my father's death."

At her look of pain and disappointment, his voice softened. "Tell me, do you trust Mackintosh? Is he a man of his word?"

Adam stiffened, caring more than he wanted to admit that she might still trust him.

"Aye." The single syllable sounded very begrudging, but Adam relaxed. Trust was a good place to start a marriage.

"Then marry him truly, stay with him where I can be certain of your well-being. Do this for me, for I cannot bear the thought of what you've already suffered."

His voice cracked, and Gwenyth's face was stricken as if only now did she realize that her valiant cousin had suffered his own hell these past weeks.

"You ask much of me."

"If I thought Mackintosh would harm you, I wouldn't ask." Daron pulled her forward. He placed her hand in Adam's.

DARON'S ACTION showed her more clearly than words that his need for revenge, his need to make up for failing to protect her, his unreasonable love for Scotland, were more important than her desire for safe haven and departure.

Blast men and their wretched pride.

Now she would be forced to a binding marriage—would they try to compel her to swear loyalty to Bruce as well? She would not. Never.

Gwenyth hated the tears she couldn't hold back, her weakness made evident. They must think she wasn't in control of her emotions. Unfortunately that was too true. And along with her emotions, she'd lost all control of her life.

She refused to accept Adam as husband. With his promise of chastity she had hope, for the union could be annulled—annulments more often than not had more to do with politics than theology. Then she would find a way to escape Moy. And Scotland.

Aye, that was what she wanted above all else.

Wasn't it?

SIXTEEN

ADAM FOUND HIS MOTHER in Angus's chamber. He pulled two stools beside his father's bed and held one until his mother was seated. Angus looked pale today and more frail than ever. Time was running out. Adam regretted the new turmoil he was about to reveal as he ignored the stool and paced instead.

"What are ye fashing yerself with now, son?" his mother asked.

"'Tis Gwenyth."

He did not miss the glance shared between his parents.

"What of her?" Angus asked.

Adam tugged at his plaid, suddenly feeling more like a bairn caught filching a sweet than a laird. "I've found her kinsman—he and his warriors are in the hall."

"Ye've captured them or given sanctuary?" Angus asked.

"Sanctuary."

Neither parent asked why, and Adam was grateful for their trust in his judgment. "Gwenyth Comyn was on her way to England and a marriage with Edward Balliol when Leod captured her."

Eva raised her fingers to her lips. "She would betray our king?"

Angus didn't give him time to answer. "Does King Robert know of this?"

"Aye. He says I must not allow them to leave Moy, especially the woman."

"Will you imprison her?"

Adam recoiled at the thought. "That is one possibility. She hasn't done anything to deserve such treatment. Yet."

Eva huffed. "Neither did our good Queen Elizabeth, yet she languishes in an English prison."

"Aye, well. Marriage can be a joy or a punishment."

Angus looked up sharply at Adam's words. "You'll punish yerself more than her, if that's what yer thinking to do."

"You may be right, Da. But if the marriage is permanent, she cannot further threaten the crown."

"Either way, ye go against her will and give her cause to hate her jailer."

"'Tis a chance I must take." He would cling to the hope of eventual reconciliation with her. To the hope that taking her to wife was indeed God's doing. For now, he saw his duty, and would not shirk it.

"Why, Adam?"

"It ends the threat to Bruce—he even suggested marriage as a possible solution. Balliol will lose much of his support without Gwenyth to give him a royal heir. And Gwenyth may well hate me, but at least it won't be because I'm crippled."

Eva drew in a loud breath, and Angus patted her hand.

Adam's words hung there, and no one spoke. Taking a seat beside them, Adam broke the silence. "'Tis a fact I've come to accept, this damaged arm. Gwenyth, for all her other faults, sees past it. I'd accept her as a wife for that blessing alone."

"Then we'll say no more of it. Do what ye must do."

Eva nodded, and Adam felt a weight lift from his shoulders. Now, one other thing remained. "Daron Comyn will pledge his loyalty to me today."

Alarm showed on his mother's face. "What will the council say to that?"

Adam rubbed his eyes. "I don't know, but frankly, I'm tired of worrying about it. I am Da's chosen successor. I can't sit back and wring my hands—I must make decisions as I see fit and live with the consequences."

Angus nodded in approval, and Adam continued. "If they want Leod to lead Clan Chattan, then I'll withdraw the Mackintosh warriors from the federation."

"I hope it doesn't come to that, but yer plan is wise."

Eva asked, "Do ye trust this Daron?"

"He'll not betray me so long as I have Gwenyth. Nay, that isn't fair. I believe the man is honorable, without such a threat."

"Bring him here so I may take his measure."

When Adam returned a few minutes later with Daron and Gwenyth, her stormy scowl said all there was to know about her disapproval. Avoiding her, Adam drew Daron forward.

"Da, this is Daron Comyn, come to swear allegiance to Clan Chattan. And to me."

Angus gave the young man a careful look before speaking, directing his question to Adam. "Ye trust the man, then?"

"I have Gwenyth's life as surety."

Daron bristled at this. "You never said . . . 'twas not our agreement at all. This is an insult. We agreed man to man, brother to brother."

"Will you go back on the agreement now?"

Daron looked mad enough to chew stirrup leather. "Nay. *My* word is good."

With a pointed look at his father, Adam reassured Daron. "As is mine. Your loyalty was freely given earlier this day, and I'll not force you now with threats against Gwenyth. My father required proof of your worth as a man, and you have given it."

Daron's shoulders relaxed. "Will you require continued proof, or can I say the words and expect them to be binding on both of us?"

Adam smiled at Daron's quick wit. "From this day forth, we are bound as laird and vassal. You are welcome here unless you prove yourself unworthy."

Adam handed his own jewel-handled dirk to Daron. Last-minute doubts assailed him. Was this wise? How would the council react?

Enough. This was only the first of many decisions he must make as laird. He refused to spend his life questioning himself.

Daron knelt, holding the beautiful and deadly weapon before him. "I swear fealty to Adam Mackintosh and acknowledge him as my rightful laird. May this very blade put me to death if I break my vow." So saying, he kissed the blade and handed it back to Adam.

Daron rose to his feet and Adam clasped his arm in a firm handshake.

Angus did likewise from his bed. "Welcome. See ye serve my son well." He scanned Daron from head to foot. "Get yerself something to eat, man. Ye look like a scarecrow."

Daron grinned. "I will, my laird." He turned to Gwenyth, who looked more bristly than a hedgehog.

"What have you done?" she hissed as Daron approached her.

Adam defended Daron. "What any man of worth would do."

"You." She jabbed her finger in his chest. "You stay out of this." She returned her anger to her cousin, but Eva barged into the fray.

"Out of this chamber with yer yelling and yer anger. Out. Spare my husband—"

"But Eva, this looks to be an interesting discussion," Angus said.

With a glare at her spouse, Eva insisted everyone leave the room and then shut the door firmly.

Trying to diffuse the tension, Adam relied on good manners to pretend nothing was amiss. "Mother, I don't believe you've been introduced to Daron Comyn."

"I am pleased to meet you, Lady Mackintosh." With perceptible patience, he said to Adam, "I would like to see to my men now, my laird. And I think, perhaps, you may have need of a private word with my cousin."

Gwenyth sputtered, but Adam tightened his grip on her arm.

DARON WATCHED as Adam and Gwenyth disappeared into the solar and closed the door. Daron felt sorry for her, for them both, knowing she and Adam must work this out between them. He was tempted to stand outside and listen, but Adam's mother saw his intent and scowled.

"Aye, my mother did teach me better, Lady Eva."

"I suspect we wouldn't have to stand very close to hear this conversation." She pursed her lips. "Come, we'll leave them to shout at each other and get ye something to eat."

GWENYTH SAT DOWN HARD, propelled onto a seat by Adam's grip on her arm. A fire burned brightly in the fireplace, but at Adam's cold visage, Gwenyth rubbed her arms. She dreaded this argument, wanted only to flee him, to flee this place. But his actions a few minutes ago foretold only too clearly that she would not leave Scotland in the foreseeable future. If ever.

She'd like to consign to the netherworld the entire male gender with their pride and love of a good fight. "Aye, every last one of them," she muttered to Adam's stiff back.

He turned. "What did you say?"

"Nothing." With relief Gwenyth noted that she was so angry

she wasn't even tempted to cry. "Why did you force Daron to swear allegiance? He and I were to start a new life. Why do you bind us to this place?"

"You know why. Daron and I can be of mutual benefit to each other. He is determined to find the beast who dishonored you as am I."

"I don't want to stay here." Especially now that Adam was threatening her with a priest.

Adam ran his hand through his hair. "And you think I don't know that?"

"Why can't you just let me go?"

"I can't. This daft bargain you made with Balliol—Gwenyth, it will only bring bloodshed. And your involvement will bring further wrath upon what's left of your clan. Surely you don't want that."

She scowled. "Why must men fight to settle their differences? Why can't you settle disputes some other way?"

"Because men like Leod Macpherson and his ilk don't understand the meaning of such an action. Nor will they be bound by an agreement not made through a show of force."

She flinched, her memories of Leod's methods only too clear in her mind. One more reason to leave Scotland. "Like Edward of England and Robert the Bruce."

"Aye, and your own father. John Comyn betrayed Bruce, didn't keep his promise. 'Tis your father who brought shame and poverty and homelessness upon you, not Bruce."

"My father had a legitimate birthright to the throne."

"Aye, and despite his enmity with Bruce, they made a pact, an alliance in order to oust Edward of England from the Scottish throne. An alliance your father chose to betray. Bruce and his wife barely escaped with their lives."

"You don't know what was said between them that day."

"I was there, Gwenyth. I heard and saw what happened."

"Bruce stabbed my father." She held back tears.

"Aye, he did. After your father drew his dirk."

She stared at him, silent in the face of the awful reality Adam dared to voice.

"I am sorry for your father's death and that my king was the means to it. John Comyn's death set off the events that may well take our country to the brink of destruction."

He came to stand before her. "One thing you should have learned from your family's painful lesson. A man's word—or a woman's—is his most important possession. 'Tis all I have, and I will not go back on it. Ever."

Adam's passionate words stirred Gwenyth. "You would die to keep your word?"

"Aye. And if I should die, Daron will protect you." He paused for a moment. "I will make a good husband, if you let me."

"I'd rather join a nunnery."

He looked as if she'd slapped him. "You don't mean it."

"I do. I have seen enough. I want no part of being a wife to any man." Even one as handsome as the laird of Clan Chattan.

He paced away and back again. "It grieves me to hear you say that, Gwenyth. But your talk of nunneries is naught but idle chatter. Bluntly put, your value as a breeder of future kings would overrule your delicate sensibilities."

"How dare you speak to me thus?"

"I dare it because it's true. If I let you go to Edward, the minute you present him with an heir, he will have what he needs to muster an attack on Bruce's crown." Holding his hand before her, he used his fingers to enumerate his reasoning. "Firstly, the pope will be on Edward's side, for there is no love lost between Rome and Bruce. Secondly, your child will have legitimate claims through both parents, and thirdly, the English will back Balliol in hopes he'll prove as incompetent a king as his father. Then Scotland will be under England's thumb again." He ground his thumb into the opposite palm to illustrate.

"But I gave my word to Edward."

"You have not willingly broken that vow, Gwenyth."

Ah, but she had, in Leod's keep. To save her life and that of an innocent man. A man who was slowly stealing her resolve and her heart.

ADAM WRESTLED with the dilemma Gwenyth presented and decided to talk with his father. He entered the room and saw that Angus seemed to be resting comfortably, for which Adam gave a silent prayer of thanks. How much longer would he be able to come to his father for advice? A cold draft swept through him as he approached his father's bedside.

"Adam. 'Tis good to see ye, lad."

Adam moved an untouched meal from the bedside before sitting down.

Angus said, "Ye look as if the weight of the world is on yer fine shoulders."

Adam grimaced. "It surely feels that way."

"Ye needn't worry. The council usually confirms the old laird's choice, especially when the alternative is someone like Leod."

"It's not that. It's Gwenyth and Daron."

"What of them?"

"I would like to give Daron some land in Altyre."

"I thought the boy wanted to live in England."

"I don't believe Daron would leave Scotland if he could find a home here."

"Those lands are a small payment if Daron's aid helps ye defeat Leod."

"You are quick to come to his side."

"Humph. I've grown fond of the maid."

"'Tis easy enough to do," Adam mused.

Angus studied his son. "I will not stand in the way of a churched marriage between you."

Adam said nothing. Under other circumstances, Adam would have no objections either. But he resented being cast as a warden for his own wife.

"She is in need of a gentle man like yerself, and ye need someone to protect. A good arrangement. And Daron's aid can stand in for a dowry."

"I'm glad you agree, Da."

"There really is no other way."

"Nay, there is not." Until now he hadn't really resigned himself to a loveless marriage. Such was not what he would have chosen.

Angus broke into his thoughts. "The council will need to be won over. After all, she is an enemy."

"Aye, but what better way to subdue her than to marry her?" he asked wryly.

"Exactly. There will probably be less objection than I received in marrying yer mother."

Adam stood and rested his hand on his father's frail shoulder. "We couldn't either of us find an easy bride, eh?"

The twinkle in Angus's eyes gave lie to his failing health. For a moment Adam dared to wish. But he must accept the inevitable.

Shaking off his melancholy, Adam said, "At any rate, I must be ready to explain my actions to the council. And to fight, if necessary."

"It will not be easy."

They clasped hands and Adam reluctantly let go. "Nothing worth having is ever come by easily, Da."

"Nay, it's not. Go with God, son."

LEOD MACPHERSON SLAMMED HIS FIST on the table and stared at Nathara. "You are certain this is not idle gossip?"

Nathara walked to the board where Leod kept his whiskey and poured several fingers of the amber liquid into a glass. Drink and Leod were a dangerous combination, but he was generally more manageable after one or two. So long as he didn't have too much. She handed him the cup. "I saw it myself. Adam is training with the sword every day and nearly bested Seamus. And the Comyn warriors train with him."

Leod cursed.

Trying hard not to sound like a jealous lover, Nathara said, "Perhaps if you'd not been so anxious to sample the woman's charms, you'd have learned who she was before she slipped from your fingers. Her ransom alone—"

"Yes, yes." Leod studied her. "I should have killed Adam when I had the chance."

"Nay," she practically shouted, then more calmly added, "You promised not to harm Adam, only the wench." Adam must live or Nathara's plans would come to nothing. "The council will not choose a murderer to lead the clan," she reminded him.

"Aye, you're right," he admitted grudgingly.

Nathara paced the room. Adam was hers, only hers. The wench must be gotten rid of, one way or another, and Nathara would be there to take up with Adam where they'd left off. If Leod could take her . . .

Leod moved to the board and poured them each a drink. He

downed his glass while she only sipped, the better to keep her wits about her. "I will marry her myself when the handfast is over. Then my son can claim the crown."

"You won't get close to her again; Adam won't allow it."

"Then Adam will die."

"But you promised. Adam is to be my reward for helping you." She felt like she was balancing on a fallen log, one that lay across a deep ravine. Somehow she must convince Leod to allow Adam to live. She must.

He grabbed her and pulled her close, his whiskey-laden breath hot on her face.

She pulled back, but his grip was too strong. "You promised, Leod. Your word had best be worth something if you expect the council members to support you."

He stumbled into her. "Stupid woman. The council will choose me." His malicious grin chilled her. "'Tis obvious Adam can't defend the clan against even a few small cattle raids."

Suddenly she feared Leod would do as he pleased, despite his promises. Leod could do what he wished with the girl, but Nathara would not allow any harm to come to Adam.

Hoping to pacify him she said, "Once you are chief of Clan Chattan, you can do as you will."

"Aye. With the manpower of the federation behind me, I will raise the future king of Scotland. My son."

She pandered to his ego. "Your plan sounds good, but what's to keep Adam from raising the future king instead of you?"

"First of all, he has no ambition." He grinned. "And secondly, he won't live long enough."

She must keep Adam safe. "You can't get close to the woman, but I can."

"What are you suggesting?"

She made a quick decision. "If you let Adam live, I will bring the woman to you."

He stared at her as if wondering if she could be trusted. "You will do this?"

"Only if you give your word, Leod."

"And how do I know you will keep your word, Nathara?"

"If I don't, you will kill Adam and I cannot abide that."

He studied her for a few minutes and Nathara despaired of getting her way.

"Bring her to me."

SEVENTEEN

THE CHAPEL AT MOY was a small room off the solar on the main floor of the castle. The only extravagances in the otherwise plain architecture of the castle were found here in this room dedicated to God. An arched stained-glass window adorned the wall above the altar. A wooden lintel and post—carved in the style of the ancients with circles, whorls, and unbroken lace patterns—lined the doorway.

Two of his mother's scented beeswax candles graced the altar. Gwenyth seemed so lost—he'd thought perhaps the familiar words might soothe her troubled spirit. But he had no idea if she'd used the book or not. He should question her, but sensed she would not appreciate the intrusion into her spiritual life any more than she'd welcomed his presence otherwise.

Adam stood before the altar, his bristling bride beside him. His earlier image of Gwenyth as a hedgehog came to mind, but though anger and resentment hung about her like a dark cloud, she most assuredly did not resemble a hedgehog.

She was beautiful—delicate facial features, full lips, and auburn hair spilling to her waist. She had protested, had not felt worthy of this custom which denoted an innocent maid. But he had insisted she wear it down, because she was innocent of what should be between husband and wife.

He wondered if she might eventually thank him for the gesture.

Judging from the scowl on her face, gratitude was not an emotion she was familiar with at the moment.

Traditionally, the marriage promises were made on the steps of the church before a crowd of witnesses. But today only Morogh, Daron, and Adam's grim-faced mother attended. Adam would announce the marriage at the council meeting next week. Until then, no one else was to know of it. There was no need to fling the news far and wide, for the marriage certainly brought little joy to anyone. Certainly not to Gwenyth.

But more importantly, the marriage would remain private because Adam feared for Gwenyth's safety. So long as they were merely handfast, those who objected could content themselves with the knowledge that the union was temporary. Vows before a priest were far more difficult to rescind. Not impossible, but nearly so. These vows that would protect her from Bruce might very well endanger her among Adam's own people. Secrecy would gain her another week of security.

Like father, like son. Neither Angus nor Adam had chosen a smooth road. Adam smiled ruefully, bolstered by this image of being so much like his father.

Adam brought his wandering thoughts back to the proceedings at hand. The priest positioned himself before them and began the ceremony. Adam watched her face as he described his dower upon her. "I, Adam Mackintosh, do give to my wife the lands and manor home of Altyre as her dower."

She stared at him, wide-eyed as he announced her dowry to him—Daron and his warriors were all she brought to their marriage. That and a deep-seated animosity toward her husband's king.

Despite his feelings for her, feelings he couldn't deny, Adam stifled his resentment at the necessity of solidifying this union. He had promised her refuge, little knowing it would lead to this. But if the handfast had delayed Balliol's plan, this marriage would end it.

Satisfied his decision safeguarded the woman and his king, Adam eyed his bride. If anything, she was even more resentful than he. She might resign herself to a life in Scotland, but would she ever resign herself to being a wife? Was he doomed to a lifetime with a woman who would, at best, tolerate the need to produce children? Could he risk rejection again and court her to win her love?

When the priest bade them be fruitful and multiply, Adam's heart leapt to his throat. Again he gazed at Gwenyth, but her face betrayed no emotion. Had the priest's words made no impact on her? There would be no feast to celebrate this marriage, no bedding ceremony, yet the marriage must be consummated to bind Gwenyth to him.

How? Without forcing her, how was he to gain her agreement? He'd promised a chaste marriage. If it was to be otherwise, she would have to allow it. He shook his head, bringing his focus back to the priest, who was looking at him expectantly.

"You may kiss your bride, Laird Mackintosh."

For a moment he thought to lift her up in his arms and hold her eye to eye, lips to lips. Aye, in a happier ceremony he'd have done just that. Joyfully. Instead he bent low, chastely bussing her cheek just as he'd done that day by the lake. *Friends.* Adam sighed, praying he would find a way to retain her friendship while becoming her husband.

Adam walked his bride to the doorway in the back of the small chapel to greet their subdued guests. Morogh and Daron murmured their congratulations before taking their leave. Lady Eva squeezed his hand and kissed Gwenyth's cheek as she left. When Gwenyth turned to follow, Adam held her back, desiring a moment alone with her. This conversation would do little to reassure her, he feared. But it could not be helped.

Her regard had softened a bit, thankfully. After pulling the door closed, he took her small hand in his and said, "This is hardly the way to begin a marriage, Gwenyth, but I must warn you. If you attempt to leave Moy, I will place you under guard within the keep. Should you actually manage to escape, let me tell you what awaits you outside my gates."

She flinched at his harsh tone, and he regretted the necessity, but she must understand what she risked if she harbored any foolish notions.

He pulled a missive from the folds of his plaid. "I have received word from my foster brother, who serves with Bruce. Your aunt, the countess of Strathearn, and her nephew Sir William Soulis, have been sentenced to life imprisonment for their part in Balliol's conspiracy against Bruce. You could still suffer their fate."

Her eyes widened in surprise. Perhaps she hadn't realized her relatives' involvement. He held the parchment out so that she might read it for herself, but she didn't reach for it. When she made no comment, he said, "I would have your promise you will stay within my walls."

Her chin came up a notch. "And if I can't give it?"

Daft, stubborn woman. "Leod also awaits you, Gwenyth." Her obstinacy drove him to prod her. "But perhaps you are conspiring with Leod to depose me as laird?"

"Nay." She shrank away from him.

He cocked his head. "You fear him, then?"

Her trembling hands gave him all the answer he really needed. "Aye."

Sorry for goading her, he gentled his voice. "He's the one, isn't he?"

She hesitated, the stubbornness gone as quickly as it came. "Aye," she whispered.

"How can you be sure?"

At her look of indignation, he hastened to assure her. "I believe you. But how do you know?"

She played with the ends of her hair, twisting and untwisting it about her finger. For a moment he wanted nothing more than to run his own hand through the length of it, to . . .

With difficulty, he reined in his wayward thoughts. "How do you know this for sure, Gwenyth?"

The pained expression on her face told him she dredged up unbearable memories to answer his question. She touched the brooch at his shoulder, fingering it as if memorizing the details. "This pin is unique, is it not?"

He would humor her; give her the time she seemed to need. "Aye. 'Twas made especially for my father when he became captain of the federation."

"And Leod's brooch is unique as well?"

"I'm sure he has more than one, as I do. But yes, he has one unique to him as laird of the Macphersons. Why do you ask?"

She looked up from the brooch. "When Leod demanded I accuse you, I believed it must be you who had . . . It was so dark." She laid her palm against his cheek. "But you had no beard, your face was tanned, and you were so kind to me that evening. I didn't know who to believe, you or Leod. And then I noticed Leod's brooch and it matched a most unusual bruise . . ."

Her voice trembled, and the hand on his face slipped away.

He gently brought her into his embrace as he fought his rage. He kissed her temple and held her close. "I'll kill him, Gwenyth. I swear it. I'll kill that misbegotten brute."

He held her until her trembling ceased and his anger subsided. And then it hit him, and he turned and smacked his palm against the stone wall.

She jumped away from him. "What?"

"If I make this known and accuse Leod, he will escape punishment because I've already been found guilty. And your life will be in even more danger. Leod doesn't like to leave witnesses."

Seeing her baffled look, he continued, "You need to know that several of my clanswomen have also suffered your fate. One still clutched a mask in her hands when she was found. Dead."

Her face turned so pale he feared she would faint. "Leod."

Reaching out to steady her, he replied, "I have no evidence, but yes, I can believe it was him."

"Why? Why does he do this?"

"I don't know." He grasped her arms to calm her. "But you understand why you must not leave Moy?"

She nodded, and some color returned to her cheeks.

He placed Bryan's letter back inside his plaid. "I have your word, then?"

"Aye."

"Good. There is another matter we need to discuss, Gwenyth." He took his hands from her arms and paced a few steps away. When he turned back to her, she seemed composed. He hoped so.

"King Robert is satisfied that marriage to me resolves your involvement with Balliol. In truth, I think he is loath to bring more harm down on you or your clan." He returned to stand beside her, wishing he didn't have to say the rest. Wishing he could erase the anxiety her face revealed. "His letter contained a command I find I cannot obey. He orders me to make the marriage binding, to consummate the vows as quickly as decency allows."

A sharp intake of breath was her only response as she stared wide-eyed at him.

Raking his fingers through his hair, he fought to keep his voice calm. "By the saints, Gwenyth, I've made many promises, but none

I am more determined to keep than my promise not to force you. I cannot do that to you, not even for my king."

She walked away and stood before the altar rail, and he thought she would fall to her knees and pray. She just stood there, staring at he knew not what. He could not make himself go to her, just as could not fathom what her response might be.

His enemy, his wife. God help him, he was falling in love with her.

He would not, could not harm her any more than he'd ever been able to harm any of God's creatures. He had never hunted for sport, but only to feed his family. And he had never killed another man, except in battle.

And he had never lifted his hand to a woman, nor would he start now.

When he thought he couldn't bear her silence a moment longer, she turned. To his surprise, her features had softened. By the heavens above, she was so lovely. Golden flecks sparkled in her dark brown eyes, and the early morning light from the stained glass behind the altar glinted in gold and red highlights in her hair. Hair that covered her breasts and fell softly, swinging now as she walked toward him.

She stood in front of him, so small, so beautiful.

He wanted desperately to kiss her full lips, to cover her in kisses. Aye, he would give her reason to be willing, but she would have to invite him. And there was little chance of that.

A wistful smile played upon her features as she looked up at him. "I will be honest, Adam. I am not happy to be a prisoner."

He smiled back at her. "And I am not happy to be your warden, lady. I would much rather be a husband." He kissed her, a far more chaste kiss than he would have liked. But she deserved his restraint. She was his wife, and he would honor her as best he could by teaching her to enjoy his touch.

Somehow. Some way.

He was encouraged when she didn't shrink from him.

"I'm not happy to wed a man who serves a king I can never give allegiance to." She stepped closer and cupped his cheek with her hand.

He leaned into her touch, kissed her palm, then said, "I understand that you would hate the man who killed your father. I won't ask you to forgive him. That is between you and God. But I will demand your loyalty."

"Yet you will not heed his order concerning our marriage." She gazed at him in wonder. "Truth be told, Adam Mackintosh, there cannot be a more honorable man in all of Scotland."

He stared at her, dumbfounded by this declaration, unsure just what it meant. "If it weren't for my overwrought honor, you wouldn't be here to begin with."

"Oh, Adam. Don't blame yourself for Leod's evilness."

"But if I'd taken you to my room, he wouldn't have harmed you."

She took his large hand in both of hers. "I will not compel you to disobey your king. I will come to you willingly, as willing as I am able, this once, Adam. More than that I cannot promise."

"Willing is the only way I'll have you, Gwenyth." He closed his eyes, stifling an urge to crush her to him. But he held himself in check. He knew this gift she offered came with a terrible price for her. Yet she offered, and only a fool would not accept.

"As willing as you are able. More than that I will not ask." He lifted her small hand to his lips and kissed the delicate fingers.

"You won't ask for my promise to remain at Moy?"

"Death awaits you outside my walls, Gwenyth. Perhaps in this one night you've granted me, I can convince you to choose life instead."

She withdrew her hand, as if distressed by his reminder of what the night would bring. "We'd best be going."

"Aye, my lady." *Before my self-discipline deserts me.*

Adam escorted Gwenyth to the keep, where she asked permission to retire to her chamber. Clearly her promise for this evening did not include a desire to spend the daylight hours in his company, and so Adam headed for the smith in hopes of finding Morogh.

He nearly collided with Nathara. "Good day to you."

"Good day, my laird." She tucked a strand of hair behind her ear with a nervous gesture, then made as if to continue on.

Curious, Adam delayed her with a hand on her arm. "We've not spoken in some time, Nathara. How go things with you?"

She edged away, glancing toward the keep. "Fine, my laird. I must go. I rode this morn and I need to wash and help your mother."

"Where did you ride?"

"Oh, just to the wood above the falls."

He'd always thought she'd be a better liar than this. Such nervousness in a woman born to an easiness in stride and conversation bespoke of deceit. "A lovely spot."

"Oh, aye. A bonny spot, to be certain." Again the agitated motion to tame her hair. "I must go, Adam. I'm late."

"Of course. I'm sorry to keep you."

She made a quick curtsy and fled.

He walked on to the smith, where he found Morogh overseeing the repair of the Comyn men's weapons. After praising the smith's efforts, Adam pulled Morogh aside. "Put a watch on Nathara. I have reason to believe she is up to mischief."

"You think she's carryin' tales?"

"I don't know what she's up to, but I'll warrant it's not good."

Satisfied that all was as it should be, Adam left Morogh and walked to the hall for the midday meal. As he strode to the dais, he was surprised and glad to find Gwenyth at the high table. She rose to greet him like a proper wife, and he bent over her hand to feather a kiss upon it, like a proper bridegroom. Aye, he would woo her and risk rejection, for she was worth the gamble.

But he'd barely begun his campaign before a shout and commotion arose to interrupt the meal. Ordering Gwenyth to stay indoors, Adam hurried to the bailey. One of the men Adam had sent to watch for cattle thieves galloped into the enclosure and slid his horse to a halt in front of them.

The man nearly tumbled into the dirt in his haste to dismount. Adam's gut clenched. Cattle raids were far too common an occurrence to incite such excitement.

Having righted himself, the man made a cursory bow to Adam. "My laird. There's been another raid."

"How many cattle?"

"Nay, my lord, only three or four beasties were lifted. They didna come for the cattle—they attacked the village at Glen Corry."

Cattle raiding was an accepted annoyance of life in the highlands, but attacking a village was tantamount to a declaration of war. Before questioning the sentry further, Adam ordered Morogh to mount a troop of men for a fast ride.

"Any loss of life, Ivar?"

"Nay, but William McBean is hurt bad. Someone tried to nab his Mary, but William ran him off."

Adam shook his head, wondering if this was more of Leod's doing. He'd thought the death of the last victim might make Leod more cautious. "Did the rest of the watch follow the trail to see where it leads?"

"'Twas no need, my laird. The fool dropped his bonnet. 'Twas a Cameron."

"Indeed." He found it much too convenient that the man was clumsy enough to leave behind his clan badge to identify himself.

Whoever had attacked the village must hope to stir trouble by such deceit. For although the Camerons were known to help themselves to Chattan cattle now and then, their laird had no reason to attack Adam's people.

Adam had to believe this was more of Leod's doing. But how could he prove it? As he mulled over that thought, Gwenyth laid her hand on his arm. "Shall I come with you?"

"Have you forgotten our earlier conversation?" She recoiled at the sharpness of his voice, and he softened his tone. "I appreciate the offer of help, Gwenyth, but I will take Nathara to tend the wounded."

"As you wish, my laird."

Morogh brought Kai to him and Adam brushed a kiss across Gwenyth's cheek before mounting the restive stallion. Gwenyth gave a weak smile then turned and walked back into the hall.

She looked troubled, and Adam regretted that he was the cause of it. But for now his duty as a bridegroom must be pushed aside by his duty as laird.

THE VILLAGE lay to the north, not far from the border with the Cameron holdings. When they arrived, Adam inspected the damaged crofter's huts and spoke with the wounded as Nathara tended to them. Only three cattle were taken, making it obvious that the people had been the target. William McBean's injuries included a broken leg, but Nathara assured him the man would recover.

When Adam had questioned the last of the victims, he ordered Morogh to gather the men together for the ride back to Moy. While he waited one of the women brought Adam a cup of chamomile tea, which he gratefully accepted.

As the warm liquid soothed him, a long-ago memory flashed through Adam's mind. Of a carefree summer day in his childhood turned to horror as Leod swung a kitten by its tail. Adam tried to rescue the creature, but Leod ran. He followed and Leod threatened to fling the kitten into a tree if Adam didn't back off. Angry and frustrated to tears, Adam had watched as his cousin walked away, the poor animal hanging from his hand.

Adam never saw that kitten again. How foolish to believe that Leod would outgrow such cruelty.

Morogh brought his horse, and they mounted up and headed home. Even Nathara was subdued as they made their way back to the castle.

As he contemplated the day's events, Adam allowed himself to wish he wasn't laird, didn't have to weigh each action and its consequences to the clan. Just a simple man with a simple life—with a wife and children and a plot of land to tend like these crofters.

He smiled at a vision of little towheaded bairns clinging to his knee, begging for a story. Of boys who would need to be taught to protect the weak and innocent in their care. And daughters who would bring laughter and joy to the clan.

Adam's reverie was interrupted when Morogh brought his horse abreast of Kai and Adam. They had reached the hill overlooking the loch just as the evening sun cast shadows to play upon the scene.

Morogh pointed to the keep. "The laird's pennant has been lowered."

Instantly alert, Adam halted his horse and Morogh did likewise. "Do you think there's mischief afoot?"

"Aye, the raid may have been a ruse to lure ye from the castle while someone attacked."

"But if the alarm was sounded in time, the castle is virtually impossible to take." Adam looked again to the rampart. Despite the failing light, the laird's flag should be plainly visible, waving in the breeze. But it clearly was not.

He felt his heart go still.

Da.

Ignoring Morogh's shouts of warning, Adam spurred his horse and galloped across the causeway. As his mount slid to a halt in the bailey, the grief-filled faces of the men-at-arms confirmed his fear.

Angus Mackintosh was dead.

EIGHTEEN

$$\approx \cdot \approx$$

THE DEATH OF HER FAMILY, destruction of her home, and Leod's cruelty had crushed Gwenyth's spirit. Daron's betrayal had seemed to be the final blow. But the death of Angus Mackintosh proved to be more than Gwenyth could bear alone.

On her knees in the chapel where she'd been married just this morning, she cried for all she'd lost. The tears came out in racking sobs and she could not hold them back. She cried not only in grief for the dead, but also for the chasm she'd created between herself and her Savior.

As she prayed she sensed that she could no longer hide from the God she had mistakenly blamed for her misfortune. In the midst of this new pain and grief, she prayed for his strength and comfort, and as the tears subsided, his peace enveloped her. God had not abandoned her, nor would he ever do so.

Father Jerard, the priest she'd refused to talk to, found her in the chapel.

"Here, lass." He offered her a scrap of cloth to wipe her eyes and blow her nose, and she took it gratefully.

"Thank you, Father."

"I sense that you were as fond of Angus as he was of you."

Gwenyth sniffed. "He was so very kind to me."

"Aye, even after he learned your true name." He looked at her thoughtfully. "Perhaps your grief today has as much to do with your other trials as it does Angus's death."

Another tear escaped. Gwenyth swiped it with the back of her hand and nodded.

"Would you like me to pray with you?"

"Aye, please."

Father Jerard's prayer eased Gwenyth's heart and she began to pray for Angus, for Adam's safe return from the village, and finally for forgiveness for doubting God's faithfulness.

Saying good-bye to Father Jerard, she went to her room. Just before sunset she heard Adam return. Thoughts of her promise to accept him as husband crowded her prayers even as she hoped that his grief would delay the evening.

ADAM LEAPED FROM HIS HORSE and went straight into the keep to find his mother. Eva's face showed strain and the telltale signs of tears, but she embraced her son and patted his back, crooning as if he alone bore the grief of Da's death.

Adam led his mother to a chair by the hearth in the great hall, sitting her down and holding her hand.

"I went to his room to tell him about yer marriage. He was resting quietly, but, must have sensed me there. When he opened his eyes, I knew the time had come."

"Did you have time to say good-bye, then?" Adam forced the words past a lump in his throat.

"Aye, we did. Yer father wanted ye to know he was proud of ye. He said to take good care of the lassie. And he asked me to give ye this." She held out a parchment with his father's seal. Adam put it inside his plaid, tucking it under his belt for safe-keeping.

Fearing his voice would betray him, Adam gazed at his hands.

Eva laid her hand on his arm. "Angus was a wise and wonderful man. And his son shows every promise of being the same."

At the moment, he didn't feel worthy of such praise. He could find no words of consolation, and so he simply sat with her until the need for solitude overwhelmed him and he left her for the sanctuary of his room.

Once inside his chamber, he barred the door and laid the letter on top of the chest where he stored his weapons. Adam dropped onto a stool, staring into the fire, fighting the grief that washed over him. Head in hands, memories flooded him, and he wept. He thought of his last meeting with Angus and praised God they had not been shouting at one another.

Aye, they had clasped hands and wished each other well. Man to man. He found consolation in the image.

When the tears stopped, Adam rose, feeling weak and ragged. He splashed water on his face from the pitcher and bowl on the table, dried off, then moved woodenly to pick up the letter and broke the seal. When his vision cleared, he read his father's shaky handwriting:

> *I know your mother will tell you this, but I wanted you to hear it once more from me. I am proud to call you my son, and I have faith that you, and someday your son, will lead Clan Chattan well. Remember all I tried to teach you, and take care of your mother.*
>
> *And Adam. Marry the lassie. It is time to find ways to bring peace to the highlands. We must learn to forgive and to forge new alliances such as the one you've begun with young Daron. Show the way, Adam, for the good of our people and Scotland.*
>
> *Peace.*

THE FIGHT AT DALRY had taught Adam all he ever wanted to know about war. He would fight to defend what was his, but he would also do anything in his power to keep the peace.

As he'd proven by marrying Gwenyth. Of course, when he was honest with himself, he admitted that he cared about her and hoped she would one day return his feelings. It was foolish to nourish any resentment, because if Robert hadn't placed her well-being in his hands, Adam would have sought some means of persuading her to remain for the full year and a day. And beyond.

How he wished he could ask his father for advice. And yet, hadn't Angus given his final say? *Marry the lassie.*

I did, Da. And in a few hours, he was supposed to do his best to bind her to him.

Adam folded the letter and placed it in his writing chest, wishing grief could be as easily locked away.

He spent the next hour overseeing the sending of messengers far and wide with the news of Angus's death.

GWENYTH CAME to the great hall for the very subdued evening meal and took her seat beside Adam. She appeared pale, and he suspected she had shed a few tears as well. He pressed her hand in greeting, and was rewarded with a return squeeze.

Neither ate much, and when the last of the meal was cleared, she turned to him. "I will await you in my chamber, my laird." Adam hoped the sadness in her voice was from grief and not anticipation of his company. He nodded, not at all sure he wanted to have a wedding night under the circumstances.

After what he hoped was an adequate length of time, Adam rose to bid his mother good night. "I don't wish to leave you here alone. May I escort you to your room?"

She patted his hand. "Thank ye, son. I shall stay here before the fire, as is my custom. I find it comforting to see that life does go on."

He hesitated, not sure if he should stay or go.

Eva smiled at him. "Go to her, Adam. Nothing would please your father more than to have ye sire his grandson tonight."

Adam felt his face grow warm. "Well, I can certainly try." He managed a grin. "For his sake."

Eva's eyes sparkled, and Adam knew his father's love embraced her still, even from the grave.

And he envied them.

Foolishly, he prayed to find that same abiding love with Gwenyth. Yet when he found himself standing outside her door a few minutes later, it wasn't hope or love, nor even duty or desire that held him there.

Just a bone-deep need to be consoled. To find respite from the guilt of his trespasses at Dalry. To find peace in the healing connection with another soul. The peace that could be found in the embrace of a cherished lover.

He braced his hands against the wall and hung his head as disappointment and grief crashed through him. Gwenyth was not a willing wife, but a reluctant one. How could he ask her for comfort when he must be the one with patience and understanding? She needed him to teach her the way of a man with a maid, and he wasn't sure he could do that tonight.

Slowly he turned and walked down the short passage to his own room where he sat before the dying fire and wept.

Sometime later, while tears still wet his cheeks, he heard the door latch lift. As he watched over his shoulder, the door opened, and Gwenyth entered his room unbidden. Traces of apprehension shone in her golden eyes, yet she walked with purpose to him.

Without a word, she cradled his head against her body, crooning words of comfort. After a few minutes, she released him and wiped his tears with the hem of her chemise. Then she held out her hand to him and said, "Come with me, Adam. Your room is cold and we are meant to sleep together this night."

With joy that she had come to him and apprehension for what lay ahead, he placed his hand in hers, stood, and followed where she led.

GWENYTH'S HAND TREMBLED as she closed the door to her chamber behind Adam, leaving it unlocked. For she couldn't bear to lock herself in a room with a man who meant to . . . no, she refused to believe Adam's touch would be anything but gentle. She had gone to find him, thinking he'd changed his mind, hoping he had. But when she'd seen him sitting there, head in his hands and full of sorrow, she knew she must give him comfort. She had promised to accept him willingly, and she would honor that promise.

The willing part was not so hard. He stood there facing her, tall and strong, his golden hair burnished by firelight. He held his damaged arm more naturally than when she'd first met him. Deep-blue eyes still held his sorrow, yet a sense of wonder also stole over his face as he stared at her. Aye, it was far too easy to be willing when faced with his physical beauty.

But it was far too easy to be frightened when faced with his size and strength. A shiver coursed through her at the memory of his bare chest and powerful sword strokes in the lists. Memories of Leod's rough hands and brutality reminded her of what she faced. She panicked, afraid she would not be able to give him what she'd promised despite her fervent prayers earlier in the chapel.

To steady her failing resolve, she clung to Adam's recent assurance that loving should be different than what she'd experienced.

Saints knew it must be, else she doubted there would be so many children born.

His eyes revealed his sadness, and she could feel his distress. A need to be comforted. And another craving she didn't understand and couldn't signify. His gaze roved over her, and the sadness was slowly replaced by a gleam of anticipation, and her heartbeat quickened in response.

"Thank you for bringing me here." Adam held his hand out to her. "Do you trust me?"

"I want to."

And then he smiled. "We have had this conversation before."

She smiled in return and gave him her hand.

He led her to sit before the fire and they talked of Angus. He seemed to want to remember his father, to tell her events from his childhood and of his father's stern but loving parenting. She shared with him her brief times with Angus, and they were content and easy with one another, despite occasional tears.

Still, she did not sit back in her chair, and she startled when he stood and stretched his hands in front of him. He lowered his arms slowly, and his earlier ease disappeared.

"We need not . . . I understand if you wish to postpone this, Gwenyth." He glanced at the large time-keeping candle on the mantle. "I've been here long enough to accomplish what is expected, and none will be the wiser."

But she could see the longing had returned to his eyes, and it struck her that he needed more than just to do his duty or satisfy desire. He needed comfort. Her comfort. Yet how could what she'd endured with Leod possibly provide comfort for either party?

There was only one way to find out, and she could think of no other man she would trust to show her.

He started toward the door.

"Wait. Adam, wait."

She stepped to him, and laying her hand against his back, gently urged him to face her. "Tomorrow—who knows if we will even have it? We can only be sure of this time, this night."

As he cradled her face in his rough hands, he smiled a smile that promised tenderness and laughter. Adam tugged her hand. "Come. Let's use this time to become comfortable with each other."

She followed him until they were once again in front of the fire. He sat down, handed her a comb, and laid his head back against the chair and closed his eyes. "I thought perhaps you might like to comb my hair."

"Comb your hair?"

He opened his eyes. "I used to love it when my mother combed my hair after a bath. I thought it might help you feel more easy about touching me. And it would ease my spirit tonight."

Amazed by his thoughtful gesture and his admission of need, she took the comb and he closed his eyes again. She glanced down at his woolen stocking and the dirk strapped to his shin.

He trusts me.

She could slit his throat and be gone before anyone disturbed the newlywed couple. But she wasn't even tempted, for the thought of any harm coming to this compassionate man tied her stomach in a knot.

Ignoring the knife, she touched his flaxen hair, something she'd often thought of doing. From the tightness of the curl, she'd expected it to feel tough and wiry. But it was surprisingly soft, and the curls sprang back into place.

Tonight she would learn what drew a man and woman together and the secrets that bound a husband and wife. Somehow, she would force her mind to forget Leod's actions and think only of Adam. And the ways he touched her heart.

But Adam kept his word and Gwenyth learned yet again that this man was a man of honor. They talked deep into the night and gave each other consolation without becoming lovers.

Sometime near morning, Gwenyth awoke to the unfamiliar feeling of Adam's big body—her husband's body—curled around her like a protective shield. As she dozed back to sleep, she knew she had never, in all her life, felt safer than she did in this man's arms.

Nineteen

Sleepily, Gwenyth pulled her head from under the pillow and answered a knock on the door. No doubt a servant bringing breakfast. "Come in," she responded. She had slept like the dead, and yet languidness filled her this morn. For the first time in a long while, she was tempted to remain abed and take a late meal in her room.

The woman cleared her throat and Gwenyth opened one eye. Then both eyes, as she bolted upright, clutching the covers to her. Her action elicited a grunt and a swiping of the blanket by Adam.

Adam! Heat rose to her face as she looked from the man in her bed to his mother.

Eva's gaze was tender and bittersweet. "I see I need not have worried. My son is safely in bed. With his wife." A troubled frown creased her face and was gone. "Best to wake him slowly, child—he's a bear first thing in the morning."

Gwenyth could only stare—words refused to form in her mind.

"I'm sorry to disturb you, but there are things to be done for the funeral. Would you send him to me—"

"I'm awake, Mother. Now go away." Adam's voice was muffled by the bedclothes, but there was no mistaking his bad humor.

"Some things never change." And with that Eva quietly left Gwenyth to deal with Adam.

Gingerly, Gwenyth left the bed and retrieved her tunic and

kirtle from the hook where she had hung it. She hastened to her wooden chest and picked up the polished mirror, inspecting her face. Not a trace of a bruise—Adam's touch had been gentle and it frightened her.

But Adam didn't frighten her. Her reaction to him did.

He'd once spoken of the bond that was formed between husband and wife. With growing alarm, she realized that unless she fought that bond, she was in danger of throwing away everything she'd come to think she desired. And for what? For the love Adam promised?

Papa, what shall I do?

For too long she'd worked to avenge her father's cruel death. Edward Balliol had offered her the means to do that. But Edward couldn't promise a home and security. And such dreams couldn't compete with the reality of Adam and the attachment she feared could be formed with him.

She wiped her tears on the sleeve of her chemise and became aware of a presence standing behind her.

Adam cradled her in his arms, his chin resting gently on the top of her head. "Hush, now. We will find a way through this, Gwenyth, I promise."

He turned her to face him, and wiped away a stray tear with his thumb. "Last night . . . Gwenyth, if you were never to lie with me, I think I'd probably die for wanting you. But there is more, much more, to marriage than bedsport. Marriage must also be about loyalty and commitment." His thumb rubbed her mother's ring.

She swallowed. "What about love?"

His smile was tender now. "I believe love comes about as a result of those other things. You'll remember I once spoke of a bond?"

"Aye." She remembered well.

He took a deep breath. "Just being with you, holding you in my arms. You are my true wife, Gwenyth. I say it is so, and I dare any man to say otherwise." He shoved his fingers through his unruly hair. "I would defy the hounds of Hades if they tried to take you from Moy."

Safety. Commitment. Home. Could she find it all here? With Adam?

His words were fierce, but in his eyes she saw a wounded man whose betrothed had rejected him. An honorable man who would marry an enemy to protect his king and then defy that same king rather than harm a frightened woman.

Did she dare to hope that love would grow out of loyalty and commitment as Adam believed? Could she trust him with her battered heart? And until she answered those questions, how would she stop herself from falling in love with Adam Mackintosh?

Perhaps it was too late.

NEWLYWED OR NOT, duty called and Adam was glad they would both have time to consider his words. He'd made his feelings clear to her, except for one detail. Of all the things he'd sought from her last night, never had he expected to glimpse the very gates of paradise. But that's exactly what he'd found, and he had no intention of stepping through them without Gwenyth.

Somehow, some way, he would make her his in every way.

But first, the care and feeding of his people still had to be seen to—work didn't wait on births or deaths or the longings of a new bridegroom. And along with the daily details the impending funeral loomed.

At midmorning he found himself in the surgery of Castle Moy, where several of Daron's men had been sent for Nathara to treat. Their time in the makeshift shelter and exposure to the elements had caused a number of them to take sick.

He stepped into the room, surprised to see Daron among those waiting for Nathara's attention. She glanced up at Adam's arrival, and he could have sworn her complexion paled. When she knocked over a vial of her medicine, Adam's amusement turned to suspicion.

"Good day to you, Nathara. I see you have no lack of patients."

"Aye, my laird." She dropped her gaze. "I am sorry about Angus."

"Thank you, lass. Do you need one of the kitchen girls to help here?"

"That would be most appreciated."

Adam noted her stiff speech, as if they had never been anything but laird and vassal. It was a good performance, he'd give her that.

Daron left his place in line to stand beside Adam.

They spoke quietly as Nathara took care of the others. Soon it was Daron's turn, and she approached them, directing a glare at Daron. "What's your ailment?"

"Nothing. I just came to see to my men."

"Well, they're fine—nothing serious." She appraised the wound on his temple. "Someone did a terrible job of stitching that for you."

"Aye, well, it was either Dougal's unsteady hand or bleed to death." Daron smiled at her, and from the look on his face, Nathara's charms weren't lost on him. But her recent behavior didn't sit well with Adam, and he considered warning Daron off. Then again, perhaps he should encourage a relationship—Daron might learn something useful.

But Nathara's next words didn't bode well for such a plan. "Too bad Dougal was competent, if sloppy. We'd have one less Comyn to deal with."

Daron's smile was flirtatious, despite the insult. "Perhaps I should show you my charming manners and change your mind."

"You have nothing to show me that I care to see."

"That's enough, Nathara," Adam ordered, taking her to task for such disrespect.

Her eyes blazed, and Adam saw attraction there as well as anger. It didn't surprise him—Daron was a well-favored man. If the attraction proved mutual, he would encourage his new vassal.

"Come, Daron. Let's take a turn at the watch."

"'Twould be an honor to keep the watch o'er your father. Perhaps now that she has no patients, Nathara would bring us food and drink?"

Adam smiled. "Aye, Nathara. Do that."

"There's food and drink laid out already."

Daron said, "Ah, more's the pity. We'll have to forego your delightful company."

Nathara glared at them, and Daron laughed as Adam guided him away. They made their way to the chapel, where Angus lay in state. A small trestle and bench sat off to the side and Adam placed his food and drink there, then murmured a thanks to the departing men who'd been keeping watch.

Then he stood before Angus, where he lay on a cloth-covered trestle, hands at his sides and a saucer of salt on his chest to keep evil spirits away. From the moment of death until he was buried, the body was kept under watch, never left alone, so that the departed's spirit could be guided to the proper place with the prayers of the watchers.

Daron came to stand beside him. "I'm sorry, Adam. I've heard only good things about your father, even from my own family. He was regarded as a fair and honest man."

"Aye, what more could you want to have said of you?"

"Perhaps that you were brave in battle?"

Adam pushed away thoughts of that day in August when he'd

been brave enough, at least as brave as a man in that condition could be. He just hadn't been competent.

He arranged the bench so they could lean against the wall and sat down. Daron joined him.

Picking at his food, Adam remarked, "'Tis a strange set of events that has us sitting here this day."

"To be sure."

"I would speak of them, if you don't mind?"

"To what purpose? Do you question the sincerity of my pledge to you?" He raised a hand to stop Adam's reply. "You should wonder at my change of heart. I think I would not trust you if you didn't."

Adam sensed a kindred spirit in Daron, a man who would keep his word and remain loyal. A man who loved his country, who perhaps regretted having supported England. "I would speak of them to understand why you pledged to me."

Daron studied his food. "I want revenge for my cousin's honor. That is the plain and simple truth."

The memory of Gwenyth's bruised face and battered body whetted Adam's own thirst for revenge, making it easy to accept Daron's explanation, but he pressed for more. "Your cousin and his father were killed by my king; your clan has been ravaged by Bruce's anger. We should be bitter enemies."

"When I've accomplished my goal, we can be again, if you like."

Adam chuckled. "I like you, Daron Comyn." He glanced at the bier and sobered. "My father fought also, and it was his fondest wish that Bruce would bring peace and prosperity and an end to our quarrel with England."

"This war is far from over."

"Aye. Perhaps it was a foolish wish, since we highlanders seem especially good at harboring a grudge."

Now it was Daron who laughed. "Oh, yes, we are good at that. Grudges and feuds and war."

They raised and clinked their tankards. Adam had noted that Daron also took water rather than ale or wine. But he made no mention of it.

"And speaking of feuds, the council will convene after the burial to decide who will be captain of the federation."

"Will you be disputed?"

"Aye, Leod will make his case against me. And I fear those grudges and feuds you mentioned will mean a rough road for me."

Daron leaned back. "How so?"

"Someone seems to have a peculiar affinity lately for Chattan cattle. Leod has convinced a number of minor chiefs that I can't protect our interests."

"Loyalty is not easy to come by," Daron observed. "You've not done yourself a favor by taking my oath, Adam."

Adam sat with his arms resting on his thighs, hands hanging between them. "Nay, I haven't. Leod is accusing you of the recent assaults on our women." When Daron jumped up in protest, Adam quickly added, "Sit down, man. I've made it clear I don't believe it and challenged him to bring me proof. Watch your back, especially now so many are coming to Moy for the funeral. Someone may use the opportunity to kill John Comyn's kinsman."

"'Tis fortunate the kinship is on my mother's side."

"Fortunate for you, not Gwenyth," Adam mused.

"Aye, she carries the burden of royal blood. Still, animosity being what it is, I'll heed your advice and guard my back. And Gwenyth's." Daron hesitated, seeming unsure how to say what was on his mind. "Bruce might very well see this association with Comyns as treachery, Adam. As a means to put your own son on the throne."

"I have no such delusions of grandeur, and my king well knows it."

Daron said, "I hope so. I would not like to see Gwenyth hurt again."

"And you think I will?"

"In all honesty, not if you can help it."

"I think we both have her best interests at heart. And securing my position is the first and most important step."

Daron agreed.

Adam studied the man he'd thought owned Gwenyth's affections. "There was a time when I thought perhaps there was more between you and Gwenyth."

"She fostered with my family—she's like a sister to me, nothing more."

"What is it you want then, Daron?"

"Well, I don't crave titles and wealth. All I require is enough land to raise some sheep and cattle and a family."

"Simple tastes, not unlike my father."

They raised a toast to Angus.

Daron asked, "And what would you have?"

He thought a moment. "The chance to lead my clan in peace. To do what I've been trained for. If Leod should be chosen, the people will suffer, for his ambitions far outstrip ours. As do the ambitions of others. Which brings me to a task you can help me with."

"Name it."

"Morogh has been keeping close watch on Nathara, but you could approach her differently."

He grinned. "You mean as man to woman."

"The idea agrees with you?"

"It would be a pleasure to spend time in her waspish company."

Adam chuckled even as he warned, "Beware, Daron. I don't trust her and her claws are sharp."

"Touch not the cat bot a glove."

"Aye, that's our clan's motto," he said with a laugh. "See you heed it well."

"I'll remember."

It felt good to laugh, and Adam knew Angus would prefer such company over sadness. He felt sure his father would also approve of the growing accord between Adam and Daron. One more thing to discuss. "I want you present at the council meeting."

"What? You'll have them at one another's throats and mine in minutes."

"I intend to name you as my captain of the guard and make it clear you have my full confidence."

"You are mad."

"I want to goad Leod to challenge me before he can assemble more support against me."

"Are you ready to fight? Physically?"

He'd told his father he would fight and die, if need be, and wasn't going to back down. The clan depended on him to keep it strong and safe. "I'll have to be."

"So there will be more bloodshed."

"Aye, some. Probably mine." He gave a rueful laugh.

Both men stared at the coffin, Adam wondering if his father would approve of his plans, and Daron praying his new laird wasn't crazy after all.

GWENYTH BUSIED HERSELF and tried not to think too hard on how much she would miss Angus. His death had not been unexpected, but had no doubt come too soon for Adam to establish a firm hold on the fractious clan. Gwenyth feared the turmoil that threatened to erupt. And Daron had placed her firmly in the middle of it.

Unsure of her reception among Adam's gathering kin, Gwenyth remained in her room. Adam had placed a guard at her door again, saying it was for her protection. She wanted to believe it, but she knew he also intended the guard to ensure her continued presence in the castle.

Gwenyth bowed her head as doubts assailed her. Hadn't she chastised Daron for his desire for revenge all the while harboring her own? Could she turn her back on promises made to her dying mother? And Edward—she'd given her word to marry him.

So many promises lay shattered in the dust. Because of Leod Macpherson.

Enough of these thoughts. She grabbed a shawl and hurried the few steps from the keep to the chapel through a light rain. She had never gotten a chance to say good-bye to Angus and would do so now.

Stepping inside the gloomy interior, she shook the water from her hair and loosened the shawl before entering the chapel. The sight of Adam and Daron, seated close together, startled her. Perhaps it was their closeness in age. More likely 'twas their sense of honor. Who could understand the bonds men forged or the reasons behind them?

They must have heard her approach, for both heads turned toward her at once. Daron rose and came to her, seeming both puzzled and anxious. Adam approached more slowly.

Daron laid a hand on Adam's arm. "I'll think about your plan and how best to make it happen." He gave Adam an unfathomable look. "And you think on the things I said, won't you?"

ADAM'S REPLY was absentminded, and he hardly saw Daron leave, for all he could see was Gwenyth. Her eyes were bloodshot and puffy.

"Are you so unhappy to be here, Gwenyth?"

She looked at him as if he'd grown an extra head. "'Tis a normal expression of grief. I don't waste tears over you and Daron and your schemes." Her voice softened. "However, I am truly sorry for your father's death. I was quite fond of him."

Tears shimmered in her eyes, and he pulled her close to comfort her in hopes that by seeking to console, he might find consolation. They stood in each other's arms, quiet and alone. Finally, with one accord, they broke apart and Adam led her to a stool.

Little outside noise penetrated the thick stone walls of the chapel, and Adam welcomed the quiet as he and Gwenyth sat in silent companionship for several minutes. The scurrying of small creatures were the only sounds.

Finally, his curiosity overcoming the desire for peace, Adam said, "Tell me, Gwenyth, you are of age—why hadn't you married before this?"

Gwenyth shifted in her seat and stared across the chamber. "I was betrothed three times, and always death or betrayal or politics ended the liaisons. Duty was ever impressed upon me until I didn't know the difference between what was expected of me and what my heart wanted."

Adam heard wistfulness in her voice. "What is your relationship to Daron, beyond being cousins?"

Gwenyth was silent for a good while, and Adam thought that perhaps she would not answer. He feared her affection for the man went beyond kinship, yet Daron had given no such indication. Mustering patience, he awaited her reply.

When at last she spoke, her voice was a whisper, as if the

thought she expressed could be heard by the dead man lying before them. "When my mother died and we were ready to flee, Daron offered to marry me. We have always been close and it would have been no hardship for me. But I refused, and now you both know why."

Adam nodded in acknowledgment. "Balliol and his plans."

"Aye, marriage to Edward and the chance to avenge my father and brother's deaths by creating a threat to Bruce's crown."

And now? What did Gwenyth want now? Did she still want revenge, and if so, what lengths would she go to get it?

Marry the lassie.

Sweet heaven, they needed to put more salt in the saucer, for Adam could swear he'd heard his father's voice. And why was Da still harping on this, and from the grave, no less? He'd married her, hadn't he?

And all but handed her my heart.

TWENTY

Nathara crept quietly through the darkened castle of Moy. Most of the funeral guests who had arrived earlier today had found a space to sleep on the floor of the great hall. But Leod had been given a chamber upstairs in the family wing.

She risked much in going to Leod's guest chamber. But Leod was still the best way to be rid of Gwenyth. He could hand her over to the king for ransom or keep her for himself, it mattered not to Nathara. Just as long as Adam would be free to marry her when the handfast was over.

She'd seen Adam with Gwenyth, and it was clear that Adam cared for his wife. Something must be done soon, before he took it in his head to make a binding union of it. That must not happen.

The stench of stale wine greeted her when she opened the door. Leod always drank, but tonight it smelled as if he'd emptied an entire jug himself.

"Come here," he ordered from the bed where he lay.

As she drew closer, the feral gleam in his eye told her he would be difficult. "You are drunk, my lord."

"Aye, but not too drunk. Come here."

She wanted to run, but she dared not leave until she exacted his promise. She must be sure that Adam was safe from Leod's hatred. And she had to protect her clanswomen.

Despite Leod's drunken state, he'd lost none of his strength or will, and he grabbed her. When she protested, he slapped her face. His ring grazed her cheek, drawing blood, and her heart sank at the knowledge she would bear the imprint for all to see.

Belatedly, she realized her own guilt in aiding and abetting his behavior. She couldn't lay all the blame on him, because it was her own desire to have Adam for herself that had drawn her to him. But she had learned that he was assaulting the village women, and it sickened Nathara. She knew he must be stopped even if it meant giving up her own ambitions.

He sat up and rested on one elbow. "When are you going to deliver Gwenyth to me?"

"Never, unless you stop the attacks on the women. I am tired of trying to mend your victims."

Leod frowned and pursed his lips. "You have no proof."

"Are you sure I don't?" Now she had his full attention and cooperation. Innocents were suffering because of Leod. Nathara realized how truly selfish she had been and how her entire clan might suffer if Leod were laird.

Shame for her behavior washed over her. Leod must be stopped.

"All right. I'll stop. Won't need to do that once I have her anyway."

"If you keep your word, I'll turn her over to you at the games."

"But that could be weeks from now."

"Aye, time to see if you mean to keep your word." And time for Nathara to woo Adam away from Gwenyth. Maybe enough time for Leod to finally be caught and brought to justice.

"Juss take her myself."

"Go ahead and try. A guard follows her everywhere. Best leave it to me."

"Fine. Juss don't fail me or your fine laird will be dead."

Nathara slipped into the hallway, intending to head for the castle surgery, where an application of a poultice might reduce the discoloration of her face. Head bowed, she darted toward the steps, running into Daron halfway down them.

"Nathara." Daron's voice sounded like a beam of warm sunshine on a cold winter day. She pushed aside the image, knowing she must avoid him until she could see how badly her face was injured.

Averting her head, she said, "Let me pass, sir."

"Come, now. I apologize for my behavior earlier. I should not have disparaged you so."

Saints in heaven, he apologized for a stinging remark?

"You are overset. What is it, lass?"

The narrow stairway made it impossible to pass by and continue on her way. He pushed against her. "Go back up the steps, Nathara." His voice was gentle, but his big body made his order an imperative.

At the top of the stairs, she attempted to move past but he grasped her arm. Pulling her before him, he tilted her head until their gazes met.

His eyes revealed his shock. "Who did this?"

Fear gripped her. Fear of Leod's rage if she told what she knew, fear of the disgust she would see in Adam's eyes; and strangely enough, she feared, too, what Daron would think.

She shook her head. "It was my fault, my laird. Do not think more on it."

Daron glanced down the hallway.

She drew in her breath. She hadn't latched the door tight, and it stood open several inches.

He saw it too, for he turned back to her and said, "Macpherson."

"Nay, my laird."

"I'll kill him."

"Nay, 'twas my fault. I should not have gone to his chamber when he was so drunk."

"You've been with him before."

"Aye." She hated to admit this to Daron, for he would surely think the worst, but it was either that or tell him the truth and that she couldn't do.

"And has he beaten you before?"

"He did not beat me. 'Tis only that our play got out of hand, my laird. This really is none of your business. I'd ask you to let me go on my way."

His grip on her arm tightened. "Why do you do this—return to him if he treats you so?"

"It suits me," she lied. Thinking the only way to be rid of Daron was to disgust him, she toyed with the lacing of his sark, twirling it in her fingers as she moved closer. "Perhaps you'd like a taste, my laird."

"Perhaps I would."

His reply shocked her, as did his kiss. But the shock came not from the harshness she expected, but from the incredible gentleness of the kiss.

She withdrew and made to slap him, but he grabbed her arm.

"Come, now, Nathara. Such theatrics are not necessary. And I can see by your actions that your interest in pain outweighs your interest in pleasure. I thought only to show you that gentleness can be pleasurable as well. Apparently you and Leod are well suited. Good night."

Nathara made her way to her own cottage, confused and bewildered by the exchange to the point where she forgot her desire to seek herbs in the surgery. She doubted Daron would have offered such kindness if he knew of her scheming to be rid of Gwenyth.

And now she must choose whether to continue her plan to be rid of Gwenyth or do what was right. Between her desire for a life with Adam and the good of the women of her clan.

She found her looking glass and stared into the polished surface at the woman she'd become. Not a healer, not a woman of virtue, but a fallen one. A woman like the one Jesus had forgiven. *Go and sin no more,* Father Jerard often urged the people of Moy as Jesus had before him. *Go and sin no more.*

ADAM ACCOMPANIED HIS MOTHER to the chapel the next morning to say their final good-byes. He watched as Eva snipped a corner from the winding sheet. Then tenderly she lifted a lock of her husband's hair and cut it off, laying it on the piece of cloth. Lovingly she folded the material around the keepsake and placed it in the purse tied to her girdle.

Having finished the ritual, she kissed his lips and Adam did the same before they wrapped the sheet around his head to ready Angus for burial.

Adam and Eva gazed down on husband and father. "'The oldest man that ever lived, died at last,'" Adam said.

Eva smiled at the proverb. "Aye, 'death is no particular' who it takes away.'"

Somehow, the familiar sayings, handed down through generations, comforted Adam, and his heart lightened under its load of grief.

The pallbearers entered the chapel with the coffin, and Adam assisted in removing Angus from the board and placing him in the wooden box.

"Are ye ready, my laird?" one of them asked.

"Give me another moment."

The men moved off to await Adam's signal.

Adam took his mother's hand. "Ian and the others want to hold the council meeting after the burial. How do you feel about that?"

Ever practical, his mother replied, "Everyone is gathered. No sense sending them all home until they've properly celebrated your father's life and welcomed you as laird."

Birth and death, the honored passages in the circle of life, were inevitable and therefore meant to be feted. Eva would take comfort from the customs and rituals of death, and she would honor her husband's life even as she mourned his passing. So it was meant to be.

Adam said a silent prayer of thanks for her strength.

"Today we will mourn, son. And then we will celebrate life in all its glory."

"Do we have enough *usqua?*" he teased.

She smiled. "Just barely, but since you're not drinking, we'll make do."

Nodding his agreement, Adam motioned the others forward. They took their places, and Adam walked at the front of the procession, his father's bier squarely balanced on the shoulders of six pallbearers. Eva followed behind with the rest of the mourners, including Gwenyth. But this morning Adam's thoughts barely registered her presence.

Angus would be buried on the hilltop overlooking Loch Moy and its castle. The Mackintosh pipers, black pennants flying from their instruments, played the Mackintosh chieftain's song while the drums beat a melancholy sound. As they wound up the hill, a new tune was begun, this one recounting glorious days in the past and hope for the future.

The future.

Tomorrow the council would gather. Would they name him captain? What tricks would Leod try?

His thoughts were interrupted by their arrival at the gravesite. Slowly the coffin was lowered into the grave as the pipes wailed a farewell to the captain of Clan Chattan and laird of Clan *Mac-antoisach*.

Adam stood there, surrounded by his kinsman, as a heavy mist enveloped them. Heads bowed and the priest praised the life of Angus Mackintosh.

Ye must keep the lassie.

Sighing in defeat, Adam vowed to start carrying salt in his *sporran*.

THE MORNING OF THE COUNCIL MEETING broke clear and sunny, an unusual occurrence, and Adam wondered if this was a good sign or bad. The bright cheery day chased away gloomy thoughts, and he held hope that he would be upheld as captain of the federation. He didn't know what kind of support Leod had been able to garner. But he believed his father had been right, that it didn't amount to enough to change the outcome of the vote.

Dressing carefully, he pulled on his best linen shirt and woolen plaid. In addition to the belt that held the plaid to his hips, he donned a leather *sporran*, a flat, purselike pouch that doubled as a place to keep small items and also protected his ability to father children. That thought made him smile in anticipation of the day when he and Gwenyth might be blessed with the gift of children.

But that day would have to wait upon the outcome of today's meeting. Adam entered the great hall where the trestles had been arranged in a circular fashion. The chiefs of each branch of Clan Chattan occupied the benches.

As Adam glanced at their faces, he wondered who was friend and who was foe. Before the day was through, he would know.

"Good morrow, Adam," Ian Shaw's voice boomed. "Come, break your fast with us before we get to the business at hand."

Shaw's warm welcome was more than Adam had hoped for, and his tension eased somewhat as he ate. Shaw had been chosen by the others to be their spokesman. Adam breathed in relief, for Ian was a good man and his father's contemporary and friend.

A quick glance around the room showed Leod was not yet in attendance, and Adam studied the others as he ate his bread and cheese. He had reason to believe most would support him on the grounds of heredity and training. And perhaps, leadership.

He would have to provide that today. Whether they followed or not, whether he became laird or not, one thing was certain. He wanted time to court his wife, to create the kind of marriage his parents had together. Adam knew such a partnership didn't come easily. But the rewards were many—

Someone dropped a tankard and the resulting crash jerked him back from Gwenyth's remembered charms. Adam looked up to see that Leod had entered the room, looking as if he'd spent the night drinking and wenching. Adam winced, hoping Nathara didn't have another victim to care for today. For all that he looked like death, Leod seemed in good spirits. What surprises did he plan?

Adam couldn't help but notice that no one made a place for Leod to sit, and he was forced to take a seat at the far end of the table. Was it his imagination, or had the atmosphere become strained?

He returned his attention to Ian and his food.

When the meal was over, servants cleared the table and Ian stood. "Gentlemen. We have seen to a proper and fitting burial of Angus Mackintosh—"

"Here, here."

"—and now we meet to affirm his choice as the next captain of the federation. As chiefs, we are required to do so. I, for one, accept Adam Mackintosh as my laird. I fought with him at Methven, and a finer fighting man has never drawn breath. 'Cepting maybe for our king." He grinned. "I suspect that with but one good arm young Adam could best many of us."

Ian's jovial response came as a welcome surprise to Adam's fears that the meeting would disintegrate into anger and contention.

Fergus Macqueen knocked his tankard on the table. "Aye, Adam proved hisself in battle and carries the scars of honor. I'll not be desertin' him now because his arm don't work quite right."

Adam rose to address them. "I thank you for these compliments. I am proud of how we all fought that day at Methven, but the scar I carry came from the ambush at Dalry."

"Makes no difference which battle, Adam," Ian assured him.

"It makes a difference to me. By now you all know the story of my foolish behavior and what it nearly cost me. I cannot forget and I don't want you to either, as you choose your laird."

Ian clapped him on the back. "Well said, lad. But you've made clear your determination to learn from that mistake. We've seen that you abide by your vows, and knowing how bad watered wine tastes, we respect you all the more."

Hearty laughter followed Ian's remark, but the respect he spoke of showed on every face. Every face except Leod's. He allowed no emotion to betray him.

"My arm will never work right; it's a daily reminder of the folly of youthful intemperance. But I've been swimming most mornings and it's stronger." How Adam would love to regain the strength to wield the claymore. For now it gave him joy to be able to use the smaller broadsword with increasing skill.

Adam watched Leod, waiting for the man to join in the discussion taking place among the others. He didn't have to wait long for soon Leod's voice rose above the rest. "But what of the recent raids? Our neighbors, the Camerons, have threatened us. They believe Adam cannot protect us, and they see what they can take."

Leod's voice was neutral, reasoned, and in control. Adam trusted him even less in this mood.

William appeared thoughtful. "Aye, that is something to consider. We may believe in Adam, but what do others think of him?"

If he was to prove his worth as a leader, he would have to speak up and defend himself, so Adam responded, "I have spoken to Lochiel Cameron. And though he's not overfond of me, he denied the raids."

"Well, of course he'd deny them. What did you expect?" Leod asked.

"I didn't expect him to admit a thing. But he has his own problems just now and doesn't need more by antagonizing me. So he gave me leave to inspect his herd for our kine."

"And?"

"And I didn't insult the man by doing so."

Many heads nodded in approval.

Leod moved to a different attack, reminding them of Adam's inability to fight and thus to protect what was his.

But someone said, "He said himself he's getting stronger. And if it comes to that he has others to fight for him."

Leod had an answering argument. "That's fine when we're talking about minor cattle raids. But what happens when the Frasers and the Grants or the Campbells figure out that our laird is not a warrior? These raids will continue until finally those others band together to overtake us."

Adam stroked his chin, fighting to maintain his calm. "Do you have proof or reason to believe they are doing so?"

"Nay, but it takes no imagination to conjure up such a possibility."

"Leod's right, there," Douglas Macphail said. "Perhaps we

should give thought to having Adam as chief and appointing a warlord to train and lead the warriors."

Adam could see where this was leading, and Leod was crouched and ready to strike at the opportunity to be appointed to the position. "You have only Leod's word that I can't fight. Indeed, he makes it sound as if I'm mortally crippled, or worse, a coward. Neither is true. I am willing to fight, and I have been training with my warriors."

He paused, careful of his words. "I can lead the men, and they will follow me, their rightful laird. How well I wield the sword is of less consequence than their trust in me to lead them well. But the idea of having someone else train the warriors has merit, and I would name Seamus to serve as warlord."

"An excellent choice," Ian said.

Others agreed. Since that tactic seemed doomed, Leod returned to his only real threat. "And what of your handfast to our enemy?"

"Her clan may be our enemy, but she is not, and that is the end of it, Leod."

"So you say. But you must find a more suitable wife once the handfast is over."

Adam wanted to throttle Leod, to fight him here and now. But his father's counsel came to mind. *Use your head, not your arm, to beat this maggot.*

"And if I choose not to put her aside?"

"You would bring Bruce's wrath upon us as it fell upon the Comyns."

Adam couldn't help but smile at the knowledge that he'd obeyed his king in this regard. But he changed his mind about announcing the binding vows he'd taken with Gwenyth. "The question today is not about whom I do or do not marry. The question is whether or not I am a fit leader. If you trust my judgment to lead you, then you must trust my selection of a wife, when the time comes."

Macqueen's voice rose above the others. "Ye've shown me nothing but wisdom and courage, lad. Ye've got my vote."

Ian said, "Adam is the rightful heir. I see no cause to deny it to him."

But Leod wasn't ready to give up. He stared pointedly at Daron, who stood against the wall behind Adam. "What of Daron Comyn? It is dangerous to harbor the old king's supporter within your walls."

"Daron has sworn allegiance to me."

There was a gasp from the men at the table.

"You heard right. Daron Comyn and his men are now loyal to me, and to Bruce and Scotland. Furthermore I have named him as captain of my personal guard." He gazed about the room, making eye contact with each man there. Now was the time to assert his right to stand before them, to lead them.

When no one spoke against him, he continued, "Clearly, Leod believes someone else should be chosen. But I am the rightful captain of Clan Chattan, by virtue of heredity, and by the strength of my one good arm, if need be. But I would prefer you to choose me because you believe me to be a fair judge and an honorable man." Adam looked directly at Leod with those words.

Leod must know he wouldn't have another chance. "I challenge you. Prove you can fight by right of arms."

"Would you have warfare, Leod? Would you see our clansmen die over such foolishness?"

"Nay, cousin. This is just between you and me."

Adam remembered their conversation the day he'd met Daron. He'd known then that only a confrontation would satisfy Leod. His father had been both right and wrong—some men would follow only if you proved you could fight.

"All right then, Leod. If that is the only way you will accept me, I will fight you. One on one."

"Nay," Shaw bellowed. "You will not fight to see who is laird. This council will make that decision. Today. Now."

With that, Ian polled each of the men, and Adam lounged against the wall with Daron.

"You don't seem too concerned, my laird."

Adam watched as Ian polled each man privately. "What good would it do to fash myself? I didn't see any support for Leod—he doesn't know when he's beaten. And if I allowed myself to act on my feelings, I'd have my hands around Leod's throat."

Daron glowered at Leod. "And mine too. He won't take defeat well, you can count on it."

Adam grinned. "And that, good man, is why you will be watching my back as well as your own."

Ian finished and banged his tankard on the table to get their attention. Without fanfare he announced, "Adam is the captain."

Leod masked his emotions, and Adam feared the anger being stifled within the man. Leod stalked toward the door, but Ian Shaw stopped him. "Stay, Leod." Shaw turned, then spoke to Adam. "I assume that you will hold a competition to choose your household guards?"

"Aye."

"It is traditional for the laird to engage in the sports with his clansmen." Shaw glared at each of them in turn. "Confine your rivalry to the hammer throw."

A feral glint lit Leod's eyes. "We shall meet in the contests, then, my laird."

Twenty-One

Torchlight blazed as Adam surveyed the great hall of Moy Castle this second evening of the competitions. Word had spread of the tourney, and people from far and near had flocked to Moy, bringing food and provisions with them. The need to accommodate so many guests kept Eva busy, and Adam was glad she had the distraction from her grief.

He'd not been private with Gwenyth since before the funeral, and he missed her. She hadn't come to see the competitions, to see her husband compete. As laird, Adam competed first in each event. Tonight he meant to extract a promise from her to accompany him on the morrow.

Though many of the sports were meant only for fun and entertainment, some tested the strength and endurance of his clansmen. Wagers were made, and much good-hearted ribbing took place. But Adam watched the events closely, as he would choose the best competitors for his personal guards.

Tomorrow, the third and final day, the only remaining events were the deciding rounds. But tonight they would make merry. The food, laughter, and the music reminded Adam of past celebrations in his home. His sisters' weddings, the births of his nieces, the death of his grandfather when Adam was a boy. On each occasion, the clan had gathered for the rituals attendant to the situation.

Now Adam walked among his guests, accepting condolences and congratulations. And not only from his own clan, but from the Campbells and Camerons, Frazers and other highland families, for Angus had been well liked by his friends and respected by his enemies.

Although relationships with some of these other clans were at times a bit strained, the laws of hospitality dictated Adam be a gracious host. But the many unfamiliar faces at tonight's *ceilidh* made Adam uneasy. He'd ordered Morogh not to leave Gwenyth's side, and he knew Daron kept watch as well.

The thought of Gwenyth brought a smile to his face and a need to see her, to speak with her. Adam searched the crowd and found her standing with his oldest sister and her family. Morogh hovered nearby, and Adam headed toward them, across the portion of the floor cleared of rushes so dancers could perform.

A piper and musicians on the flute and *bodhran* played a lively tune while a half-dozen men danced, feet making an intricate pattern as they pranced around two swords laid crosswise. The trick, as Adam well knew, was to complete the dance without bumping the swords. If a warrior touched a sword, it was said to be an omen of a wound or even death.

The music ended, and before Adam could move on, Fergus Macqueen grabbed his arm. "Come, my laird. 'Tis past time ye danced the swords for us this evening."

"Aye, join us." Another man clapped him on the back while a third pushed a tankard of ale in his hand.

Adam handed the drink back and scanned the room once more as Fergus cackled. "The lassie will wait on ye, ye fine, braw laddie."

Knowing they would not rest until he acquiesced, Adam shrugged, grinned, and said, "Aye, she will, for I'm a fine figure of a man." His friends guffawed and slapped his back in admiration and approval. Hoping his wife would move closer to see better, Adam allowed his men to guide him to the swords.

Each of his mates took a stiff guzzle of ale, and the musicians began the familiar tune. Within minutes Adam's haste to speak to Gwenyth receded as he reveled in the dance. Performed almost entirely on the toes, it required a proscribed order of steps and leaps, and Adam lost himself in the challenge of the movements and in a skill he'd always excelled at.

The people crowded close, too close, and someone accidentally bumped against his back, breaking Adam's concentration. A gasp rose from the onlookers as his left foot nudged the blade of the top sword. Determined to finish without another fault, he pushed aside the distraction and continued.

When the music ended, the applause and congratulations were robust, as if to overshadow the portent. No one said a word about his touch of the blade, and Adam shook off his apprehension. 'Twas naught but a superstition anyway. He excused himself and strode to where Gwenyth stood, hoping to dispel the hint of foreboding the dance had evoked.

"Greetings, wife." He didn't have to force the smile that accompanied his words, for he truly delighted in seeing her here among his clan.

"My laird."

The sound of her dulcet voice struck a cord within him, crowding out these past several days of cool politeness between them.

Cool because he'd been unwilling to face her rejection. Unwilling to know for sure that she would not commit herself to this marriage. And yet what did he expect? Nothing had changed. Leod would take her or kill her if given the chance, and Bruce had not rescinded the order to hold her.

Even though she smiled at him, he believed she put on a

show—a brave smile, here among her enemies. He curtailed the impulse to pull her into his arms and kiss her and asked instead, "Are you enjoying the festivities?"

"AYE, INDEED." The sight of Adam gracefully leaping and moving between the sword blades had impressed Gwenyth to no end. How could a man of his size move so precisely in such a small space?

Glancing up at Adam, she hoped he couldn't tell what she had been thinking.

He was grinning and wiping the sweat from his forehead with his sleeve. "Why haven't you come to watch the athletics?"

"I've been busy helping your mother."

"Aye, and I'm sure she's thankful for it. But I'd be pleased if you would attend tomorrow."

He sounded a bit like a small boy hoping for a favor, and his eager, open request for her company was impossible to resist. "Aye, then. I'll come if it would please you."

He beamed. "I shall escort you."

Controlling her features so as to hide her delight in the prospect of Adam's company, she nodded and smiled.

Adam was called away to dance another round, and Gwenyth studied his broad back as he walked away. Each day it became more and more difficult to withhold her affection from him. Kind, generous, and honorable to a fault—surely she could create a satisfying life with such a man, despite their differences.

She had been praying, asking God to help her resolve her need for revenge with her need for the love and security Adam promised. So far, no answer had come, but she was hopeful.

As Adam disappeared into the crowd, Gwenyth's attention snagged on the man who had just entered the hall. Although she'd felt safe enough this evening, the many strangers in the hall made her anxious. And now Leod added to her apprehension.

She slipped away to her chamber, and Morogh followed her.

"I'll be outside yer door through the night, my lady," he said. "But lock the door all the same."

She did not hesitate to slide the bolt home.

DARON WATCHED LEOD enter the hall and accept a tankard from a serving girl. Gwenyth and Morogh left soon after. He'd watched Gwenyth's encounter with Adam, and they seemed to have parted amiably. Actually Adam had looked like a bairn on a holiday.

The thought made him smile.

He turned back to his task for the night—keeping a close eye on Nathara. He'd danced with her once, and he planned to do so again as soon as the musicians played another folk tune. Until then he occupied himself with watching her flirt with every man who came within range.

That thought did not make him smile.

The bruise on her face had faded quickly, or perhaps she had disguised it with some womanly art. Daron controlled the anger that accompanied the thought of Leod striking her. Despite her admission that she'd gone to him willingly, Daron held only scorn for a man who would hit a woman.

But Nathara did not dally with the fellow who stood with her now. She faced him, hands on hips, then her back stiffened and she pushed her hands against his chest. Daron quickened his steps, never taking his eyes from the two, fearing the man's reaction. He recognized him as the archer who had bested everyone in today's competition.

By the time Daron was close enough to hear, the man concluded the discussion with a courtly bow and a quiet, "As you wish."

Daron breathed a sigh of relief just as Nathara whirled around and charged into him. Steadying her with his hand, he demanded, "Who was that?"

"No one," she bit out.

"Did he refuse your favors, then?"

"My favors are no concern of yours."

"Ah, but they are, fair Nathara."

She eyed him suspiciously. "Why?"

He dared not let her know of Adam's order to keep her under watch, and the only other excuse he could muster was to feign interest.

"Who is he?" Daron asked with more jealousy than he'd planned.

Nathara smirked, but there was a touch of desperation in her voice along with the flirtation. "He's the archer who won today's match."

"Aye, I know that. Why did you have cross words with him?"

"You'll have to ask *him.*" She pushed past Daron, and he let her go. What business was it of his whom she chose to meet later? And how was it possible that he, Daron of Buchan, was interested in a woman who passed her favors around as if on a platter?

Foolishness.

He shook his head, then followed discreetly, suddenly hating the order to follow and see for himself what she was up to. Not because he cared what she did. No, he followed her because Adam asked and no other reason.

Thus assured of his motives, he trailed her. She went directly to her own cottage, and though he watched well into the night as the music faded and the castle quieted, no one shared Nathara's home with her this night.

As the night deepened, Daron pulled his plaid tighter about his shoulders and settled in for an uncomfortable night of

contemplation. Who was the mysterious archer, and why did he
have heated words with Nathara? A vague uneasiness plagued
Daron as he dozed.

When dawn finally broke, he rose stiffly at the approach of the
man who would keep Nathara under watch for the morning.
Before he broke his fast, Daron searched the castle and grounds for
the bowman.

He was nowhere to be found.

GWENYTH STARED out the arrow slit in her chamber, looking
down on the gathering of clans. Despite her grief at Angus's death,
she had been reluctant to keep company with those who'd come to
mourn, preferring to remain in the kitchen or helping Eva instead.
And this morning, a gnawing sense of anxiety, a feeling of dread,
held her captive in her room.

Last night she'd promised to join Adam at today's festivities,
despite her reluctance to mingle with the many strangers within
the walls. Leod Macpherson was here—she'd seen him last evening
and fled the hall to avoid an encounter. The castle and grounds
were swarming with those who might wish her harm.

Adam arrived at her door, looking incredibly handsome in his
best plaid, held at the shoulder with the rampant cat brooch. "Come,
we'll stroll amongst my clan." She could swear she actually saw his
chest puff with pride. "And I'll impress you with my prowess."

She stifled a giggle, draped her *arasaid* around her shoulders,
and took his proffered arm. "I am ready, then."

Thin sunlight filtered through a cloud-filled sky, but no mist
or fog hung in the cool air. Gwenyth pulled her plaid closer as
Adam led her to the area of the outer bailey set aside for the
caber toss.

Gwenyth had not seen such a competition for many years, but she remembered it vividly. A poplar tree was cut to a length twice as tall as a man, and the bark stripped from it. The men took turns seeing how far they could throw the massive pole. The trick was to heave it end over end and get it to land as straight away from him as possible.

The competition was already underway, and Gwenyth couldn't hide her amusement at the balancing act required in order to juggle the upright spar into position. Once satisfied, the man tossed it forward, and the giant tree flipped in midair before it tumbled and bounced just slightly off-center.

The crowd cheered as the smiling fellow carried the pole back for the next entrant.

She turned to Adam. "You were able to compete in this?"

"Not very well. I was eliminated in the first round. But 'tis the laird's duty to attempt each sport."

She grinned at his sheepish admission. "Tell me again why they do this?"

Adam moved them to a better observation point, then stood behind her. His arm nearly encircled her as he pointed, and she relaxed into his solid chest. His breath hitched before he said, "See how the pole is notched along one side? A man who can toss the log against the wall of a fortress with the notches facing up can then climb the pole and breach the wall."

"How clever." She felt safe as cares and duties fled in the simple bliss of a beautiful day with an agreeable partner.

"But I have also seen the skill used to toss a limb over a rain-swollen creek." His breath grazed her cheek, and she pulled away slightly, afraid to show her reaction to his nearness. But a shiver betrayed her, and he pulled her close again.

"Ah, then it is a very practical skill," she teased.

Tongue in cheek, he answered, "Aye. Perhaps I should teach you."

She laughed, relaxing as Adam guided her to a pavilion for something to eat. They sat at the makeshift table and devoured bannocks and savory colcannon stew before heading off to watch the hammer throw.

Everywhere they walked, Gwenyth was greeted with obvious curiosity and shy respect. But there were also other glances that clearly displayed animosity. She shivered.

Adam touched her hand where it rested on his arm. "I thought the hot stew would warm you, wife."

"'Tis not the air that chills me."

"Aye, I've noticed the stares." He halted. "Do you wish to return to your room?"

"Not without seeing Daron." A stubborn part of her refused to cower from those few people who did not want her here. "No one has threatened me, and somehow I doubt they would risk your wrath to bring me harm."

"I think you're right. Come, let's find Daron."

They walked past the hammer-throwing event. "Were you eliminated in this event as well?" she asked.

"Aye. Barely managed ten feet. However," Adam bragged, "I am still among the leaders in the stone toss." He guided her to where that sport was taking place.

It didn't take much imagination to see how this event came to be. Gwenyth could remember her brothers and cousins tossing rocks into the loch, seeing who could throw the farthest, who could heft the heaviest rock. She smiled at bittersweet memories of so many whose lives ended much too young.

She offered Adam a tentative smile, pushing her memories aside. As they approached the other athletes readying themselves, Gwenyth saw Daron among them.

Daron came to stand with them. "As laird, Adam makes the first throw—he's really very good at this," Daron admitted. "So far only Seamus and I have bested him."

Throwing the stone only required the use of one arm, and Adam was obviously enjoying his success. Gwenyth watched as he made his second throw and the distance was measured. There were many admiring sounds, and Adam grinned.

His grin widened when he caught her eye, and she smiled back, unable to resist the warmth of his obvious affection for her. Seeing him standing there so pleased with himself and looking more handsome than any man had a right to, she wanted nothing more than to move into his arms and promise him anything . . . everything.

But he had made her his wife and imprisoned her with the words. Not a prison formed of love and attachment, but the walls of his keep and the enmity of his king.

And yet . . .

What had he said when he told her about love and loyalty? He expected both from her, but he'd given her no words of love. But didn't actions speak louder than words?

And yet. What if? But no. She sighed.

Daron and the others finished their throws, and to her surprise and delight, Daron was declared the winner. Adam strode toward them, and Gwenyth braced for the onslaught of emotions his presence seemed to bring.

Clapping Daron on the back, he winked at Gwenyth. "If I'd known he could beat me at the stone toss, I'd have refused his vow of loyalty."

Daron grinned. "Should I have held back and let you win?"

"Never," Adam responded, his voice full of good cheer.

In high spirits Daron joined them, and the three of them moved about the grounds. By late afternoon the competitions were finished, and a loud bell sounded.

Adam's cheer visibly faded as he said, "'Tis time to name my personal guard." He led them to a small rise, indicating she and Daron should stand there while he made the announcement.

ADAM'S JOY in Gwenyth's company and the day's festivities abruptly ended in anticipation of what lay ahead. He dreaded the naming of his guard, for Leod had done well and made no secret he expected to be chosen. How could Adam invite a man he couldn't trust into his inner circle? How could he explain if he did not?

The answer eluded him.

Leod approached him. "My laird, I propose one final contest, all in fun and in the name of sport."

Uneasy, Adam said, "And what would that be?"

"I would prove myself worthy to be in your guard. And you may show our clansmen how well you can wield a sword."

"You want to fight me?"

"Just a friendly display of swordsmanship. Show everyone how 'tis done."

The hair on Adam's neck stood on end. He remembered their confrontation that day in the fog and Leod's bold challenge at the council meeting. He did not trust Leod—what was the man up to? But surely he wouldn't try anything dishonorable here, in front of everyone.

Ian stepped between them. "My laird, I must insist upon a private word with you."

Morogh appeared ready to murder Leod where he stood, and although Adam understood their desire to protect him, he resented the implication.

Ever since the council meeting, Adam had come to believe that the men he admired and respected had chosen him more for what was in his heart than for his sword arm. He didn't have to prove himself to them. Nor did he need to prove anything to himself.

So why even consider Leod's challenge? Perhaps Leod's request for friendly sport was his way of acknowledging Adam as laird. Or perhaps it was treachery. There was only one way to find out. Adam resigned himself to ending their feud Leod's way. And should Leod turn on his laird in front of the clan, he would not live out the day.

Forcing a smile and amiable tone, Adam said, "Leod, if you agree, I will meet you as soon as I have finished with Ian." To the crowd he said, "I will announce the guard at the conclusion of our sport."

"As you wish." Leod tipped his sword in deference and was soon lost among the crowd.

TWENTY-TWO

Although most of the nearby clansmen seemed in accord with Adam's decision, Ian nearly dragged Adam away from the others. "Of all the stupid, ill-conceived, witless ideas. I should take a strap to you myself. Your father . . ." Ian muttered and sputtered until they'd reached an empty tent. "Are you crazy?"

"Nay. But I think Leod may be."

"All the more reason not to fight him, Adam. What if you are wounded?"

"I will recover."

Ian's face contorted. "Blast the optimism of youth."

Adam smiled grimly. "Leod's threats must end, Ian. All my life he has bullied anyone weaker than he. I cannot allow it to continue." He did not want to fight Leod or anyone. But this confrontation had been a long time coming, and Adam was determined to end it today, once and for all. "And when I beat him, I'll have reason not to invite him into the guard."

Ian puffed in exasperation. "If you beat him."

Before Adam could chide the older man for his lack of faith, someone cleared his throat outside the tent. Adam looked to the opening to see Morogh. And beside him an anxious-looking Gwenyth.

Morogh stepped closer and jerked his head. "Come, Ian. Let these young people have some time together."

Ian balked, but Morogh grabbed his shirt. "Come on." The two men left, Ian grumbling and protesting all the way.

GWENYTH CAME to stand before Adam and stared into her husband's azure eyes. She saw steadfast determination there. Still, Morogh had begged her to intercede, to use her feminine charms if need be to change Adam's mind.

She lowered her eyes, scanning the dirt floor of the tent. Anxiety and foreboding had shadowed her all day, and now it was clear to her that she was not the one in danger. And her heart nearly stopped at the realization Adam might be hurt or killed before this day was over.

Gazing back up at him she said, "You must not fight him, Adam."

"Do you fear for me then, wife?"

"I do." The admission came easily, far easier than acknowledgment of how much she cared for him. "Why must you do this? You have already seen the truth of your father's advice. The council chose you."

His tender regard told her he appreciated her opinion. "Leod is responsible for those other assaults, Gwenyth. I can't prove it, but I know it. I must avenge them." He cupped her cheek with his palm, his gaze steady. "And you."

"Let Daron do it," she pleaded, knowing the argument to be futile.

"Leod challenged me."

She pulled away from his touch. "You will be hurt or killed." *And it will be my fault for forcing you into this marriage.* Another life cut too short. Merciful heaven, when would it end?

"And what of Daron? Ah, you are not so sure I can best Leod, but Daron can?" His voice hardened. "'Tis only meant for sport—Ian won't allow us to fight to the death." He tilted her chin upwards. "You have so little faith in me?"

"Of course not. I distrust Leod."

"As do I." He brushed away her tear with the pad of his thumb. "Have you come to care for me, then, love?"

"Aye," she whispered and flung herself into his arms, drinking in his gentle strength and the rich sound of his voice. The intensity of her feelings for him came as a surprise. Or perhaps they'd been this strong for some time, and she had fought against them.

She feared for him, not only because she feared the loss of his protection, but because she'd come to accept his belief that they were meant to be together. Who could know or understand God's reasons? It was useless to deny it. But he spoke of loyalty, and what she needed to hear were words of love before she could trust completely.

"Well now. Have faith. In me and in God." He lifted her face, then bent and kissed her, a sweet kiss of promise that quickly deepened into desire. He pulled away, his breathing as unsteady as her own. "You will be safe, no matter what, for Seamus has pledged to protect you, to marry you if need be."

"You have given me away?"

"Only if I am dead, Gwenyth. Only then. And only because doing so ensures your life and keeps you safe from Leod's reach. And Robert's."

She shook her head, both amazed at his foresight and praying his preparations were unnecessary. "I should be angry with you, but all I feel is fear. Please be careful, husband."

He observed her, his expression guarded. "And you will be waiting for me?"

"Aye." A day ago, an hour ago, she might have hesitated. But when faced with the possibility of losing him, everything became very clear. She cupped his cheek. "No matter what condition you are in or how many parts are maimed or missing."

He favored her with a smile, the one that could melt a frozen river, the one her heart could not ignore. "And that vow of chastity you coerced from me?"

She grinned. "I will try to forget it, my laird."

"Truly?"

"Aye."

He pulled her close and kissed her brow, her nose, her eyelids. "Ah, Gwenyth. Dare I hope you will become my true wife soon?"

She pulled away, just enough so she could look into his eyes. He would fight to rid the world of a bully, a man who would harm the weak. This husband that God had chosen for her had honored her in many ways. And now he would risk his life against a man who knew nothing of honor or loyalty.

"You needn't fight Leod to gain entrance to my chamber."

He looked startled but recovered quickly. "But I would gladly fight a hundred men for that privilege, did you but ask."

"Would you not fight at all, if I asked?"

"I wish I could grant that boon, love. But the differences between Leod and I must be put to rest. And my wife's honor and that of Leod's other victims must be avenged."

"Is there nothing I can say or do to persuade you against this folly?"

The gleam in his eyes was unmistakable, and she felt herself blush. He pulled her against him. "Aye, lass. You are temptation itself."

"Then let me tempt you," she whispered, her voice unnaturally husky.

"Adam, lad." They parted hastily as Morogh strode into the tent, forcing reality back with resounding finality. "Has she convinced ye not to fight?"

"No. I will meet Leod on the field. Now give us a moment," Adam growled.

Morogh groaned but wisely retreated to stand by the doorway.

ADAM RESENTED the intrusion almost as much as he resented Gwenyth's questionable avowals of affection. Was it all just a means to change his mind, or did she truly care? He pulled Gwenyth close again and quietly asked, "You were supposed to convince me not to fight?"

"Did I not succeed?" Her voice was light, despite the worry clearly evident on her face.

He raised her chin so he could look into her eyes. "I will want to finish what we started here, my lady."

"Then see you stay in one piece, my laird."

"No protests? No begging?"

She held his gaze with gentle affection. "Leod must be stopped. I know 'tis selfish of me, but I am tired of living in fear of him. Of living in fear that all I hold dear will be taken from me, again. Please, promise you will keep Daron close-by."

All I hold dear. Adam smiled, knowing now without a doubt that she would be waiting for him. "I will. 'Tis supposed to be a gentleman's fight, but—"

"I don't trust Leod, either. He knows nothing of fealty."

Adam embraced her, pulled her soft body close, and lost himself in her sweetness. He didn't know if those emotions could be improved upon, but he wanted a lifetime with this woman to find out. If he survived this encounter with Leod, he vowed once again to court this woman as she deserved to be, to teach her all the ways of love. To entice her to come to him freely.

"Lady Gwenyth, send the boy out here."

Adam grinned down at her, rolling his eyes and mouthing the word "boy" in mock exasperation.

"There is no boy in this tent, Morogh," she challenged, then raised on tiptoe to whisper, "Only an honorable man." With a kiss to his cheek, she pulled away from him.

At this moment, Adam felt the full force of dread. The day he'd known must come was here. He held no illusions that Leod would keep the contest friendly. Would Adam die just as he found hope of winning Gwenyth's heart? Or would the promise of her love give him the strength he needed to accomplish his task?

He took Gwenyth's hand and led her to the tent's exit. Stepping through, he said to Morogh, "Come then. 'Tis time."

With Gwenyth's arm tucked safely in his own, Adam walked toward the agreed-upon area. He handed her to Morogh. "Keep her safe."

Reluctantly he put her out of his thoughts and concentrated on the task ahead. Because it was to be a friendly display of swordsmanship and not a fight as such, none of Adam's men would join him to protect the weaker arm.

Leod stood some twenty feet away, his sword at the ready. Adam donned his leather hauberk—the same one, now skillfully repaired, that had no doubt saved his arm the last time he'd fought. But unlike that last fight, Adam's mind was clear, his body strong. He gave thanks to God for bringing him safely to this day, and asked for his blessing. *Thy will be done.*

Adam took his sword from the lad who held it, then carefully unsheathed it. 'Twas a fine weapon, shorter and lighter than the claymore, but deadly nonetheless.

Caressing the hilt, he hefted the sword, reminding his brain and muscles of the differences in fighting style required for this weapon. He swiped the air, warming his body for the exertion to come.

Leod was smiling and jesting with the crowd. For a moment, Adam considered that perhaps the man meant no harm after all. But that sixth sense, the one that could save one's life when in danger, warned him not to believe Leod's jovial behavior. Indeed, when the man finally turned to him, only darkness shone from his eyes.

And it was directed at Adam.

He allowed himself a quick search of the crowd. Gwenyth stood well back, Morogh close by her side. Morogh would not let her come to harm. Dragging his thoughts from such distraction, he looked to where Leod stood. If Leod did not prove himself loyal, Adam would kill him. Gwenyth's life and the future of his clan were at stake. He turned his full attention to Leod.

Leod circled and Adam followed, feinting and thrusting, in no hurry to clash. Adam recalled everything he could remember about Leod's fighting style. And reminded himself that, sport or not, Leod would test Adam's weak left side.

Indeed, the other man's first attack was a flurry of thrusts to Adam's left, which he managed to defend. Leod's surprised reaction was gratifying, and Adam allowed himself a moment to celebrate that small victory. They were well matched, always had been. Now they engaged in full, two-handed swings and arm-numbing blocks, and sweat rolled down Adam's face. As he'd anticipated, Leod made repeated attacks to Adam's left, forcing him to use the arm over and over.

Fatigue set in, and Adam struggled to take the offensive and bring Leod's attack to the right. Leod smiled in silent acknowledgment and pressed harder.

Adam was thankful for the time spent swimming, for it had undoubtedly strengthened his whole body. But would it be enough?

Leod's blows came faster, and with sudden awareness, Adam saw that the other man had changed the rules of the game. No longer were they putting on a show—Leod was fighting to win, just as Adam had known he would. The spectators must have noted the increase in intensity, for Adam heard Ian call a halt.

But neither Adam nor Leod complied, and no one was foolish enough to step close to the swinging blades.

GWENYTH WATCHED in mute, frightened fascination as the two men fought. Their display inspired awe, for both were skilled warriors. She thought Adam fought well, but as the skirmish continued, she feared she could discern a growing weakness in his left arm. Just as Seamus had once intensified his bout with Adam, Leod now did the same.

Gwenyth gasped. Ian Shaw was shouting at them to cease, but neither man would be first to put aside his weapon. Leod drove Adam back, and the crowd quickly dispersed to give room.

But she moved closer, aware now of Nathara just behind her and Morogh but a step away. A quick glance at his face showed that he, too, realized Leod's intent.

Adam recovered from the charge and slowly pushed Leod back. Grim determination shone from his face, and she knew he would not relent. And Leod seemed equally resolved to cut Adam down.

Fearful now, Gwenyth's heart raced.

A brave man tugged at Leod's sleeve, trying to deter him. Seeing it, Adam gave way, saying something she couldn't hear. But Leod shook his head, yanked his sleeve free, and lunged at Adam.

Adam lurched back, stumbling as he misstepped, and Leod moved in. Gwenyth stifled a scream. *God, please protect him!*

Adam regained his footing quickly, but not before Leod drew blood from Adam's thigh. Ian's continued shouts for them to cease echoed around them, but Leod snarled and continued the fight.

Out of the corner of her eye Gwenyth saw Daron at the edge of the crowd, sword drawn. Others had done the same, and Gwenyth feared more blood would be shed before this was through.

Without taking her gaze from Adam, she pleaded, "Morogh, do something."

"Naught to be done, lass," he said in a resigned voice. "This has been coming since those two were lads."

"Well, one or both of them may not live past the day."

"Aye."

Please, God, let Adam live. With a jolt, Gwenyth recalled her fervent prayers for deliverance in Leod's hall. And how Adam had been the answer to those prayers. Yes, God had given her everything she'd prayed for and until today, she'd been too blind to see it. *Adam.*

His face showed the strain, yet still he fought well. Leod, on the other hand, seemed to taunt his adversary and twice left himself wide open. Adam did not take advantage.

Gwenyth couldn't bear to watch but couldn't turn away. What would happen if Leod won? What if he killed Adam? The prospect of a world without Adam, and Leod still alive, didn't bear thinking.

As the men struggled on, Gwenyth remembered Adam smiling as he played and splashed in the loch, moon-blessed on the parapet, the honorable man who would move heaven and hades. . .

For her.

Be strong, my love.

Adam slipped on the now matted grass, caught himself before

he fell, then feinted left. The quickness of the move must have caught Leod unaware, for Adam's next thrust sent Leod's sword sailing out of his hand to land several feet away.

Gwenyth sighed in relief. It was over.

Leod made a mocking bow, then scanned the trees on the hill behind the crowd.

Gwenyth wrenched her gaze from Adam, following Leod's stare, as did Nathara. Movement in the trees caught her eye, and she heard Nathara scream at the same time Morogh shouted, "Watch out, lad!"

Adam twisted in response to the warnings, and Nathara barged forward, shoving Gwenyth's tiny frame against her husband's mountain of a body. Her shawl slid from her shoulders as Adam grunted in pain. Surprised and confused, Gwenyth stepped back to assure herself that Adam was unharmed from the unknown danger Nathara had sensed.

Seeing Adam's pained expression, Gwenyth quickly dropped her gaze to where her plaid hung suspended from an arrow imbedded in Adam's arm. Her stomach lurched, but still she had the presence of mind to reach for the dirk strapped to his leg. Gently she cut away the cloth to reveal Adam's left arm, pinned fast to the leather hauberk and useless.

Blood dripped to the ground and stained Adam's kilt while Morogh and several others raced into the woods in pursuit of the assassin. Nathara clung to Leod's back, pounding him with her fists and blistering the air with her rantings. He broke from her hold to run like the coward he was, but Seamus and Daron tackled him and brought him back, one on either side, to face Adam.

Gwenyth pressed her hand against Adam's back. "Come, my laird. Let me tend to your wound," she said.

"I'm not finished here, wife."

"Aye, you are," she said, somewhat desperately. "Let the others do what must be done."

He shook her off, rage and pain making his actions less than gentle. She nearly fell as she backed away from the enraged laird of Clan Chattan.

"Bring his sword and let him go," Adam ordered, pointing his own weapon at Daron.

"Nay, my—"

"Do it."

Adam stood his ground, his face contorted with rage and determination, and none dared gainsay him.

None save Daron, who now stood between the two, Leod's sword in hand.

Adam growled, "Give him the sword."

Daron glared at Leod as he said, "You've bested him, my laird. Leave the rest to me."

"I'm going to kill him." He turned to Seamus. "Break off the arrow."

Seamus moved to do his laird's bidding and Gwenyth ran to stop him, grabbing hold of the giant's arm and hanging fast like a dog with a disputed bone. "You must not. If you disturb it the bleeding may increase."

Adam shook his head as if to clear it. "You promised to accept me no matter how damaged, Gwenyth. Now go, and let me finish this."

The tenderness in his voice did nothing to allay her fear, but clearly he was determined. She fought tears as she did as he asked, flinching at Adam's grunt of pain when the arrow snapped in Seamus's hands.

Daron, still holding Leod's weapon, implored, "He doesn't deserve to die a warrior's death, Adam." He turned to Leod. "I'm of a mind to settle this myself. You've dishonored my kinswoman and paid an assassin to kill my laird."

Leod didn't deny either charge. Instead he smirked, seeming to defy Adam into finishing what would be a lost cause, wounded as he was. "Aye, Adam. How does it feel to know I had your lady before you? Or have you even bedded her?"

Adam roared and despite his wounds and pain, it took four men to hold him from advancing on Leod. Gwenyth held her breath, for clearly the effort had cost him. Pain etched his features, and still the blood seeped. Every instinct urged her to go to him and mend his wounds. But he'd made it clear he did not appreciate her interference, nor would she give him cause to resent her.

He must end this his way. She only prayed he would not insist on finishing the fight. He'd proven his mastery with the sword by disarming Leod—the fight should have ended then, would have ended then if not for Leod's treachery.

Daron spoke the words that formed in her own mind. "You have bested him, Adam. His sword is here in my hand, and you still hold yours. The fight is won."

"I must avenge Gwenyth's honor."

Gwenyth stepped close. "Do not die to avenge me, my laird, I beg of you. I could not bear to live with your death on my conscience." *And I cannot bear the thought of spending my life without you.*

"I want him dead."

Daron nodded. "Aye, and he deserves it. But Leod has forfeited his right to die an honorable death."

Adam seemed to hear the words this time, and Gwenyth stepped forward to go to him. But Ian blocked her way. "Let the man be, my lady. He'll need your care soon enough. But not just yet."

Gwenyth bit her lip. Ian was right, but Adam's blood formed a puddle on the ground at his feet, and she feared his strength drained away with it. But the rage and determination never left his features despite his pain, despite her plea.

The crowd parted, and Morogh and two others hauled a man wearing a scabbard of arrows to stand before Adam.

"You," Daron shouted as he accosted the archer.

"Hold, Daron." Adam stepped forward, still holding his sword. He confronted the man. "Silence will buy you a swift death. Confess and I will show mercy."

The bowman licked his lips and glanced quickly in Leod's direction. Gwenyth knew that Adam wanted the man to name Leod, to give proof of his cousin's treachery so all would know his death was justified above and beyond Adam's need for revenge.

And if Adam didn't allow his wounds to be tended soon, he might well follow Leod to the grave.

"Save your mercy, Adam." Leod gestured to the now trembling archer. "The idiot was supposed to have better aim."

A gasp went through the crowd as Leod's confession sealed his fate. All that remained was the question of who would kill him. Adam advanced, sword arm raised.

The men holding Leod moved away, and Leod stood still. Alone. A man without honor.

"Bring his sword," Adam growled at Daron.

"Don't do this, my laird. He is gambling that you will give him another chance to kill you."

"Bring it."

GWENYTH ALTERNATED between praying for Adam's sanity to return and railing against the stupidity of men.

Adam saw Daron's reluctance and knew his friend had every reason to fear. Adam could feel himself weakening as the blood oozed from his wounds. Still, he had the strength and the desire to plunge his sword deep into Leod's treacherous heart. But

Daron was right; Leod had indeed forfeited the right to such a death.

Daron returned to his side, Leod's sword in hand. With a clarity that belied his diminishing energy, Adam saw what must be done. In winning the sword fight—a fight that Leod had suggested for sport and then turned into a battle—Adam had proven himself as a warrior.

Now he must prove he also had a laird's wisdom, the wisdom to back down from a fight that was already won. And the wisdom to allow a loyal liegeman to seek his own revenge.

Adam leaned on his sword to keep from swaying. "There is no death more ignoble than to die by one's own sword."

Daron's eyes widened in understanding.

Adam nodded. "Do it."

Without hesitation, Daron spun and plunged Leod's own weapon into his chest.

With a shout of surprise that quickly became a gurgle, Leod slid to the ground as Gwenyth averted her eyes from the sight. She took no joy in any man's death, but she could not stop the relief that flooded through her.

Adam lived.

She ran to him, waiting until Daron and the others lowered him to sit on the ground before grasping his hand. His eyes were glazed and his breathing quick. Now that she was close, she could see that the arrow had also penetrated the leather and entered his side.

Fighting back panic, she glanced frantically for some way to move him. From seemingly nowhere a trestle materialized, and Seamus and Daron laid Adam on it. Half a dozen men jockeyed for the privilege of carrying their laird into the castle as his life's blood left a trail upon the thin, rocky soil of Clan Chattan.

TWENTY-THREE

GWENYTH SENT NATHARA for her medicinals, and Eva hurried ahead of the entourage to prepare Adam's room. By the time Seamus and Daron placed Adam on his bed, he was unconscious.

If the stubborn man hadn't insisted on leaking blood for unnecessary minutes—minutes that had seemed like hours to Gwenyth—he wouldn't be so pale. Or so still.

Grimly, Gwenyth directed the men to cut away the hauberk so she could pull the arrow through the flesh of Adam's upper arm. She allowed the wound to bleed freely to cleanse it, despairing over each additional drop of lost blood. Nathara and Eva prepared a poultice, which they tied tightly to cover both the entrance and exit wounds. Thankfully the bleeding quickly stopped.

Adam's lack of consciousness was a blessing, for even so he groaned with pain when Nathara removed the arrowhead from his side. The hauberk had prevented the point from going too deep. But even a shallow wound such as the one on his thigh could fester, and the women knew it. Once the wounds were bound with a poultice, nothing more could be done.

Nothing but pray.

Eva dismissed a subdued Nathara before turning to Gwenyth. "Get some rest, lass. I'll watch over him for a few hours."

"I won't leave him."

Eva hugged her. "He has survived worse. And he has more to live for this time."

"Then we shall not lose hope." But what did Adam have to live for that he hadn't had after Dalry? A woman whose loyalty was questionable, just as before. She had promised to accept him no matter what. Would he cling to her vow as he fought to overcome his wounds? Gwenyth hoped so. She pressed Eva's hand as the woman left her alone in the chamber with her husband and her newly regained faith.

To make the time pass, she worked on the tapestry she'd begun recently. The design was a familiar one, and the task went quickly. She fought back tears as she prayed that Adam would live to see it.

But by morning Adam's body was hot to the touch as his fever-wracked body labored to heal itself. Gwenyth had slept fitfully by his side, waking throughout the night to cool him with gentle bathing and attempting to get him to drink a fever-reducing tea. But most of it had dribbled down his chin and wet the bedding.

At first light Eva entered the room followed by two servants, one carrying a tray and the other a pail of cool water. Ignoring the food, Gwenyth took the bucket from the girl and dipped a cloth into it. She replaced the cloth on his forehead with the cooler one.

Laying her hand on Gwenyth's shoulder, Eva said, "Ye must eat, child. I'll bathe him."

Reluctantly Gwenyth gave over the cloth, knowing Eva needed to feel useful, to believe she could make a difference. Gwenyth empathized. Never had she felt so ineffectual, not even while nursing her mother during her final illness.

Gwenyth forced a few bites of bread and cheese past her lips then washed it down. Closing her eyes, she prayed the prayer she'd offered countless times in the past hours. *Please, God, let Adam live.*

The day passed as Eva, Nathara, and Gwenyth took turns

bathing the heat from Adam's body only to have it return. By the next morning, his breathing was shallow, and Gwenyth's prayers grew desperate.

Don't let him die not knowing that I love him, she begged. For there was no doubt that she did love him. More than the memory of her father, more than any need to seek revenge on a king. Enough to release the past and face the future with hope.

Exhausted from her emotional turmoil and needing to be close, Gwenyth climbed onto the bed and lay beside her husband, clinging to his hand and the sound of his labored breathing.

ON THE AFTERNOON of the fourth day, Gwenyth roused from a restless sleep at Adam's side. She stirred the fire and added fuel to heat water for sorrel wood tea.

She changed the dressings on his wounds and managed to get some of the tea down his throat. He rested easier, and the fever seemed to be leaving him. For the first time in days she dared to believe he would recover, and she whispered a prayer of thanks.

By the end of the week, Gwenyth caught herself almost wishing Adam's fever would return. At least then he'd be unconscious. And quiet. Then she grinned. He was a querulous patient, but he was alive; and judging from his increasing attempts to leave his bed, he'd soon be on his feet.

She approached his chamber, carrying the midday meal, curious at the lack of orders and bellowing. Balancing the tray, she opened the door to find him sitting by the fire while his page shaved him.

"So that is how to keep you quiet—hold a razor to your throat," she teased, all the while averting her eyes from his bared chest. She'd certainly seen it while sponging him to cool his fever. But somehow he was much more imposing with that devilish smile gracing his mouth.

Ah, that wonderful, delightful mouth. Heavens, when had she turned into a wanton? She felt her face blush, and Adam's laugh confirmed he'd noticed the telltale color.

He dismissed the lad and indicated she could set the tray on the small table in front of him. "Will you join me?" he asked. "There's enough for two."

"Aye, thank you."

Gwenyth sat next to him on the bench and picked at her food, smiling when he urged her to take more. Would he tell her now? Tell her that not only would he move the very earth for her, but why. Would he say he loved her?

She gave herself a mental shake. She looked at him, at the twinkling in his eyes and the warmth of his smile, things she had feared never to see again. She vowed to be patient.

And then he kissed her.

He pulled away, wincing as his arm brushed against his bandaged abdomen.

Gwenyth jumped to her feet. "Adam Mackintosh, you are the most difficult patient I've ever had to deal with."

"And that's the thanks a wounded husband gets for defending his lady's honor?"

She dropped to her knees in front of him. Taking his large callused hand in hers, she whispered, "I died a thousand deaths, Adam, to see you lying there so still." Tears sprung to her eyes, and he wiped them away.

"Ah, Gwenyth, I didn't mean to make you cry." He tilted her face up to him. "I have not forgotten the words we spoke the day of the fight."

"Nor have I."

"And I am most anxious to finish what we started." He stood, tugging at her to come with him, and she complied. His lips brushed hers, then he kissed her thoroughly, leaving no doubt what he referred to.

But do you love me?

He swayed and clutched the mantle for support.

She helped him to sit down. "I'm afraid you aren't well enough to collect on my promise to forget that vow of chastity."

Ruefully he said, "I feel weaker than a babe."

"Come, you need to get back into bed and rest."

He must have been tired, for he didn't protest, leaning on her and allowing her to guide him. She settled the covers over him, then took the tray and promised to return later in the day.

Perhaps in time he would come to love her. And if he said the words, then Gwenyth would know that she could trust him completely and leave the past behind. But having seen her world collapse around her once before, Gwenyth would not declare her heart until she was sure. Only thus could she protect herself.

ALL THOSE who had gathered for the funeral and the games had returned to their homes to tend their crops. Gwenyth and Eva planned for Adam's investiture ceremony, which would now be held in conjunction with Michaelmas and the end of harvest.

July slipped by quickly as Adam regained his strength. By Lammas and the end of haying season, he seemed his old self, but despite his avowal of impatience, he never once asked Gwenyth to join him in the huge four-poster bed where she'd nursed him back to health.

Somehow, this second brush with death had changed him, and Gwenyth was no more sure of her future now than she'd been when she first arrived at Moy. But that wasn't entirely true. Now she knew that all she'd ever wanted was a home, a safe place to love and be loved. A place where her heart could dwell.

Castle Moy had become that place. She'd found a home where she'd least expected it—in the heart of a highland laird.

One day as she worked on the tapestry she was making for Adam, word had come that Edward Balliol had fled to France, his designs on the crown defeated. She prayed for his well-being but no longer desired the match with him. No doubt, when circumstances warranted, he would make another attempt, and Gwenyth had had enough intrigue and its attendant upheaval.

She was content, despite the lack of intimacy with her husband. But one day, when they walked through the orchard, she approached the subject.

"Your arm has healed well, my laird."

He flexed his elbow. "Aye, so it has." He grinned. "I've taken up swimming again."

She swallowed. "So Morogh told me. But there are other activities you have avoided." Try as she might, she could not hold back the embarrassment of being so bold, and she felt her face grow warm.

He stopped walking and faced her, taking her hands in his. He lifted her palm and kissed it. The warmth of his gaze and the sweet touch of his lips made her want to surrender her heart, her mind, her soul. Surely he would not treat her thus if he did not love her?

"Most couples require time to know one another before engaging in the intimacies of the bedroom," he reminded her. "I am giving us that time."

"But we have been handfast for nearly six months."

"A situation neither of us chose." He drew her close and bent to her ear. "Patience," he murmured. "In a few days the clan will gather for the investiture. And you must decide whether you truly wish to be married to the captain of Clan Chattan."

"I—"

He traced a finger across her lips. "You must decide if you will give your heart along with your body, Gwenyth. I'll not rush you. If and when you come to me, it will be freely, I swear. And I ask you to give me a few more days to court you as you deserve."

He smiled. A smile she couldn't resist if the devil's own hounds were chasing her. And she knew that whatever he asked, she would give him, even if he never said he loved her.

"As you wish, my laird."

GWENYTH'S TENDER SMILE as she yielded to his request nearly undid his well-laid plan, for it gave him hope her surrender would be as complete as his.

But for now he would be patient. Only a few more days until Michaelmas and his investiture. A few more days before he would lay his heart open and risk rejection. The courting of his wife took a daily toll, and Adam's patience was wearing thin. But she deserved to be courted, to be cherished, and he'd stay true to his plan if it killed him.

And every time he looked at her, the ache in his heart nearly did.

So he forced his attention away from her face as he strolled with her through the orchard, making inane conversation about the harvest, the fish he'd caught yestermorn, anything to take his mind off of his fantasies.

Finally admitting defeat, he escorted her to the keep and with a hasty adieu, hurried to the lake—the very cold lake—for a swim.

THE MORNING of Adam's investiture dawned with the usual fog, but by the time of the ceremony, the sun broke through and cleared the sky. A large platform had been erected in the bailey so that all could watch as Adam took the solemn oath that would guide him as captain of Clan Chattan. Gwenyth sat with Eva and Morogh as the others found seats or standing room.

The audience hushed as Seamus led Adam and the priest onto the stage. Seamus wore a claymore strapped to his back and a skean dhu at his waist, with a shorter knife tucked into the garter holding up his wool stocking. He looked every inch the formidable warlord.

And Adam simply took her breath away. Healed now from his wounds, he stood tall and proud. The folds of his great plaid were held at the shoulder with his father's brooch and were belted around his lean hips with a wide, leather belt. He wore no weapons, symbolic of his trust in Seamus to protect him.

Gwenyth's attention wandered as the priest spoke of Adam's solemn responsibilities. A sharp poke from Eva's elbow brought her back.

"What is it?"

"The priest just reminded Adam of his duty to provide an heir, and now Adam wants ye to come up there with him."

Panicked, she squeaked, "Why?"

"I don't know, lass, but he doesn't look too patient. Go on with ye." And she gave a gentle nudge.

Knees weak, thoughts in turmoil, Gwenyth stood before her husband, the most powerful chief in the northern highlands. And surely the most handsome man in all of Scotland.

He took her hand, then faced the crowd. "Twice I have spoken vows with this woman, once as a handfast spouse, and again with a priest. Both times against her will." He smiled at her. "And against my will as well."

Whatever did he plan to do? She implored him with her eyes to give some hint of what was to come, but he only shook his head and graced her with a tender smile.

"Gwenyth Comyn should be my enemy. But she and her cousin have reminded me that a Scot's only real enemy is a dishonorable man, no matter what his birth."

She glanced at the crowd and saw they had moved closer to hear. And still she didn't know why she was standing beside Adam, why he hadn't yet taken the oath.

"Trust me," he mouthed.

She smiled and relaxed. She trusted this man as she trusted no one else on earth. He'd proven worthy of her confidence in him many times over. Aye, she trusted Adam Mackintosh with her life. And, yes, with her heart as well.

To the crowd he said, "Before I take the vow to be your chieftain, I will marry this woman properly, in front of witnesses, with both of us willing." Then he spoke for her ears only. "If you are not willing, you are free to leave. With Balliol out of the country the king has lifted his sanctions against you. You may seek an annulment on the grounds you were coerced."

She had no time to show her surprise, for he leaned closer and whispered in her ear. "I'll not keep you here against your will and have you resent me and my touch. I love you, Gwenyth. I only wish it was enough to hold you."

A weight lifted from her heart. "Who said it wasn't?"

He gazed at her, his heart written there upon his face for anyone to see. "Gwenyth?"

"I love you, Adam."

As if drawn by the magic of these newly admitted feelings, Gwenyth leaned into his embrace. His lips found hers, and she wrapped her arms about his neck. This was the man she trusted, with her very heart and soul. Soon she would trust him with her body as well.

The priest cleared his throat, and they parted. The look in Adam's eyes promised he'd not wait long to repeat the kiss.

Adam faced his clansmen once more. "Now is the time to voice your objections to this marriage. Now, before I take the oath as chief, while you can still choose another. For I will have Gwenyth as my wife."

She drew in her breath. "You would refuse to be laird?" she whispered, incredulous.

Facing her, holding her hand, he blocked her view of his anxious clan, effectively shutting out the rest of the world. "I would."

"I couldn't let you do that."

"You couldn't stop me."

Her remaining tension melted and she laughed and shook her head. "You are impossible."

With a wicked grin, he agreed. "Aye. Will you marry me anyway?"

"Again?" she teased.

His voice was thick as he replied, "For real, this time. In the name of love, honor, and loyalty."

She threw her arms around his neck. "Oh yes, Adam. Yes."

He kissed her thoroughly, then with a cocky nod of satisfaction he turned back to the waiting crowd. "Well?" he bellowed.

Not a soul raised an objection.

A beaming Adam nodded to the priest, who bade them kneel. Then Gwenyth and Adam promised, for the third and final time, to cleave only to each other, forever. When the priest asked if they wished to exchange rings, Gwenyth glanced at her finger where her mother's ring still rested.

She looked in Adam's eyes. "Once I promised you my loyalty for a year and a day. Today I promise that and more. Forever."

His eyes shone bright, and she could swear his hand trembled as he waved to Seamus, who stepped forward and placed another ring in the priest's outstretched palm. He blessed it, then gave it to Gwenyth. There in her hand lay a replica of her mother's circlet, large enough for Adam.

Tears stung her eyes as she fixed it on his finger and watched him push it into place while the priest reminded them, "The ring is a sign of God's eternal, never-ending love. 'Tis a circle of honor, and it symbolizes a love that even death cannot destroy. God bless you both."

Gwenyth didn't hear the rest—couldn't hear or see anything or anyone but the man she loved and trusted, with all her heart.

At the end of the ceremony, they rose to their feet and Adam escorted her to stand beside Seamus, whose bemused look mirrored Gwenyth's own fluttering emotions.

Adam moved back to kneel once again before the priest. His voice was strong as he made his pledge to Clan Chattan. "I will uphold and defend my clan with my honor and my life, so help me God."

And then it was over, and they were surrounded by everyone wishing them well. Emotions ran high, and Gwenyth saw Eva wipe her eyes. Propelled away from her by back-slapping clansmen, Adam nevertheless managed to make eye contact with her. He smiled and winked and said, "Later."

LONG AFTER MIDNIGHT, the sounds of celebration drifted from the bailey to the huge bed in Adam's chamber. Later had finally come, when trust and need overcame reluctance and two had become one.

Gwenyth pulled away from Adam's embrace and chuckled at the evident look of disappointment on his face. Certain of herself, certain of the man she held in her arms, Gwenyth had gladly surrendered heart, soul, and body to her husband. Adam's gentle patience had dimmed the distant memories of Leod's cruelty. She did not fear the future, for Adam would never betray her.

"Tell me about this tapestry you made for my wedding gift. 'Tis beautiful—Daniel in the lion's den, isn't it?"

"I made it to remind me of all that you've taught me, beloved. But none of it would matter had you not reminded me of the most important thing of all."

"And what is that?" Adam asked.

"Victory always belongs to those who do God's will. No matter how difficult the situation, you must trust God."

"Aye, sometimes it is hard to know his will, or knowing it, to obey. But it has turned out well for us."

His bemused gaze turned most definitely hungry, his grin roguish. "This last lesson will take many sessions. It can't all be taught at once."

"Then pray we have many years to continue my education."

He pulled her into his arms. "Is this the same woman who so reluctantly accepted my attentions until now?"

"Nay," she whispered. "That woman was a hurting creature who knew nothing of the power of love to heal."

As his head bent to seal their love with a kiss, he murmured, "To everything there is a season . . ."